Bexley's BIKER

ROYAL BASTARDS MC

MISTY WALKER

Bexley's Biker
Copyright © 2021 Misty Walker

Cover Design: Lou Gray
Photo: Adobe Stock
Editor: Novel Mechanic
Proofreader: Sassi's Editing Services
Formatting: Champagne Book Design

ALL RIGHTS RESERVED. This book contains material protected under International and Federal Copyright Laws and Treaties. Any unauthorized reprint or use of this material is prohibited. No part of this book may be reproduced or transmitted in any form or by any means, electronic or mechanical, including photocopying, recording, or by an information and retrieval system without express written permission from the Author/Publisher.

This is a work of fiction. Names, characters, places, and incidents either are the product of the author's imagination or are used fictitiously, and any resemblance to actual persons, living or dead, business establishments, events, or locales is entirely coincidental.

To all the MC bikers who hang out at Maverik ... thanks for not making it weird when I gawk at you, wondering what your story is. I can't help it.

PLAYLIST

"I Wanna Be Your Slave" by Måneskin
"You've Really Got a Hold On Me" by Smokey Robinson & The Miracles
"I'm not Pretty" by JESSIA
"Make This Go On Forever" by Snow Patrol
"Love is a Battlefield" by Pat Benatar
"Beggin'" by Måneskin
"Save Your Tears (Remix)" by The Weeknd (with Ariana Grande)
"Take it Easy" Eagles
"Give Me a Reason" by Portishead
"Still Don't Know My Name" by Labrinth
"I Feel Like I'm Drowning" by Two Feet
"if i were you" by blackbear feat Lauv
"Stay" by The Kid Laroi & Justin Bieber
"Cough Syrup" by Young the Giant
"Nasty" by Bryce Fox
"Everlong" by Foo Fighters
"Go Fuck Yourself" by Two Feet
"Do I Wanna Know?" by Arctic Monkeys
"flagpole sitter" by Elohim & AWOLNATION
"Time Of The Season" by The Ben Taylor Band
"#1 Crush—Nellee Hooper Mix" by Garbage
"idfc" by blackbear
"Changes" by blackbear
"Leave Before You Love Me" by Marshmello (with Jonas Brothers)

ROYAL BASTARDS CODE

PROTECT: The club and your brothers come before anything else, and must be protected at all costs. **CLUB** is **FAMILY**.

RESPECT: Earn it & Give it. Respect club law. Respect the patch. Respect your brothers. Disrespect a member and there will be hell to pay.

HONOR: Being patched in is an honor, not a right. Your colors are sacred, not to be left alone, and **NEVER** let them touch the ground.

OL' LADIES: Never disrespect a member's or brother's Ol'Lady. **PERIOD.**

CHURCH is **MANDATORY.**

LOYALTY: Takes precedence over all, including well-being.

HONESTY: Never **LIE, CHEAT,** or **STEAL** from another member or the club.

TERRITORY: You are to respect your brother's property and follow their Chapter's club rules.

TRUST: Years to earn it ... seconds to lose it.

NEVER RIDE OFF: Brothers do not abandon their family.

Dear Reader,

While I did extensive research on the laws that pertain to Khan's arrest, I took certain creative liberties in order to tell his story the way I wanted. Do not use this book for legal advice.

Bexley's Biker is a dark romance and contains violence, gore, domestic abuse, knife play, blood play, rough sex, alludes to rape (though the act isn't described in any way), and general bad behavior.

There is no cheating or other woman/other man drama.

The Royal Bastards are bikers, and this book is a dramatization of what I think a 1%er club might look like. Read it for the escapism and entertainment of a good woman falling for a bad man, not for relationship inspiration.

Read the books you like and don't let anyone shame you for it.
XOXO,

Misty Walker
ROMANCE AUTHOR

Bexley's Biker

PROLOGUE

Khan

The guard leads me down a long hallway, my foam sandals clacking against my feet with each step. The cuffs around my wrists and ankles squeeze the joints painfully, but I'd never ask for them to be loosened. That would make me appear weak, and weaknesses like that are exploited when you're locked up.

We stand in front of a closed door until a buzzer sounds, unlocking the door to a private room. Inside, sitting at a shiny stainless-steel table, is Bexley fucking March, the club's defense attorney kept on retainer.

The sexy as hell brunette is wearing a fire-red dress suit, with a deep V showing off her long neck and ample cleavage. I want to bury my face in those tits.

Hell, I want to suffocate in them.

I used to be known for chasing young women looking for a good time. Now all I crave is Bexley's feisty personality and exaggerated curves.

I want to watch her ass jiggle while I fuck her from behind, feel her thick thighs squeeze my head while I eat her out, and grip onto her padded hips while I sink into her pussy. Then after we're sated, her body warm and naked against mine, I want to argue and fight over trivial shit.

Jesus, fuck. I need to get out of this place. My dick can't handle the celibacy.

"Wes," she bites out like my name's a curse word, but I ignore it and focus on her pouty red lips.

What I wouldn't do for her to leave lipstick stains on my dick after sucking me dry.

My cock chubs in my cotton prison uniform, leaving nothing to the imagination. And if the wide-eyed expression Bex has is any indication, she notices.

Her throat clears. "Have a seat."

The guard gives my shoulder a hard shove, making sure I remember who's in charge. On the streets, I'd break his neck for doing something like that. But in this place, I have to play by the rules and not make waves.

At least that's what Bex says.

I plop down in the plastic chair, feeling the legs bow under my weight. I freeze, waiting for them to snap in half, but it must be my lucky day because they hold strong. I'm a big guy, tall and muscular, and I've been known to break furniture.

The guard lifts my hands from my lap and drops them on the table. The sound of the metal cuffs clangs against the stainless-steel table and echoes through the room. Then he secures my shackled wrists to a ring on the table and my ankles to a similar ring in the cement floor.

"That's unnecessary," Bex says.

"My job is to keep you safe, Mrs . . . . ?"

"*Miss* March," she corrects.

"Does that mean you're single?" he flirts.

I roll my eyes. He's wasting his time.

Bexley's **BIKER**

Bex knows it, and I know it, yet when she spots my reaction, she leans over the table and traces a black painted nail over the swells of her breasts seductively. "Are you asking me on a date?"

I growl, low and menacing. This game she's playing is a personal attack on me, not a genuine interest in him. She knows I want her, and I'm pretty sure she wants me too. She's just too stubborn to admit it.

This guy doesn't stand a chance. He's a wannabe douche on a power trip who couldn't keep her satisfied. Bex is commanding and strong; the key to winning her over is tricking her into thinking she's in charge. Not making her feel like the weaker sex because he wears a uniform and has a pair of handcuffs and a badge.

"That's enough." The guard pulls out his baton and takes a threatening stance. I hold up my hands as much as the cuffs will allow, and he tucks it away, turning back to Bex. "We can talk about this date when you're finished with him. I'll be right outside the door. You sure you're okay?"

"We'll be fine. Wes will be a good boy, won't you?"

Would it kill her to use my road name?

"A regular Boy Scout," I reply, keeping my gaze on her.

The guard nods and leaves us alone. Bex pulls a few files out of her briefcase and stacks them neatly on the table. If my hands were free, I'd toss them on the floor if only to watch her head spin. I fucking love messing up all her perfection.

"Whatever you're thinking, don't do it," she says, without lifting her eyes.

"Wasn't thinking about anything other than how beautiful you look today, darlin'."

"Ha." She laughs humorously, then taps a finger on her chin, a pensive look on her face. "What is it? You want to knock my papers on the floor, don't you?"

"Don't know what you're talking about," I fib.

"Are you trying to tell me you don't get off on annoying me? Let's count all the reasons you're full of shit." She lifts a finger for each of my recent crimes against her. "You gave Roch's dogs my brand-new pair of Manolo Blahniks to use as chew toys—still trying to figure out how you got them out of my car since you were with me the whole time. Then there was that time you intentionally spilled motor oil on my Mercedes. Even though you claim it was an accident, I know the truth. Or, how about the time you tripped me, and I sprained my ankle?"

"It's not my fault you didn't see my foot." I smirk.

"Whatever. I didn't come here to argue about your schoolboy crush. I'm here to talk about the pre-trial next week."

"Is there a problem?"

She scowls at me, causing two lines to form between her eyes. I bite my lip to stop myself from telling her. She'd run out of the room and to the nearest plastic surgeon for another round of Botox if she knew.

"You were caught on camera, stealing a van that was later used to blow up a building. Yeah, I'd say there's a problem."

Of all the things I've done, it pisses me off that stealing that van is the thing I got busted for. We stopped a human trafficking ring by using that van to blow up the storage unit. Not that I can use that as my defense.

"So, how do we get out of it?" I need to keep my head on straight with these steep charges I'm facing.

"You can't. The best I can do is try for a plea deal, and even that's a long shot because of your extensive record."

"Would the plea deal get me out on parole?"

Her lips, so plump when she arrived, are now a flat line. "Wes, you're not hearing me. You're facing a minimum five-year sentence and fines in the hundreds of thousands."

Her words hit me like a ton of bricks. Five years behind bars? I'd lose my mind.

Memories of all the times I was locked up on drug charges flood my mind. Detoxing in a cement cell is a special kind of torture. The cold sweats, constant shivering, and body aches from withdrawal were only intensified by the frigid temperature of the facility.

Each time I was released—sober—I swore I'd never return, but it was a lie I told myself. Within a week, I'd be back to shooting myself up with heroin if I could afford it, or meth, when I couldn't.

It was a vicious cycle Goblin's old man finally freed me from. He was serving time for gun charges and took a liking to me. He explained what the Royal Bastards were about and said they were always looking for new members, especially big motherfuckers who knew how to shoot a gun, like me. He said if I stayed clean for a month after I was released, to stop by the club.

It was a tough month, but I was determined. The day I stitched the Prospect patch on my cut was one of the proudest of my life.

The club is the best thing to ever happen to me. Loki and I quickly became closer than brothers, and now I'm the vice president. Of course, I won't be for much longer if I can't get these charges dropped.

"What about bail?" I ask, my mind figuring out how to make the footage of me stealing that van disappear.

"I'm going to ask for house arrest. I'll claim you need to work to pay for my representation." She taps her lip with the end of her pen. "You guys still have the construction business, right?"

I nod. We started a phony company years ago to clean our money. I keep Loki, our Prez, Goblin, our enforcer, and Roch, our Sergeant-at-Arms, on the payroll, and we take on bullshit jobs for appearances while also cleaning our cash.

"Okay then. It's settled. I'll work on getting you out on bail.

You'll be released for at least six months, and we'll put together your defense during that time."

"Thanks," I say, meaning it.

I like to razz the girl, but she's saved my ass more than once, and I appreciate it.

"Are you doing okay?" she asks, concern lacing her tone. "Anyone bothering you?"

I smirk, the seriousness of the moment leaving me. "You worried about my safety, Bex?"

"You *are* in jail."

"Darlin', have you seen me?" I twist my arm to the side and flex. Since my hands are chained to the table, I'm only able to show off my triceps, but they're still impressive.

"You're not indestructible."

"The only weakness I have is you," I flirt.

"God. You can't be serious for longer than two minutes, can you?" She huffs and gathers her things, tucking them away in a bag that probably costs more than everything I own put together, including my bike. The girl loves her designer bags.

"Did Loki ask you to give me any messages?" I ask. Prez hasn't seen me, and I understand why, but I'm feeling disconnected from my club. I need to know what's going on.

"He said to tell you the footlong Italian sub is on ice, but the six-inch was left out in the open. Not to worry, though, because Tulsa is hungry and will finish it before it spoils." She cocks her head to the side. "Whatever that means."

It means Anthony's dead and Max got away, but Koyn's crew will take him out soon. Good. I fucking hate I wasn't there to help take them out. Maybe if I had been, Max's body would be out in the middle of the desert alongside his dad.

The Corsettis have been a pain in our ass for a long time. The oldest Corsetti brother, Dom, abducted Loki's woman. He paid for that with his life. Anthony, the younger Corsetti brother, retaliated by sending his son, Max, after Roch's woman.

The world will be a better place with them underground.

"An Italian sub sounds so fucking good," I groan. "That'll be my first meal when you get me out of here."

The food here sucks, and there's never enough to fill a man my size up.

She glances at her glitzy watch. "It *is* lunchtime, and that sounds yummy. I think I'll go get one right now. With onions and peppers. Maybe a drizzle of oil and vinegar. My mouth is watering just thinking about it."

With our eyes locked in a stare, she licks her upper lip suggestively.

Fucking hell.

"You're a cruel bitch, you know that?"

She beams. "Yep, I know. See you next week. Don't drop the soap."

Strutting over to the door, she sways her hips, and my eyes catch on her juicy ass. I can't look away.

She pounds on the metal door, and the guard holds it open for her.

"How about next Friday night for that date?" he asks.

"What's your number? I'll text you."

"Do you have a piece of paper?"

"Just tell me. I'll remember."

I chuckle, knowing she has no intention of ever calling the poor sap.

"555-2703."

"Got it. Talk soon." She pats his chest, and I listen as her high heels clack down the hallway.

"Goddamn, she is sexy as hell," the guard says, confidently strutting into the room to unlock my cuffs.

"Don't know what you're talking about, Boss."

"Yeah, you do. I saw the way you looked at her. You want her." He crouches and unlocks my feet. "A woman like her doesn't want a con, though. She wants someone with a decent job who has the balls to deal with criminal assholes like you."

I rise to my full height, looking down at him. I'm six-foot-eight and two hundred and fifty pounds of solid muscle. I could sit on this twig and break him.

"Don't worry, I'll take real good care of her." He grips me by the arm. "You think she likes her ass fucked? A chubby girl like her probably has a loose pussy."

Without considering the consequences, I ball my hands together, creating one large fist, and swing to the side, connecting with his jaw. The force of it sends him skittering, eventually landing on his ass. I stalk over and crouch next to him. Holding his hands up in defense, he cowers like the little bitch he is.

Like that could stop me from ending him.

"You listen to me. You touch a hair on her body and swear to God, I'll send you straight to Hades. And your bitch mom, who's letting you live in her basement? It'll be her ass that gets fucked by every one of my brothers."

His face turns an ugly shade of red. I was guessing about him living in his mom's basement, but his reaction says I'm spot on.

"Back the fuck up, inmate," he growls, but it's all for show. His hands are shaking, and there's a wet spot in the front of his pants, telling me he pissed himself.

"Not until we have an understanding." I kneel on his neck, cutting off his air supply.

He chokes and sputters comically but nods in agreement.

"I'd like to go to my cell now, please," I say.

Officer Dumbass gasps for air as he struggles to stand up. As soon as he's upright, he takes me by the arm again.

Only this time, we both know who's in charge.

And it's not his pathetic ass.

A soft man like him couldn't handle Bex. She needs a challenge, someone to verbally spar with who doesn't back down. She can't win without a fight, and Deputy Dipshit would get butthurt at the slightest raise of her voice.

But I have no problem taking her shit and throwing it right back at her. I'm damn good at it, too. When I say something that makes her eyes narrow and her lips purse tight, I can practically smell her sweetness dripping between her thighs.

All because of what *I* do to her.

Not this loser.

Bex doesn't know it yet, but she's mine. The second I get these charges against me dropped, I'm coming for her. And there'll be nowhere for her to run.

Chapter ONE

Bexley

I lean against the hood of my diamond white Mercedes AMG GT and check the time on my cell.

He's late.

To at least feel like I'm being productive, I scroll through emails, but none of the words register, so I lock the screen. My mind is too preoccupied with Inmate #347685, who is taking his damn time getting out here.

Pushing off the car, I pace back and forth, spinning my phone in my palm. How much can one man annoy me when he's not even in my presence?

The answer is a lot because I'm about to leave his ass in county lock up.

Determined to do just that, I slide onto the smooth black Nappa leather and start the car. One of his boys can come get him. I'm not a damn taxi service.

I throw the car in reverse and nearly jump out of my skin when I hear tapping on the passenger window. I glance over to see a man-child squishing his whole ass face against the window and blowing his cheeks out.

Ladies and gentlemen, I give you my client, a dangerous misfit outlaw with the maturity of a toddler. And the body of a Viking warrior, but we don't need to mention that.

I roll the window down and give him my best scowl. He grins and leans his very big head, covered in very big hair and a very big beard, inside my car.

Everything about this man is extra.

"You leavin' without me, darlin'?"

"I was about to," I say coolly, pressing the button to roll the window back up, not caring when it traps him inside at the neck because he didn't duck out in time.

"Not funny, Bex. Unroll the window," he says.

Instead, I let off the brake a touch.

"Bex," he growls, walking sideways as the car inches forward.

My foot lifts a hair more.

"Swear to fuck, darlin', you don't push your foot on that brake and unroll this window, I'll have you over my knee with those sexy as hell jeans down around your ankles and your bare ass up in the air."

That should scare me, right?

I roll my eyes and push on the brake while unrolling the window. After freeing his head, he jerks open the door and performs what can only be described as an act of contortion to get his enormous body inside my coupe.

"You made me late," I say, peeling out of the parking lot.

I know I should have a little more respect for the law since we're in the jail parking lot, especially considering the cops around here know me and hate me. After all, I'm the person who works to release the criminals they arrest. My job is literally to undo everything they do.

But this car is so sexy when she goes fast.

"Not my fault," he grumbles. "Deputy Dipshit decided his last act of dominance over me was a cavity search before they sent me on my way."

I laugh so hard, an unattractive snort slips out.

"Now I wish I would've written his number down when I was visiting you. He deserves at least a hand job for that act of genius."

I expect a snarky comeback, but instead, the car becomes unexpectedly quiet. I glance over and see a red-faced man glaring menacingly at me.

"What?" I ask, confused.

"Don't even fuck around about that stuff, Bex. You're not allowed near that asshole's dick unless it's to cut it off."

Now he's pissing me off. I've never been, nor will I ever be, a club slut. Not that I'm shaming because *my body, my choice* and all that, but I lived my life in a man's shadow once before, and I'll never do it again.

A man like Khan is bigger than life, in size and ego. He needs a woman who's okay standing in the dark.

That's not me.

"Did you just say I'm not *allowed*?" I huff. "Like you have any say in what I do."

"You wanna play this game?" He rubs his thumb and forefinger down his scruffy jaw. "How about this? You go near him, and I'll fucking slit his throat. And that'll be on you."

This time his threat isn't laced with humor; it's full of something that sends ice through my veins. For having just been released from jail, he sure is cranky ... and something else I can't put my finger on.

"I'm not going anywhere near his two-inch dick, okay?"

I hate backing down to him, but there's too much tension, and we have a half-hour drive ahead of us. Our banter is usually the most pleasurable part of being around him, and that's only because I enjoy arguing. Not today, though. Something's off.

He shifts in the seat uncomfortably. I can't blame him; his knees are nearly crushed to his chest, and he doesn't strike me as someone who regularly attends yoga.

"Could you have bought any smaller of a car? This thing is like a go-cart. And why is the roof so fuckin' low?" He pounds his fist into the roof, denting it. "I don't know how you drive a cage all the time."

"Versus the death trap on two wheels you drive?" I point to the damage he caused. "And you're paying for that."

"At least you can breathe on a motorcycle. I can't fucking breathe in here." He tugs on the collar of his white T-shirt.

"Hold on," I say and roll his window down.

Sweat's beading on his brow, and his complexion is flushed and clammy. He doesn't look so good.

I thought he was using an expression, but maybe he really can't breathe. I pull over onto the shoulder of the highway, worried he's seconds from throwing up all over my expensive interior. Before the car's in park, Khan throws the door open and gets out.

What the hell is wrong with him?

I step onto the dirt shoulder, only for my hair to fly in every direction from the desert wind. I'm spitting strands of hair out and tying it back in a ponytail when I spot Khan. His hands are on his head, and he's pacing back and forth, muttering something to himself.

I approach cautiously. I've been the club's defense attorney since before Khan even joined up, and these guys are all the same—short fuses and volatile behavior. But they keep my bank account very happy.

"What's going on, Wes?" I ask with a tone that says I'm bored.

He doesn't answer or acknowledge my existence.

"Wes!" I shout.

Still no answer.

"If you don't answer me, I'll have no choice but to call Loki and tell him you're having some kind of psychotic break."

Not even a look my way.

"Fine. I'm calling him." Pulling my phone out, I unlock the screen. I don't know if Loki will care or what he'll even do, but I have no other options and no time to deal with this.

"Put the phone down," he warns.

"Then tell me what this is and how we can speed it along so I can get back to work."

"Jesus Christ, Bex. Can you give me a goddamn minute?"

His expression puts a small fissure in the ice block I keep around my heart whenever Wes is near. He looks lost.

I don't know this side of him. It's confusing and disturbing.

Awkwardly, I pat him on the back a few times and say, "It'll be okay, bro. Some guys enjoy cavity searches. If that's something new you just found out about yourself, I can see how that would be confusing."

He doesn't laugh or hurl an insult.

What the hell?

"You're a pain in the ass. You know that, right?"

He storms over to a fence surrounding the miles of fields in front of us and rests his forearms on top of it, showing off his broad shoulders, tapered waist, rounded ass, and tree trunk thighs.

Goddamn.

I step back to admire him, but I can't even enjoy it because he's over there having a crisis of faith or something.

Walking over to join him, I mimic his position, staring into the field of God knows what. I think they're weeds, but hell if I know.

My gaze shifts upwards, and I count clouds while wondering how long this will go on when he breaks the silence. "Told myself the last time I was locked up, it wouldn't happen again. I've got some real bad memories of that place, and being back inside really fucked with my head."

I want to shoot out a quip about how maybe he shouldn't break the law then, but something in his tone has me holding back. I actually feel bad for him.

"Yeah. I have a few places like that myself."

"Have you ever gone back?" he asks.

"No, and I never will." I turn around, resting against the fence and hooking my high heel on the bottom rung. I knew I should've worn flats today. I have to expect the unexpected when I'm around this man.

"Keep it that way. Speaking from experience, it fucking sucks."

"Something traumatic happen last time?" I can't help but want to know more about this enigmatic man.

"Not one thing specifically. I don't know how much is in my file you carry around, but I was a junkie for a lot of years, and each time they locked me up, I went through withdrawal. Nothing worse than having the cold shakes, feeling like you have fire ants crawling all over you and gnawing on your flesh, while also being trapped in a dank cement cell and screamed at by the guards."

"Does it make you rethink your career path, maybe?"

I can't help it. I'm a smart ass by nature.

"No. How else would you be able to afford that car and those heels if it weren't for me?" He smirks.

Phew. He's back. I can't take introspective Khan, Vice President of the Royal Bastards MC. Never thought I'd say this, but I prefer man-whore alpha Khan, Vice President of the Royals Bastards MC.

At least with that version of him, I know what to expect.

"You want to go grab tacos from Roberto's?" I ask.

"You buyin'?"

"Sure, but I'm billing you for it."

"Bitch."

"Jackass."

He throws an arm over my shoulder and pins my head under his armpit before rubbing his knuckles on my scalp. I swat at him and kick his shins.

"Knock it off," I gripe.

He releases me. "That's payback for nearly decapitating me back there."

"Drama queen."

Twenty minutes later, we pull into the trashy-looking restaurant that serves the best tacos I've ever had. I order four carnitas tacos with rice and beans on the side. Khan orders twelve, hold the rice and beans.

We take our feast to a table and settle in. I wiggle in my seat, doing a little dance at the corn tortilla-stuffed goodness. Unwrapping the first one, I take my first bite, moaning at the explosion of flavors. When I wash it down with a swig of my forty-four-ounce Coke, I catch Wes staring at me, his mouth agape.

"What?" I ask around another bite of taco.

"I don't think I've ever seen you eat."

"We aren't friends. We don't share meals."

"You like food, huh?" he quirks a bushy brow.

"Don't start with me. I think it's obvious I like food." I motion up and down my body. My curves have curves, but life is too short to worry about calories. "I won't apologize for not looking like one of your many fuck toys."

"I wasn't saying it like that. You know I think you're hot."

Either from the spices in the tacos or his words, my skin heats. I don't like it. I need to shut it down.

Bexley's **BIKER**

"I'm not giving you a discount for complimenting me. You have a type, Wes. Everyone knows it. If the girl can't double as a hundred-pound barbell, you aren't looking twice."

I've heard the talk around the clubhouse about how funny everyone finds it that such a big man has a kink for tiny women.

"Then you understand why I'm so intrigued. You said it. You're not my type."

And there's the ego and the reason I keep him at a very far distance from my heart and my pussy.

He's an asshole playboy.

"I'm not letting your backhanded compliment stop me from enjoying these tacos." I take another big bite, letting the juice drip down my chin and not bothering to wipe it off before going back for more.

Wes shakes his head and brings his own taco to his mouth, eating half of it in one bite. Even his mouth is big.

"Did they fit you with a tracker?" I bunch up a wrapper and toss it on the tray.

He lifts his leg and pulls up his jeans to show me the black box attached to his ankle. "I registered my job sites, and since I thought they might frown on me living at the clubhouse, I'm moving in with Loki."

"Is one of those job sites the clubhouse?" I ask.

"We're doing renovations in the basement. It wouldn't be responsible if the general contractor didn't show up to inspect his guys' work." He smirks.

"You better hope they don't find out you're full of shit."

"That's the beauty of it. We really are renovating the basement. Normally it would be a two-week job, but I foresee a few unexpected issues, prolonging the process."

"Can you please just stay out of trouble for a while? You're getting down to your last chance before they lock you up and throw away the key. If that doesn't already happen with this last stunt," I say.

"You worried about me, darlin'?"

"I'm worried about the club not keeping me on retainer because all of you fools are locked up."

"You *are* worried about me." He points a teasing finger my way.

"Not on your life."

"You like me."

"I can't stand you," I hiss.

"You want me."

"Why do you say shit like that?"

"Because when I do, the little vein in your forehead throbs, your cheeks pink up, and if I were to reach in your panties right now, we both know what I'd find."

I squeeze my thighs together, feeling for myself what he'd find. There's a puddle between my legs.

Fuck. Shit. Damn. This is getting out of control.

My appetite gone, I jump to my feet and carry my tray to the trash. Without a second look, I march out the door, climb in my car, and leave his ass at the restaurant.

I peel out of the parking lot feeling smug, but when I glance in my rearview, I see him standing on the sidewalk, doubled over in laughter.

Asshole.

Chapter TWO

Khan

"How's it going, brother?" Goblin, our enforcer, gives me a back-slapping hug.

"Good now that I'm out of the pokey," I say, taking a seat at the long, living edge wooden bar top.

I trace a finger over the spot I carved my initials into the day I patched in. I have history here. I'm finally home.

"I heard they approved you to move in with Prez. Cracked my shit up they think that's the most stable environment for a man on house arrest."

"Thank you, U.S. Justice System." I rap my knuckles on the bar, signaling to Miles.

"Good to see you back, Khan. What can I get you?" he asks.

"A beer and a shot."

I watch to see if the kid remembers my alcohol preferences. Like the suck-up he is, he pulls out a can of Bud Light and pours a shot of Hennessey, then sets them in front of me with a proud smile.

"Good man," I say, lifting the shot glass to my lips and

swallowing it down. Fuck, I needed this. "What's been going on here?"

"Nothing now that Max and Anthony are on a permanent vacation. Runs have been smooth sailing, keeping Miguel happy and the money flowing in."

It pleases me to get confirmation that Max and Anthony Corsetti are in Hades. Those two fuckers are responsible for my current predicament.

Bitches be trouble.

"That's good. We'll need the cash to make my problem go away," I say, chugging my beer.

"We got your back. You won't go down for this." Goblin takes a deep inhale of his smoke, letting it out in fat rings. "Want one?"

I grab the pack and light up, moaning as the nicotine fills my lungs. I traded for a couple smokes while locked up, but it was nowhere near my pack-a-day habit. I have what they call an addictive personality. I probably shouldn't drink, but alcohol was never my vice. Now, offer me a loaded needle of black tar heroin, and I'd kill your family dog for it.

"Church," Loki calls out.

"Let's do it." Goblin hops off his stool, and we file into the Chapel.

Inside the windowless room, with a hand-carved wooden table, sits a guy I haven't seen in a long time, Coyote.

"What the hell are you guy doing here, brother?" I ask, bumping my knuckles against his.

"Heard you were in some hot water," he says.

I laugh. "And in case things go sideways, you want to be around to take VP from me?"

It's funny because Coyote's a nomad for a reason. Dude can't even sleep inside the clubhouse when he visits, let alone settle down in one spot. I'm surprised clothes aren't too confining for this guy.

"No, man. Not looking to do that. Just thought the club could use some extra support," he says, but there's more to it. I can tell by the haunted look in his nearly black eyes.

"So, does that mean you're sticking around?" Moto, our Road Captain and resident gear head, asks, taking his seat at the table.

"For now," he says.

"We have an extra room," Sly, our treasurer, says from where's he's seated next to Moto.

"I'll pass on that." He turns to Loki. "If it's okay, I'll camp out in the yard."

"Fine by us. Just be careful of all the landmines out there. Roch's dogs don't exactly flag their shit," he says.

"Thanks, bro." Coyote leans over the table and shakes Loki's hand.

"You're the one who's helping us. You're right. With Khan needing to keep his nose clean, we could use it."

I fucking hate being the odd man out. The next few months are going to be torture.

"Let's get this meeting started." Loki pounds the gavel, and all nine of us quiet. "Miguel needs us to make a run to Northern Oregon. Moto, who's up?"

"Bullet, Goblin, and Roch."

"You guys good with it?" Loki asks the three brothers, who all nod. "Okay. Ford will drive the van."

"What are you running these days?" Coyote asks.

Questions like that usually raise hackles. But Coyote's been an honorary member for almost as long as I've been around. He's trusted and has always been loyal.

"That's right," Loki drawls. "You haven't been around since we took out Dom, right?"

"The Corsetti asshole?" he asks.

"We didn't get a chance to explain when you got here, but Corsetti had taken our gun business from us after the big ambush that knocked off a bunch of members and ol' ladies." He frowns, and I know he's thinking about his mom getting killed during that gunfight. "But after we removed him from the situation—thanks for helping with that—we got control of the gun business back."

"Now you're back to running for Miguel?" he asks.

"Yeah."

"Nice. I can go on the run if one of you would rather stay behind," he offers.

We all look at Roch. His girl, Truly, moved in recently, and from what I heard while I was locked up, they haven't come up for air very often.

He nods, trying to be his normal stoic self, but I see the difference in him. The deep frown lines on his forehead aren't so pronounced anymore, and his normal frown has perked up into a flat line. I'm happy for my brother. He's had the weight of the world on his shoulders for so long, he deserves some good. And Truly's definitely something good.

"That settles it. Coyote, you're in, and Roch, you don't have to quit fucking your girl for a few days. Everyone wins." Loki flips open his Zippo and lights a smoke.

"Since I'm staying out of the business until all the legal shit clears, I'd like to get the basement finished up. I listed the clubhouse as a job site, so there's a chance the cops might pop in for a visit during business hours. As long as I'm not wearing my cut and I can prove work's being done, there's not a whole lot they can do," I say.

"That means no club business while Khan in on the premises. I don't like the idea of the police thinking they can show up whenever, but we need the added space, and we've been putting it off for too long." Loki taps his cig on the side of the ashtray. "Use the prospects or whoever else you need to get it done."

"Budget?" I turn to Sly, who's slick with numbers.

"We still have Birdie's dad's payout assigned to renovations, so don't go crazy, but there's enough."

"Then I have one last question," I say. "How many stripper poles do we want down there?"

My brothers beat their fists on the table and holler. Everyone except Roch, who, even though he's getting regularly laid now, still doesn't have a sense of humor.

"That's all I got for today. We're having a cookout tonight in honor of Khan being a free man. Make sure all you fuckers are there. I'm looking at you, Roch," Loki says, slamming his gavel and adjourning the meeting.

Hell yeah.

I need a party to get me feeling like myself again. Jail fucked with my head, and I haven't been able to get right. Maybe after some booze and a buffet of women, I'll feel normal again.

I check the temperature dial clipped to the smoker, seeing the meat is nearly done. I've got a good buzz going after day drinking with my brothers and catching up.

Now it's late afternoon, and I only have two hours left before I have to be back in Tahoe at Loki's house in the woods. It's time to crank up the party. I need to get laid, or at least have a good option to take back with me. Although Birdie would probably cut my nuts off if I brought patch pussy to their house.

Fucking house arrest.

"Hey, Bex!" Moto greets, and I whirl around.

Walking out the back door and onto the patio is none other than my lawyer, dressed in the fanciest pair of white shorts I've ever seen. They look like those trousers she always wears, only these end just below her ass and not at her ankles. Up top, she's wearing a low-cut shirt with a blazer over it. And, of course, she has on those dangerously high heels that accentuate her calves and make her hips sway dramatically when she walks.

Her long brown hair is curled at the ends, and she has on her signature red lipstick. The same color I've pictured smeared on my dick so many times, I've lost count.

A quick glance at Loki tells me this is a setup. Ever since he found out I have a... what? A crush? That's too juvenile for how I feel about Bexley. No, it's not a crush.

This is me maturing and wanting more than a quick lay from the women I've been with. Being locked up again was a harsh reminder that my life could be over in the blink of an eye and when that happens, I want to know I went after the things I want.

I stalk over to her, stopping to grab a beer out of the cooler. I pass it her way. "Didn't know you were going to be here."

"Loki invited me," she says, unscrewing the top off the beer and taking a sip.

I watch in fascination as her lips wrap around the mouth of the glass bottle. It only solidifies the dirty fantasies I have of her in my brain.

"She deserves to celebrate more than you do. She did all the hard work." Loki swings an arm around her shoulders.

In my head, I know he's happily engaged to Birdie, who would do some gnarly shit to his junk if he cheated on her. But an animalistic place inside me ignores logic and fills me with the urge to kill my best friend for daring to touch what's mine.

"Chill, bro. You're turning red." Loki slaps me on the chest and walks away.

"Are you drunk?" she asks, lifting to her tiptoes and sniffing what I'm assuming is my breath. Her face pinches. "Oh my God. Are you stupid?"

"What are you talking about?"

"You can't drink. If they do a piss test on you, you'll be back in jail, and there won't be anything I can do about it until the trial." She smacks me upside the head.

I rub at the spot she swatted at. "Alcohol isn't illegal."

"I hate to repeat myself, but are you stupid? Didn't you listen to anything the judge said?"

"He had lettuce between his two front teeth."

"So?" she asks incredulously.

"So, it was distracting."

She shoves the beer into my chest. "I can't do this with you. I pulled strings to get you out, and this is how you thank me."

She turns to leave, but I grab her arm, stopping her.

"I didn't know. I won't drink anymore. Shit, woman."

"Don't give me attitude. I'm not the fuckup here."

Ouch.

"Listen—"

"No, you listen. Maybe this whole boyish behavior was cute when you were in your twenties, but it's not anymore. Grow up and stop being such a goddamn idiot." She looks down at where I'm still holding her arm. "Let go and never put your hands on me again without my permission."

My hand falls away, and I stare at her, stunned. We fight every time we see each other, but there's always an underlying teasing nature to it. That's not what this is.

"Sorry, Bex. You know I'd never hurt you."

I'm a lot of things—and most of them ain't good—but I never do anything without consent.

She pinches the bridge of her nose. "No, it's not you. I mean, it is you, but in this case, it's not *only* you."

"You want to talk about it?"

"No. I just want to have a beer, eat some food, and go home to soak in my tub. Think that can happen without us killing each other?"

"Sure, darlin'. Grab a plate, and I'll feed you my meat." I wink.

She folds her arms, pushing her fat tits even higher, and leans away from me, knitting her brows. "Does that really work for you?"

"What?"

"Those corny pick-up lines. The way you pull chicks, I thought you'd have better material."

"Shut the fuck up and sit your ass down. I'll bring you a plate." I shake my head as I move back to the smoker. I dish up a little of everything: a hamburger, a hotdog, brisket, steak, and pulled pork.

This'll keep her pretty mouth busy.

"Dinner's up," I shout to everyone and watch the frenzy ensue as I walk back over to my annoying lawyer. I set the plate down and sit next to her.

She wiggles in her chair the same way she did when we had tacos. It's the cutest damn thing I've ever seen.

"This looks so good. You smoked all this?" she asks before picking up the hotdog and sinking her teeth in it. Ketchup collects on the corner of her mouth, and I have to fight the urge to lean in and lick it off.

"I'm a barbecue master." I steal the chicken drum off her plate, stick the whole meaty end in my mouth, bite down, and scrape the meat off with my teeth as I pull the bone out.

"You're barbaric."

"You're sexy," I say, sweeping my thumb over her lower lip to collect the glob of sauce. I hold her eyes as I suck it off.

"Gross." Her eyes pull down, her nose wrinkles, and her upper lip curls.

Goddamn, I love her bitchiness. It makes my cock rock hard.

This feisty woman will be mine.

Chapter
THREE

Bexley

I mostly contain my enjoyment of the meal Khan made as we both pick away at my plate. But I slip when I place a piece of perfectly cooked steak in my mouth and moan.

"Gotta say, I love watching you eat, darlin'." Khan's gaze fixates on my mouth.

"Can't say I care," I say, chewing loudly in yet another attempt to turn him off.

It's a wasted effort because the deep wrinkles appear on the outer corners of his eyes, and he flashes me an amused smile.

Fucking hell.

He leans in and murmurs, "You'd care if it was my cock I was feeding you."

My fork falls to the table in surprise as his dirty words make my clit throb in need.

"I can tell you like that idea. You blush beautifully."

I clear my throat and reach for my fork. It doesn't matter how my body reacts to him. I can't give him what he wants.

"You're a criminal and my client. I have no desire to be anywhere near your member."

He guffaws. "You're especially feisty today. What rich girl problems have your panties in a twist today?"

Right before I walked into the clubhouse, I received a cryptic text that said, "See you soon," and I can't figure out if it's a wrong number or if my psycho ex has finally found me.

Since I can't tell him any of that, I straighten my posture and sneer, "Nothing an outlaw biker needs to worry his pretty little head over."

I expect him to throw out a returning insult. Or laugh at my sass. But he does neither of those things. Instead, his penetrating gaze bores into mine as though he expects to find the truth behind my lie. He won't. I'm a master of disguise. I have to be. It's what keeps me alive.

Thankfully, the moment is interrupted when Loki stands up and pounds a fist on the picnic table, gaining everyone's attention.

"It's been a shit year. We lost a brother," he says, referring to Jake, who lost his life protecting the club. "And we went to war twice, but we're stronger for it."

The crowd hoots and hollers, pounding their fists on the tables, startling me. I've been here on business many times, but never socially. Looking around, it's clear to see that I don't fit in. The guys all have on jeans and their leather cuts, and the women are scantily clad, accentuating all their assets. Even Truly and Birdie, who don't come from this life, have on stylish and sexy dresses.

Me? I'm wearing trouser shorts and a blazer, both white. Which turned out to be an especially stupid choice given I'm sitting on a dusty plastic chair in the middle of a backyard that is full of dog shit and torn-up grass.

I don't do casual.

Loki swipes a hand through the air, silencing them. "And we're growing."

Birdie stands up next to him, smiling big, with tears in her eyes.

Oh god. I really shouldn't be here.

I move to stand, but Khan chooses that moment to wrap his abnormally strong arm around the back of my chair, not allowing me to move.

"You're knocked up?" he shouts, moving his arm up onto my shoulders. I pick his hand up from where it's resting dangerously close to my boob and toss it off.

Birdie's face falls at his suggestion. "No, asshole. Loki asked me to marry him, and I said yes." She plucks a ring from her pocket and slides it on her finger. "We're getting married!"

Truly jumps up and rushes over to her friend. They both visibly swoon over the ring. I'm short on friends at the moment, so seeing how close they are makes me jealous.

Roch clears his throat and stands, preparing to say something. This oughta be good. The man doesn't orate. Truly leaves Birdie and returns to his side, tucking herself into him. It must feel good to know you've found your person.

I wouldn't know; the only men I'm with are gone before we even exchange names.

"Pregnant," Roch says simply, scratching the back of his neck.

He's not one to mince words. Of all the brothers, he's the most perplexing. He looks like he belongs on the cover of *GQ*, not in a biker club with a bunch of outlaws. But look closer, and there's no mistaking the devil that lives inside him.

Eyes widen in all directions, everyone freezing in place.

"You're pregnant?" Birdie calls out in a high-pitched tone. Truly nods, tears welling in *her* eyes now.

Fucking hell. I don't do emotion.

Suddenly, everyone's on their feet, congratulating Loki and Birdie on the engagement and Truly and Roch on the baby. Even Khan leaves me to join the excited crowd.

Of all the ways I thought tonight would go, it never crossed my mind I'd witness an engagement and a baby announcement. These guys better watch out. If I were one of their many enemies and saw this, I wouldn't be afraid of this family-friendly biker gang.

Khan tosses Birdie over his shoulder, making Loki punch him in the gut, knocking the air from his lungs. He sets Birdie down, not all that gently, before doubling over, expelling a loud, pained breath. Everyone else watches on, laughing their asses off. Even Roch.

They're a family, and I don't belong. I only came because Loki asked me to, and I knew it was a bad idea.

I give my plate of food a longing stare, bummed I can't finish it, before grabbing my purse from the back of my chair. Careful not to draw attention to myself, I stand and walk around the side of the clubhouse to leave.

I'm opening the door of my car when I hear my name being called. I expected Khan to chase after me since his main goal in life is to irritate me, but it's not him. It's the beautiful bombshell, Birdie, who is Loki's *ol' lady*. Or whatever they call their women.

"Wait up, Bex!" she calls out, expertly maneuvering through the gravel lot in heels.

Everything about this woman is perfect. Her cute little button nose, her naturally blond hair, and her thin frame with the perfect amount of boobs and butt. She's every man's wet dream, and on top of all that, she's nice and a good person.

I have no idea how she fell for the scary president of a biker gang.

"Sorry I didn't say goodbye. I have some work to do back at the office," I say.

"Okay." She nods her head. "I just wanted to make sure you were okay. You ran off like your butt was on fire."

"You noticed that, huh?"

"I did. I also noticed a very large man looking pretty sad about it."

"Who? Khan? Psh." I wave her off. "If he's at all upset about me leaving, it's because he won't have someone to argue with."

"I don't know. I think he likes you." She grins.

"If that's how he treats the people he likes, I think I'd rather he hates me. Maybe then he'd leave me alone."

"Is that really how you feel?"

No, I think we have unexplainable chemistry that freaks me out because I have a traumatic past that has left me untrusting of everyone and everything.

I keep that to myself and instead say, "He only thinks he's interested in me because I don't fall at his feet like all the other girls. He wants a challenge, not me."

"Maybe. We'll see." There's a challenging glint in her eyes I don't like.

"Well, I better head out. I have work." I hook a thumb over my shoulder.

"What are the odds he walks away from this?" she asks, surprising me when her expression turns serious.

I lean a hip against my car and fold my arms. "Honestly, I don't know. Speaking as a friend of the club, if they get ahold of the footage, he's golden. But as his attorney, who knows nothing about their plan to steal the footage, he's screwed but I'll work hard to get him a reduced sentence."

"I'm begging you. Please do everything in your power. I have resources these guys don't have because of my dad, so if there's anything you need to grease any wheels or whatever, do it and let me know. I'll do whatever it takes." Her face hardens to stone. "He doesn't show it, but Loki is having a hard time with all this.

He feels responsible, and the guilt is eating him alive. Not to mention knowing his best friend and brother might have to go away for a while. He needs Khan. We all do."

"I swear, Birdie. I'll do whatever I can. But I'm not some shady lawyer who makes back-alley deals. I fight fair and square. Whatever the guys do on their own time is on them," I say.

"I get that. But these guys are my family, so understand that if I think things are going down a road that doesn't help Khan stay here with us, you'll be out, and I'll find someone who will do *whatever* it takes." Her truth burns like a fire behind her eyes.

I don't take offense. She has something to lose. I know what that feels like and the lengths a person will go to protect themselves and those they love.

"I understand."

Her demeanor goes from dark and serious to happy and cheerful in the blink of an eye. "Good. Glad I cleared that up. You sure you have to go? There's enough food back there to feed an army."

"Yeah. I better go figure out our loophole to get Khan off, so I don't get fired," I joke.

"I like you," Birdie says. "You've got spunk."

"Thanks. I can tell we're well-matched in that aspect."

The pride I feel at seeing my gorgeous office never gets old.

Walking inside, there's a plant wall with a backlit sign that reads, "March Law Offices." When designing this place, I went for modern sophistication, and my designer delivered just that. I love the grandeur of the rich wood floors and sleek lines of the modern furniture. Add in the homey feel from the plants, and I feel more comfortable here than I do in my downtown apartment.

Bexley's **BIKER**

I lock the door behind me since it's a Sunday, and no one is dumb enough to come into work on a weekend except me.

When I sit at my desk and flip on my computer, I can finally breathe after the awkward barbecue. I may be inept at some things—socializing, making friends, and dating—but work isn't one of them. I'm a damn good attorney, and that's something no one can take away from me.

Bringing up my email, I see a few from Marcy, my secretary. I scroll through the first one telling me about the meetings I have scheduled for next week, knowing I spend my weekends preparing. I flag it to go over later and move on.

In the next one, she asks how I feel about starting up a "Potluck Tuesday" to boost morale.

Potluck Tuesday?

Receiving a paycheck twice a month isn't enough to boost their morale? I know watching my bank account grow is enough of a morale boost for me to show up to work every day.

Is having a work ethic not a thing anymore?

I type out a quick response, informing her there is zero chance of that happening, and hit send.

Organize a potluck on your own time.

I'm sure my employees call me a bitch behind my back when I deny them things like holiday parties or fucking potluck Tuesdays, but I don't care. We're here to do a job and get paid.

I pay my employees well and offer substantial benefits, but I require a professional atmosphere. There's no room for drama or gossip within these walls. Since getting too friendly with employees breeds that drama and gossip, I forbid it.

After answering any pertinent emails, I dial up my voicemail, a pen and notepad poised and ready to write my messages.

The first two are clients looking for updates about their cases. I'll call them back on Monday. The third is from a public defender who's been trying to get into my pants for years now.

I hit delete on that one because I don't date, and even if I did, it wouldn't be with his slimy ass.

I hit next and listen to the fourth message. "March Law Offices? Seems like you're doing well for yourself, *Sienna*."

I slam the phone down, ice running through my veins and a chill climbing up my spine. Now I know who that text message was from earlier.

How did he find me?

It's been ten years since anyone has called me by that name, and hearing it again sends me back in time. Back when I was stupid, naïve, and trusting.

I'm not that person anymore.

I paid for a new identity. An expensive one that was supposed to guarantee my anonymity. Untraceable, according to the man who ran a Postal Express from the front of his store and a whole host of illegal things from the back. Everything from guns to a whole new life.

I opted for one of each.

I go back to my computer and click onto the security camera footage, carefully checking vantage points and motion alerts. There's been no movement inside or out and no cars creeping through the parking lot. That means he's only found me virtually. But it's only a matter of time before he or one of the creeps he keeps on his payroll show up at my door.

Last time I ran from him, I had nothing. No car, no house, no possessions of any kind. Everything I had, he gave to me. And, as he spelled out for me every day, whatever he gave me, he could just as easily take away.

So, I left it all behind.

I can't do that this time. I have a beautiful office, an equally beautiful apartment downtown, and people who count on me. Disappearing again will be more difficult, if not impossible.

My heart pounds so loudly, I can't hear anything else except the steady thumping. Pressure builds in my head and chest, squeezing my insides and making me feel as though I might explode.

I can't run again.

Fucking hell.

I close my eyes and take a calming breath in through my nose and out through my mouth. Over and over again.

I can flee the country. Hide in plain sight among the millions. Maybe India or Ecuador. Find an unknown village somewhere and start over. I won't be able to practice law, but there are other things I can do to occupy my time.

All while living in constant fear.

I can stay here and face my demons. I don't even know what *he* wants from me. Maybe he wants nothing and only wanted me to know he's keeping tabs on me.

Yeah, right. Since when is he known for his forgiving personality?

The thoughts spin around my mind for so long, I'm dizzy. Before I know it, the sun has gone down, and my office is shrouded in darkness. I shut down my computer and lock my office behind me. I still don't know what I'm going to do, but I know I can't do anything this late at night or from this location.

Fucking hell.

Chapter

FOUR

Khan

I wake to the sound of the river that runs along the backside of Loki and Birdie's cabin. When he built this place, I thought he lost his edge, turned soft, but waking up to this has changed my mind. This is fucking heaven.

I climb out of bed and stretch my arms over my head. My joints pop and creak as I move, reminding me I'm no spring chicken anymore.

I throw on some clothes, grab my smokes, and step outside. The best part about this house is the French doors in both the master suite and guest room that I'm staying in. It brings the outdoors in, as they say on those *HGTV* shows I like to watch on mornings when I have a hangover and need to chill the fuck out.

Birds chirp, squirrels run along the edge of the creek, and the chilly morning works better than a cup of coffee to wake me up as I sit down on a patio chair and light up. With my cig dangling from my lips, I tie my hair back and relax into the padded seat.

"Good morning," Birdie chirps, stepping onto the deck from her room. She sets one of the two cups of coffee she's holding down in front of me on the patio table.

"Mornin'."

"How'd you sleep?" She takes a seat across from me.

"Like a fucking rock."

"That mattress isn't the best. Your room was being used for"—her cheeks pink—"other purposes when we found out you'd be moving in. We ran out and grabbed the first bed they had in stock."

If she only knew Loki's told me all about their kinky games with the human-sized birdcage he locks her up in.

"Darlin', any bed that isn't a bunk bed and has a man named Bubba sleeping above me is the best bed I've ever slept on."

She grins. "I see your point."

Never had a sister, but Birdie has filled that place in my life. Her and Truly both.

"Anything fun happen after I left last night?" I ask. This whole curfew thing has me feeling like a child. It sucks.

"No. It was pretty tame. You know you're the life of the party." She slaps my arm.

"Not anymore." I lift my ankle up and hike up the leg of my jeans, showing off my new electronic jewelry.

"You won't have to wear that for long. Bex will get you off."

Bex will get you off. I like the sound of that.

"She's gonna try, but I like my chances of solving the problem better."

She eyes me suspiciously. "I don't even want to know."

I chuckle. "Wasn't gonna tell you."

"Now that we're talking about Bex," she says too casually. "What's going on with you two?"

"You mean my future wife?" I ask.

She chortles. "You're going to have to work harder to get

her to marry you than you'll have to work to get that tracker off your ankle."

"Ain't that the fucking truth. What did you say to her after she ran off, anyway?"

Feel a bit like a chatty schoolgirl, but I'm dying to know.

"I asked her what your chances are of clearing the charges. Then I threatened her if she wasn't successful." She covers her face with her hands.

"You goin' dark on me, Birdie?"

"What can I say? You assholes are rubbing off on me."

"If I go down for this, it won't be because of her," I say gently.

"I know. I just hate how out of control this all feels. Loki tricked me into thinking you boys are untouchable."

"Nah. Not untouchable, just hard to reach." I give her shoulder a squeeze. "Don't want you to worry about me. But if there's any way you two can have that wedding before my court date, that'd be cool."

Thinking about my best friend getting married without me by his side makes me fucking sick.

Birdie goes from lighthearted to dead ass serious in a heartbeat. "Are you *that* worried?"

"Nah, I'm joking. Even if I have to bust my ass out of the state pen, I'll be there."

She nods. "Good. Because we want a Halloween wedding."

"Sounds good, darlin', and thanks for this," I say, lifting the steaming mug to my lips and taking a sip.

"You're welcome. You need anything before I leave for school?"

"Nah, I'm good. Loki already gone?"

"Yeah. He wanted to be there when the guys left on their run."

"Good man. Sure am glad you two have each other."

"Stop it," she scolds, circling her finger in my direction. "This whole pensive vibe you have going on is unacceptable. It's not you."

I stretch my legs out and rest my hands on my head, taking in the view. "I'll be fine. I've got my brothers, my club, and a girl who needs chasing. Plenty to keep my mind busy."

She studies me for a minute before saying, "You're a good guy, Khan. Bex would be lucky to have you." Then she stands up and disappears back into her room.

I'm not a good guy, and Bex deserves a hell of a lot more than me. But fuck if I don't want her anyway.

From inside, I hear my phone chirp. I find it on the nightstand and see Bex's name flash across the screen.

Speak of the devil.

"Yeah?" I answer.

"Are you busy?" she asks.

"Not particularly. Why? Are you calling to apologize for ditching me last night?"

"Uh, no. I stand by that decision. Where are you?" She sounds frantic and out of control; Bexley March is always in control, so it raises my hackles.

"Loki's house, but I'm getting ready to head out to the clubhouse."

"Okay. I'll meet you there."

"Everything all right? What's this all about? Did something happen with the case?" The panic that's always teetering on the surface rears its ugly head. Never used to be this way before prison came knocking at my door.

"No, no. Nothing about the case. I just need your help with something."

"What's that something?"

She sighs. "I need you to do some digging on someone. Like a background check or something."

"I don't know anything about computers, but Sly's a whiz at that sort of shit. Who is he?" I ask, unable to stop myself.

"His name is Martin Alexander. Last time I saw him, he was living in New York—"

"Hold on, let me grab a pen," I interrupt, digging through my bags until I come up with a pen and a receipt. "What's his name?"

"Martin Alexander. Last time I saw him—"

"Yeah, yeah. New York. I got it. How long ago was that?" I scribble the name and location down.

"Ten years."

"Someone I should be concerned about?" I ask.

"No. I just need to know where he's at and what he's been up to." I hear her car door shut and an engine roar to life. "I'm heading to the clubhouse now."

"Might take me a minute to get there, still need to shower. Why don't you pick up doughnuts and coffee from Dough Boys first?" I grin, knowing what's coming next.

"I am not your waitress or delivery girl. If you want doughnuts, stop and get them yourself."

There's the fire that was lacking from her voice at the beginning of the call.

I push even further. "You work for me if I remember correctly."

"You pay me five hundred dollars an hour to keep your pathetic ass out of prison, not to go through drive-thrus."

"How long do you think it takes to go through a drive-thru?"

"Khan, I don't have time for games today," she warns.

"Maybe ten minutes if you hit the morning rush. What's the math on that? Do I need to convert to decimals, or is there an easier way?"

"It's eighty-three dollars and thirty cents, asshole. Plus expenses, so a ten-dollar box of doughnuts plus gas would make it right around ninety dollars," she spouts off like it was the easiest thing in the world to figure out.

I lower my voice to a near-growl. "You're sexy when you do math."

"You're so fucking annoying. I'm hanging up now. See you when I see you."

"Don't forget those doughnuts. I'll round it up to a C-note so you can get yourself something too."

I hear an aggravated shriek before the line goes dead. I laugh so loud, the birds scatter from the trees.

Fucking love irritating that woman.

I walk into the clubhouse, feeling oddly detached from the place I've called home for many years now. My brothers are busy doing everything they normally do during the week, but it's different because I'm not part of it. I hate it.

"Khan, my man," Sly greets from where he's perched at a table with a laptop in front of him, sipping coffee.

"How's it going?"

"Good. Just doing a little digging on the guy you asked about. I know you said you were only after some background level of digging, but I couldn't help but go deeper. This guy's a fucking asshole." He turns the laptop to show me, but I'm distracted by the front door opening and Bex sauntering in.

She's dressed in a tight, knee-length black skirt that follows her every curve, and her black, silky, button-down blouse is undone enough to show off the delicious swells of her breasts. Her makeup is flawless, and her pouty lips are coated in a bright pink color that pops against her dark features.

My dick chubs instantly, and I shift to adjust its position in my jeans.

"Are those doughnuts?" Sly asks, pushing his chair back and moving in on the pastries Bex holds out to him.

"Hey, those are mine." I lean back on my chair until I'm on two legs to try and swipe them, but Sly holds the box just out of reach.

"Fuck off. I'm the one working while you're sitting around doing jack shit." Sly flips the lid of the cardboard box open and stuffs a glazed doughnut in his mouth. Something catches his eye, and he hands the box over to me before saying, "Petra."

I turn to take in the woman who's been staying with us for a few months now, after we found her drugged out of her mind in Anthony Corsetti's house. Seems he kept his wife that way intentionally, and it did a massive number on her psyche, leaving her skittish and timid like a mouse.

"Hey, girl," Bex says.

Petra gives her a tight smile, taking small steps toward the bar.

"Want a doughnut?" Sly asks, all too eagerly.

She shakes her head no and tucks her long, hair behind her ears. I've picked up on her moods based on how much of her face she shows. Sometimes her hair nearly curtains her entire face. Those are the times she doesn't want to talk or be involved in what's happening around the clubhouse. But sometimes, like today, it's tucked behind her ears and showing off her face.

She's pretty, but not in the same obvious way Bexley is. She's more ethereal with her pale skin, black hair, ruby lips, and sharp cheekbones.

"How about some orange juice?" Sly suggests.

I can't quite figure out what his end game is with her. Ever since I can remember, he and Moto have tagged-teamed all the women they're with, but that's dried up lately, and both seem to be overly involved in the mouse who now lives here. They'll be thoroughly disappointed when they find out she's not a tree worth climbing.

The girl's afraid of her own shadow; she's not about to sleep with two bikers.

"Yes, please," she says.

Sly rushes to do her bidding, pouring a pint glass full of juice and sliding it over to her on top of the bar.

"Thanks." She holds the glass with two hands as though it's too heavy and disappears back down the hall where her bedroom is. Sly watches her go with longing in his eyes.

"Is he into her?" Bexley whispers as she sits next to me and snags a doughnut covered in pink frosting and sprinkles.

"Dunno." I shrug, taking a bite of my second pastry.

"How much were you able to find out?" she calls out to the love-struck biker still staring down the hall, snapping him out of his trance.

"A lot, actually. How do you know this guy?" Sly strides back over to his laptop and taps some keys.

"He's someone from my past."

Sly glances nervously at her, piquing my interest.

"From what I can tell, he's a real piece of shit."

"He is," she agrees.

"Over the last ten years, he's had multiple domestic violence allegations, but his victims always changed their stories before official charges could be filed. He was living in upstate New York until two years ago," he says.

"And where now?" I dig my pack of smokes out of my pocket.

"Reno." Sly turns the laptop to face us, showing us a screen full of text. "He's running for district court judge in the next election."

"He's what?" Bexley gasps.

"He's currently a state magistrate judge. Surprised you haven't seen him around," Sly says.

"My clients typically commit federal crimes and aren't seen by state judges. If they go to court at all." The chair makes a scraping noise against the hardwood floors as she pushes back from the table. "I need to go."

"Who is this guy?" I ask.

"No one important. Thanks, Sly. Can you email me the full report, please?"

"Sure thing." He taps a few keys. "Done."

Bexley hightails it out the door, but my steps are much bigger than hers considering our size difference and the sky-high heels she's wearing.

"Wait up," I call out.

"I don't have time for this, Khan. I need to go." She opens her car door, but I shove it closed again.

"Not until you tell me what this is about."

Suddenly her shady behavior earlier makes sense. She's scared.

"If I tell you, will you let me go? I really do have a meeting to get to."

I cross a finger over my heart. "Promise."

"Martin Alexander is my asshole husband."

What the fuck?

Chapter
FIVE

Bexley

"Martin Alexander is my asshole husband," I say. I leave off the fact that he's technically still my husband, and the last time I saw him, he put me in the hospital.

"He's a judge?" Khan asks, squinting against the sunlight.

"He was back in New York, and apparently, he still is here in Reno."

"Why is he here, Bex?"

"I don't know. That's why I needed Sly's help." I teeter back on my heels. It's a dumb thing to do considering I have on stilettos, but I like the feeling of balancing on something so precarious. It's as close to danger as I get these days.

I guess not anymore since Martin's in town.

"What kind of asshole are we talking about?"

"The kind I felt the need to run away from. Now, if you'll kindly remove your paw from my car, I need to go." I pry his fingers off my car and bend them back until he winces and pulls away. He doesn't go far, though.

"He hurt you?" He brushes my cheek with the back of his hand, genuine concern in his eyes that only serves to piss me off.

I'm not the scared little girl I once was. I can take care of myself now. No broody biker necessary.

"That's private information."

"If this guy came here to hurt you, then you better get over yourself real quick. I can't help if I don't know the entire story."

"It doesn't matter what his intentions are because I won't be here to find out."

"What do you mean you won't be here?" His eyes narrow on me.

I dig a piece of paper out of my purse. "This is the phone number for Louis Montgomery. He's one of the few criminal defense attorneys I trust to take care of you. Call him."

I open my car door, but before I can get in, Khan slams it shut again.

"You aren't going anywhere," he growls and crumples the card before tossing it to the gravel. "And I'm not trusting my case to someone else."

"I promise Louis is good. Almost as good as me. You're in capable hands."

"Fuck Louis, and this has nothing to do with my case. You don't have to run from shit when you have an entire MC on your side."

I glance at my watch. Before coming here, I called an old client of mine, Nick. Two years ago, he was up against felony identity theft charges, and I got him off. He owes me, and I have an appointment with him in thirty minutes.

"Get out of my way, Wes. Now." I shove his solid chest, but he doesn't move an inch.

"Darlin', I swear to fuck if you don't get your ass inside so we can talk this out, I'll carry you in there myself."

We stare each other down, both of us unflinching. For as

stubborn as he is, I'm ten times worse. Before I have time to react, he makes good on his promise by squatting low and tossing me over his shoulder.

"Put me down. Now!" I kick and squirm, but even though I'm no waif, I'm no match for his size.

"Settle down." He swats my ass like I'm a goddamn child.

"Fuck you, Wes. Put me down."

He ignores my shouts and carts me into the house. I assume he'll set me down in the open space that serves as their bar, dining room, and entertaining area, but he marches right past there and continues down the hall.

Fucking hell.

I don't stop struggling, even kicking my efforts up a notch when he releases the hand on my ass holding me steady to fish for a set of keys in his pocket. But again, my efforts are wasted. He's too big and too strong. After getting the door unlocked and open, he kicks it closed behind us and tosses me on a bed.

I've never been past the front area of the enormous house, so my eyes immediately scan the room. It's small and disgustingly messy. Empty beer bottles and ashtrays full of stamped-out cigarettes litter every flat surface. I can't even see the floor under all the dirty clothes and trash.

"Please tell me this isn't your room." I turn my nose up and pretend to dry heave.

"Yeah, what's wrong with it?" He looks around, clearly not seeing what I do.

"You are a garbage human being, you know that?"

"Sorry I didn't have a chance to tidy up before I was arrested and taken to jail."

"The fact you spent even one night in here with it looking like this proves how repulsive you are." Something on the ground catches my eye, and I jump to my feet. "Is that a used condom?"

His eyes follow where I'm pointing, and he reaches down to grab it and toss it in the trash. "There. All better."

"Oh my God, if you don't let me out of here, I'm going to scream."

The fucker laughs, howling like I said the most ridiculous thing ever. I'm dumbfounded at what's so funny.

"Fuck, babe," he says, his hysterics dying and his expression losing all humor. "You think anyone out there is going to come running because some bitch is blubbering in my room?"

"You're a misogynistic asshole," I spit out, burning hot rage filling my blood.

I know this macho guy act is just that—an act—but the fact he would even say something like that makes me sick. I shove past him and open the door.

"Ah, Bex, don't go. I was joking. You know if the guys heard you scream, they'd kick my ass."

I flip around, standing in the hallway and folding my arms. "Do I know that? Because according to each of your arrest records, none of you are the most stand-up bunch of men I've ever met."

His face hardens. "Don't even joke about that shit. Our wrap sheets are full of violence, but not one of those charges has come from hurting a woman."

I almost feel bad for even suggesting it because he's right. The Royal Bastards are outlaws who break as many hearts as they do laws, but they'd never lay a hand on one who didn't literally ask for it.

"Listen very closely. I don't need any of you to handle my shit. I'm a big girl and have been taking care of myself for a very long time. This thing I have going on? It doesn't concern you."

"I heard you out, so now you listen to me. If you had your shit handled"—he makes air quotes around handled—"then you wouldn't have to run. No one should let anyone have that much control over their life."

Shit. He's right. But when the man you trusted enough to marry chooses violence *and* is a well-respected judge, leaving was my only option.

"I don't trust you," I admit.

He closes the distance between us and tucks a strand of hair behind my ear. "I know, darlin', but you have to trust someone. I'm asking for that someone to be me."

How in the hell did I go from wanting to kick his teeth in to considering his offer? I must be stupid.

"Come on, Bex. Tell me the whole situation, start to finish, and I'll come up with a solution. You don't like my offer, I won't stop you from leaving. You like my offer, you stick around. Yeah?"

I sigh and close my eyes, mulling it over. I don't want to skip town. I've made a life for myself here. I may not have friends, but I have my blood, sweat, and tears in my law office. I worked hard for it, and I don't want to give it up.

"Fine. I'll hear you out. But not inside your bedroom. There aren't enough vaccinations in the world to keep me from contracting something in there."

"Fair enough. Come on." He breezes past me, his heavy boots pounding down the old wooden floors.

I follow, still unsure if I should waste time explaining everything to him. But if it'll save my business and keep me in town, it's worth a try.

He leads me down the stairs and into the basement that's currently under construction. Drywall dust, screws, nails, and tools litter the floor. I carefully step around them, not wanting to ruin my eight-hundred-dollar shoes. Khan walks over to a piece of furniture covered in plastic and yanks it off, revealing an ugly futon. He plops down on it and pats the space next to him.

"I can't sit on that. It'll ruin my clothes."

"Miss Priss, get your stubborn ass over here and sit down." He brushes off the fabric, sending dust floating in the air. "There."

I perch myself on the very edge—limiting the amount I have to actually touch the nasty thing—and cross my legs. When I turn to Khan, I notice his eyes are fixated on my thighs where the fabric has ridden up.

"Eyes up here," I say.

"Darlin', I know I've made it obvious to you, but goddamn, you are one fine lookin' woman."

"I didn't come down here to be sexually harassed. Do you want to talk, or can I go?"

"I'm not harassing you. I'm appreciating your form."

"Whatever you have to tell yourself."

"Fine. So, what's up with this Martin asshole?"

I debate how much to tell him but ultimately decide on the whole truth. I have nothing to lose.

"I met Martin when I was in college. He was a visiting professor for my political law class. He was older, mature, and fascinating."

Khan makes a *pft* sound. "If you're into the boring professional types."

"Well, I was. We hid our relationship for the first three months, but when my professor returned, and Martin was no longer my teacher, we started dating out in public. I fell fast and hard. He showered me with gifts, took me on trips, and was nothing but a gentleman. He proposed on our six-month anniversary, and I said yes."

"Sounds like a fairytale."

A small smile creeps across my lips because I still have some good memories, no matter how things ended up.

"It was. But then we got married, and I moved into his Manhattan condo, and slowly things changed. He no longer wanted me to go out with my friends, and when I convinced him to let me, he picked my outfits. His control over me was a slow-moving virus. I didn't realize how sick we were until it was too late." My nose stings, but I hold back the tears. "The only thing he did approve of was going to law school."

"What happened after that?"

"He began asserting his control over me in *different* ways," I say.

"Like how, Bex?" he growls.

"Why does it matter? All you need to know is it got bad. Bad enough for me to find someone who could give me a new identity, and then I ran. First to Vegas, then here."

"It matters because I need to know."

"He used his physical advantage to keep me in line."

Wes growls, actually growls.

"Your real name isn't Bexley?" He pulls a pack of smokes from the inside of his cut and lights up.

"It's not."

"And he found you anyway?"

"Seems like it," I say, waving at the layer of smoke settling above my head from there being no ventilation in this room.

"Must have some powerful pussy if he hasn't forgotten you all these years."

"And one other reason," I say hesitantly.

"What's that?"

"When I left, I stole a sizeable amount of cash to set me up in my new life. He was dirty and accepted cash bribes for more lenient sentences. He kept all of it in a safe in his office. There was almost three million in there. Do you have any idea what three million dollars in cash looks like?"

"Can't say I do." He lets his spent cigarette fall to the concrete ground and stomps it out with his boot.

"Bricks and bricks of hundreds, just sitting there. I didn't know how much I would need." My eyes must've been saucers when I finally cracked the code on his safe. It took weeks of testing new combinations before I finally typed in the right one."

"How much did you take?"

"Like I said, I had no idea how—"

"How much, Bex?"

"All of it. I took it all. With that amount of money, I thought I could buy the best identity, make it so no one from the past could find me. Not even my friends or what little family I had."

"You stole a few mil from this guy? No wonder he's spent a decade tracking you down. Gotta be honest, I've killed people for less."

My shoulders slump, and I wrap my arms around myself. Khan, seeing my reaction, reaches around my back to bring me to his side, but I jump to my feet, not wanting to be touched.

"Now you know why I have to run. I have money saved and"—I pace the floor, my heels clacking—"I won't be stupid and stay in the country this time. And I'll keep moving from place to place."

"You can't keep running. You'll run out of money eventually, and then what?"

"I don't know. I'll figure it out."

"What if you paid him back?" he asks, casually resting his ankle on his knee as though we're discussing the weather.

"He's not after just the money. I embarrassed him. His perfect little wife left him and took his money. I know him. He wants me, and he wants revenge."

"I'll take him out. I've done jobs like that before." He shrugs.

My steps falter, and the hand that was running through my hair freezes in place. "I'm going to pretend you didn't admit that to me."

"You already know we aren't Boy Scouts. If we were, we wouldn't need you."

"We have an arrangement. You tell me only as much as I need to protect you."

"Attorney-client privilege, baby."

"That doesn't mean I want to know about it. *And* that only counts for crimes committed, not future crimes like talking about killing my ex."

"I'm pretty sure you wouldn't tell anyone if you hired us to kill your ex." He tips his head to the side.

"No one is killing anyone. I uphold the law, not violate it."

"We can talk in code if it makes you feel better." A sly smile breaks across his face, and he leans forward. "Do you want us to take out the trash? We've taken out lots of trash before and are really good at it."

I roll my eyes. "That doesn't make it better."

He stands to his full height, which is well over a foot taller than I am. I'm sure he's intimidating to a lot of people, but I know him too well.

"Listen, don't run yet. You can stay here at the clubhouse in my old room, and I can put a prospect on you. Meanwhile, Sly can do more digging, and we'll see if we can bury this guy the legal way. If he was taking bribes before, he's probably still doing shady shit."

Although the idea has a certain amount of appeal because I really don't want to leave this life behind, I can't imagine staying in this bad boy frat house.

"I don't want to live here, and your room is disgusting."

"I'll have Sissy clean it."

Sissy and another girl, Tabitha, live at the clubhouse with the guys. From what I gather, they cook, clean, and take care of *other* needs the guys have. I couldn't do it, but they are here on their own accord and seem happy, so who am I to judge?

"Don't be an asshole. You're a grown-ass man who is perfectly capable of cleaning up after himself."

"But I don't want to."

"What is my life right now?" I ask nobody, my hand going to my forehead. "Sad thing is, I was getting comfortable in my life. I wasn't constantly looking over my shoulder. I felt safe. Now look at me. I'm a scared mouse moving in with a biker gang to protect myself."

What's worse is I know I have no other choice. I have to do this. An image of my broken body flashes through my mind. Martin had taken me to a gala, and while he was off schmoozing, a man approached me. The conversation was benign, and I made sure to let him know who I was married to.

It didn't matter. Martin saw, and the second we got into the car, the abuse began. I wish I could say I left after that. But I didn't.

Noticing my sudden switch in mood, Khan softens his reply. "It'll be okay. Swear it. I'll clean this place up, and you'll be safe while we figure this shit out."

"I'm scared," I admit.

"I know, darlin.'" The arm he wraps around my shoulder feels like a security blanket I want to wrap myself in.

I duck out of his hold and clear my throat. "Fine. I'll move in. But you have to clean this place up all by yourself."

He holds out his hand, grin fixed firmly in place. "Deal."

Reluctantly, I place my much smaller hand in his. His skin is chaffed and rough, making me wonder how it would feel against the softest parts of me.

Fucking hell.

"Deal," I say.

Chapter SIX

Khan

I grab some trash bags from the pantry in the kitchen and make my way to my room. After not having spent much time here lately, it feels weird stepping back into the life of the Vice President of the Royal Bastards. Other than Church yesterday, I've been absent from all club business and all the perks.

My dick has had no attention in a long fucking time. I could've had Sissy or Tabs give me a blow job last night—Lord knows they offered—but after Bex stormed off, I couldn't get my head in the game.

This bitch is messing with my mojo. Proven by the fact I'm cleaning my fucking room.

After being inside Loki's nice house and in a room that smells good and doesn't have shit all over the place, I see what Bex was bitching about. Before now, I didn't give a shit. The girls I fucked didn't give a shit either. They gladly climbed on the dirty blankets and spread their legs for me, and I was too lazy to care.

I didn't care about a lot of shit until I got arrested. It was a quick reminder of how quickly my life could be over. If I died today, I'd be disappointed in my life. I've done nothing meaningful.

"Get to it," Bex orders from where she's perched in the doorway.

"You gonna stand there and watch me?"

"Sure am." Her satisfied smile annoys me. Somehow, I think she's getting the better end of the deal.

I don't know why I was adamant about her staying in town. I mean, I like the girl, but there are plenty of girls out there. Why should I care about her?

That's not true.

It's just the constant rejection talking. But my ego can take the hits until I wear her down. She's worth it.

No other girl makes me feel anything other than horny. Not that Bex's banging body doesn't make my dick hard because it definitely does. But it's her attitude that turns me on in a way I've never experienced before.

It's easy to find a chick who'll let me bang her into a mattress; it's harder to find a chick who'll argue with me and stand up for herself.

It's fucking hot.

I walk around the room and dump ashtrays, gather bottles and cans and everything else I don't want to keep, and put it all in the trash bag. It fills up quickly before I move onto the next bag. After the trash, I gather dirty clothes into a hamper and set it outside my room.

"Why are you putting it there?" Bex asks.

"Because that's how Tabs knows it needs to be washed."

She shakes her head. "Uh-uh. Nope. You're doing your own laundry too."

"I don't know how to do laundry," I admit.

"Time to learn, big boy. I'll make a self-sufficient man out of you if it's the last thing I do." She heads down the hall, waving for me to follow.

Picking up the basket, I trudge after her, rethinking our arrangement. Throwing some trash away is one thing. Laundry is a whole other.

"This is a washing machine." She points to one of the appliances in the laundry room.

Our clubhouse was an old brothel house in the 1920s when Reno had a red-light district, and the layout reflects that: one large area where men would enter, have a drink and pick their girl, a bunch of smaller bedrooms where the girls stayed and fucked their clients, and two bigger areas to accommodate a kitchen and laundry room.

"I know what a washing machine is," I say.

"That makes you not doing your own laundry worse. Separate your clothes into colors. Whites, dark, and colored items all need their own load."

"Not going to happen, darlin'." That will take all damn day, so I open the lid and dump everything in, whites and darks alike.

"Fine, but when all the wife beaters you seem to love so much come out dingy, don't come crying to me. Dump a scoop of this in." She hands me a plastic cup full of detergent. "Now turn the dial to extra heavy and hot to kill all the germs swimming around on your nasty drawers."

"I wear clean underwear, Bex. I'm not gross."

"Your room says otherwise. Now close the lid and hit start."

I do as she says, instantly hearing a rush of water fill the drum.

I'll admit I'm spoiled. There are privileges that come from being a good-looking, charming giant of a man. One of those is getting chicks to do shit for me. From the time I left home until now, there's always been someone around to do my bidding. That's why it surprises me I'm proud I did it on my own.

I don't get praise from Bex, though. Instead, she hightails it out of there to no doubt boss me around more back in my bedroom.

"Do you keep extra bedding around here?" she asks.

"In the hallway closet."

"I wasn't asking so I could do it for you. I was insinuating you to do it yourself."

Like a petulant child, I stomp down the hall and find some black sheets and a black checkered comforter from the closet. I unfold the fitted sheet back in the room and hold it up, trying to make sense about which corner goes where and eliciting a condescending laugh from Bexley.

"Tell you what, I'll make your bed, and you can take these disinfectant wipes and wipe down"—she motions around the entire room—"everything."

She pulls open the curtains and cracks a window, then gets started on making the bed. Before now, I would've just tossed the flat sheet and blanket down and called it good, but she takes the time to put the fitted sheet on and tuck everything in.

Not realizing it, I stand there and watch her, impressed she can maneuver around so easily in that skirt and those heels.

"I don't see any disinfecting happening," she says, bent over the bed, folding the top part of the sheet over the comforter.

"Right."

I must use a thousand of those wipes going over every surface until she deems the space sterile. After running a mop over the wooden floors, I'm finally finished.

"Is this fit for a princess or what?" I ask, draping an arm over her shoulders.

She slides out of my hold and says, "It'll do."

I laugh because what else can I do? Hours of hard work for a passable response.

"Why don't you go back to your apartment and get your stuff while I talk to Loki about your new living arrangements?"

"Oh, okay." The fearful expression from earlier returns. I can't stand to see this side of her.

"Duncan'll go with you. You'll be safe with him."

Duncan's technically a prospect, but only because we haven't had a chance to patch him in. After all the shit that went down with Roch, and then I was arrested, it was decided to not patch anyone in until I was out. Now that I'm a free man, it's only a matter of time. All three of our current prospects, Duncan, Ford, and Miles, have more than proven themselves.

"You can't come?" she asks hopefully.

Hearing the vulnerability in her tone makes today worth all the work. She wants me to protect her, not the club.

"Wish I could, darlin.'" I hold up my ankle.

"Right. I forgot about that."

"I'm a phone call away. Something bad happens, I'll gladly go back to jail if it keeps you safe."

"Don't be an idiot. You hate jail." Her self-confidence returns, and she pushes me out of the way and struts out of the room.

There's my girl.

I trail behind her, spotting Duncan and Miles at the bar. "Duncan, can you take Bexley to her apartment so she can collect a few things? She's moving in for a bit."

"Sure, brother." He turns to Bex. "Bike or van?"

"Van," I say, not waiting for her response.

If she's going to be on the back of anyone's bike, it'll be mine. Just thinking about her pressed against the kid on his bike makes my blood boil.

"Probably better anyway. I don't travel light." Bexley walks out the front door.

Duncan's brows raise. "She's a feisty one."

"She's gotten herself into some bad shit with a bad dude. Don't let her out of your sight and make sure you clear every room in that apartment before she even steps foot in it, you hear me?" I narrow my eyes on him. "Anything bad happens to that woman, it's your ass."

"Got it." He pulls his piece from the holster, checks how many rounds he has loaded, then tucks it away.

Watching them pull out of the parking lot has me feeling pathetic. I can't protect her. I can't even go to the grocery store. I'm allowed at the clubhouse during the day only because it's considered a job site, and in less than four hours, I have to be back at Loki's house.

I head inside and look for Loki, who I find in the Chapel, pouring over a stack of papers.

"You got a minute."

"For you, brother? Always." He pushes the papers to the side and leans back in his chair, placing a cig between his lips. I join him, lighting my own smoke.

"Bexley's married." The words are bitter on my tongue. If she's going to be married to anyone, it should be me.

"No shit?"

"No shit. Over a decade ago, she ran from the abusive motherfucker and took three mil in cash from him."

Loki whistles. "Not chump change."

"Nope. And he found her even though she changed her identity and has been cautious."

"Damn. What's she going to do?" he asks, blowing out a lungful of smoke.

I know Loki would do anything for me, no matter the reason, but I still lie about my reason for wanting to keep her close.

"I offered her my room for now. I need her to get these charges dropped, but that won't happen if she's clear across the continent in hiding. I didn't mean to do it without asking, but—"

"It's not a problem. I'll tell the guys to cool it with the parties and patch pussy."

"That won't make them happy," I say.

"Goblin doesn't notice anyone without a college education because he wants a decent conversation after they fuck, Roch and I are off the market, and Sly and Moto are caught up with Petra for some reason. I don't think anyone will mind."

"Truth."

It's only hitting me now how much the dynamics around here are changing.

"Who is this guy? Anyone we need to worry about?" he asks.

"Maybe, maybe not. He's a judge from New York City who moved here and is running for district judge."

He whistles again. "We better keep it quiet we're protecting her. We have enough heat from the law right now."

"Nuff said."

He gives me a knowing look. "You realize you aren't trying to keep her around only for her profession, right?"

"What do you mean?" Am I that transparent?

"What do I mean? I mean, you've been following her around like a lovesick biker since you patched in."

"She's hot." I shrug.

"No, that's not it. I've seen how you are with other women. It's not like how you are with her. She treats you like gum on the bottom of her shoe she can't scrape off, and still, you don't relent."

"Did you grow a vagina the second you put a ring on Birdie?" I scoff.

Loki chuckles. "Big, bad Khan's in love."

"I'm not in love, asshole. Yeah, I want to fuck her, but that's where it ends. I'm not the settling down type like you pussies." Lies. All lies. If I could convince Bex to marry me tomorrow, I would. And we haven't even fucked.

"Say what you want, that woman has a hold on you."

"If we're done swapping tampon tales, I got shit to do." I stand up and walk out, listening to Loki laugh all the way to the bar.

"How's it going, baby?" Sissy asks, setting up some cold cuts and hoagies for lunch.

"Fine. How are you?"

"Can't complain. Are you hungry? You haven't gotten your appetite back since getting out." She sets mustard and mayo out on the bar too.

"I could eat." I take a roll, stuffing it full of meat and slathering it with mustard.

"Your appetite for other things hasn't returned either." She licks her bottom lip suggestively.

"Been busy and having to leave every night for the middle of fucking nowhere doesn't help either." I take a big bite of the sandwich.

"I saw you cleaned your room. Do you want to go mess it all up with me?"

I carefully consider my next words. The last thing I need is Tabitha or Sissy to be pissed at me, but they should know where I stand. We've used each other for sex over the years, but that shit has ended.

"That's not going to happen anymore. I got Bex now."

She smiles, showing no signs of hurt. Thank fuck.

"Things are going well between you two, then?" she asks.

"No." I laugh. "But they will be."

"No one can resist you for too long." She squishes my cheeks between her fingers.

I brush her away, laughing. Truth is, they've become family over the years.

We found Tabitha in a fucking politician's closet after we killed him. She was eighteen, malnourished, and had been abused for years. We tried to put her back with her folks, but she didn't want anything to do with it. She begged to stay with us, and we let her.

Sissy was a waitress at a bar we used to hang out in. One day, after getting shit-faced at her bar, we invited her to the clubhouse. She never left, and we never asked her to. She made herself invaluable to us by becoming a house mother or some shit.

No one was thinking about sex back then, but eventually, when you put two beautiful women in a house full of men, it's bound to happen. Though none of us would give a shit if they didn't want to.

"Will you tell her that? Because she doesn't seem to be falling for my charms," I say.

"That woman looks like she's been battling the world her whole life. Give her time."

"Or she needs to be bent over and spanked," I say.

"I'd like to see you try." She laughs and disappears into the kitchen.

I finish off my sandwich and am about to go downstairs when my burner rings. I pull it out of my pocket and answer.

"Yeah."

"Gotta problem, Khan. Bexley's place has been tossed," Duncan says.

Shit.

Chapter
SEVEN

Bexley

I stick my key in the front door of my apartment and push to turn it, but the door opens like it wasn't even latched, let alone locked.

Fucking hell.

"Wait. Let me check it out." Duncan squeezes past me, gun drawn. "I mean it. Don't come in until I tell you it's clear."

I nod, fright freezing me in place. I couldn't go inside if I wanted to. Through the open door, I can see shit everywhere. My furniture is toppled over and cut open, glass from vases and framed art is covering my wood floors, and there's a red "Ur dead bitch" spray-painted across one wall.

I lift my hand to my mouth to hold in the shriek threatening to release. I wait for what feels like an hour for Duncan to tell me it's clear, the whole time wondering what I would do if there was someone in there.

I have no weapons, and I don't know how to defend myself. I'm pathetic, relying on a man to keep me safe. Something I swore I'd never do. Yet did I take self-defense classes once I settled in Reno? No. I got complacent, convinced my new identity would keep the Boogie Man away.

I was wrong.

"It's clear, Bex. You can come in, though you might not want to see what's been done to the place," Duncan calls out from somewhere deep in the apartment.

I listen as Duncan calls Khan to tell him the situation. I know it's Khan because his deep booming voice can be heard from clear out in the hall.

I stare at the threshold for long seconds, willing myself to move, but my uncooperative feet won't allow me to.

"Bex? You okay?" Duncan pops his head out the door, startling me. "Whoa, whoa. It's okay. It's me. You're safe."

"Am I?" Stupid tears well in my eyes.

"Why don't you tell me what you need, and I'll grab it for you?"

I clear my throat, swallowing the emotion down. "No, thank you. I can do this."

I step one foot in front of the other until I'm in my open concept kitchen, dining room, and living room. It's unrecognizable. Fluff from the furniture is littered all over everything; no piece of furniture has been left untouched.

My glass coffee table is in shattered pieces, crunching under my feet as I step further into the space.

I feel violated. It makes my skin crawl to think about people in my personal space. Nothing in here was especially sentimental, but it was mine. Things I worked for and picked out myself. And now it's all gone.

"I think they were looking for something," Duncan says, kicking a chair out of the way.

"I think you're right."

Of course, he's right. Martin wants his money. I don't blame him. If someone stole that kind of money from me, I'd move heaven and hell to get it back. But he doesn't deserve it. He owed it to me after everything he put me through, everything he took from me.

"The blood was a nice touch." Moving to my bedroom, Duncan drags a leather-gloved finger over more writing that says, 'U know what you did.'

"Blood?" I croak.

He touches his finger to the tip of his tongue. "Pig blood, maybe?"

"You licked it," I say, dumbfounded.

He shrugs, so nonchalant. Like he tastes blood every day. Maybe he does.

After looking around, I walk into my closet to pack some clothes, but I realize that's not possible.

"Let's go," I say, walking out of my room.

"What about your stuff?"

"There's nothing worth saving."

"Well, shit," he says after assessing the situation for himself. "They slashed everything. What about toiletries and crap?"

He steps into the en suite but returns seconds later.

"Trashed?" I ask.

"Yep." He smiles sadly. "Does this mean shopping?"

"Not really in the mood, but can we swing by a drugstore so I can pick up a toothbrush?"

"We've got all that shit at the clubhouse. Sissy and Tabs can probably loan you some clothes too."

"Thanks."

The drive home is somber, unlike the ride over where Duncan blasted hard rock, banging his head to the beat. Now the van is silent, save for the road noise.

From my periphery, I catch Duncan glancing over at me every few seconds.

"I think you're in shock, babe. You look a little green."

I turn and look out the window. I am in shock. I can't believe this is all happening so fast. Yesterday I was Bexley March, badass attorney. Now I'm back to being Sienna Ryan, frightened victim. I hated that woman. She was weak and pitiful. She put up with way too much without fighting back.

"You have questions. I can practically hear them stirring around in your head. Go ahead and ask," I say.

"Who's after you?"

"My husband."

"You're married?"

"Yes. I stole some money from him and ran," I say, then amend, "A lot of money."

"You think he's come to collect?"

"Yes."

"Now I see why you're moving in. But don't worry, we've got your back. Khan won't let anything bad happen to you."

I turn to face him, studying the kid. He has the youthful look of someone in their early twenties, and if you stripped away the leather and grease-stained jeans, he could pass for a college student.

I wonder what his story is, but my mind is chaotic enough right now. I don't need someone else's trauma floating around in there. But I make a mental note to ask him when things settle down.

Duncan parks in the gravel lot outside the clubhouse, and before I can even open the door, Khan is there.

"I'm so sorry, darlin'. You okay?"

I nod even though okay is not even close to being accurate.

"Come on. Let's get you inside."

For once, I let him hold my hand and pull me inside. I'm too tired to fight. Cleaning Khan's room and then seeing the destruction in my apartment has left me exhausted.

He leads me to his room and sits me down on the bed. It

smells good in here, and I realize he lit a candle while I was out. Jasmine and iris, if I were to guess. Floral and feminine.

"It's all gone. Everything. They took a knife to my Tempur-Pedic mattress, slashed my clothes, wrote in blood on my walls, and destroyed my furniture."

"I sent Duncan and Roch to clean it up and get it out of there," he says.

"What about the police? They'll want to dust for fingerprints or something, right?"

"Do you think it's a good idea to call the cops?" he asks skeptically. "Because yeah, what he did was illegal, but so is buying a new identity and stealing three million dollars. You have no idea if he cleaned that money and covered his trail. You'd be incriminating yourself as much as him. Plus, we have no idea who he's paid off."

I rub a hand over my forehead. "You're right. I don't know what to do. This is only the beginning, Khan. You don't know him. He gets his mind set on something and doesn't give up."

"I know the kind. Loki's cool with you staying as long as you need, and Sly's already gotten to work finding out more about him. We got your back, Bex."

"Can you teach me how to defend myself?" I lift my gaze to his.

"Would that make you feel better?"

"Yes. It would."

"Then, yeah. I can teach you vulnerable areas to attack if you ever need it."

"Thanks."

"Gotta ask you a question. Where's the money?" he asks hesitantly.

"Somewhere safe. I'm not an idiot. It's not in my apartment or at the office."

My money is in a safe deposit box at the Grand Sierra

Resort Hotel and Casino downtown. Their security is top of the line since it's the high rollers who ask for a box. No one is getting my money.

"That's good. Smart."

My phone buzzes in my handbag, and glancing at the screen, I see it's Marcy.

"Hello," I answer.

"Hey, boss. Are you coming in today?" she chirps.

"No. Sorry I didn't call. It's been a busy day."

"There are two men here to see you. They don't have an appointment, which I told them they needed, but they're insisting." Her voice turns to a whisper. "I think they're cops."

Fucking hell.

"I'll be right there." I hang up and stand.

"You can't leave, Bex. Not right now."

"My secretary said there are cops at the office."

He jumps to his feet and blocks my path. "Whoa. I can't let you go without backup. Who knows who they really are?"

"Then come with me. You're allowed to go to my office."

"Send a Royal Bastard, who's on work release, with you to meet the cops?" he asks in a tone that suggests I'm an idiot.

And I am because he's right. That's a stupid idea. Plus, if Martin is behind this, seeing a Royal Bastard will clue him in on where exactly I am.

"Goddamn it," I curse. "I don't know what to do."

"Call her back. Tell her to let them know if they want to talk to you, they need to schedule an appointment. Tell her to get their business cards so we can figure out who they are."

I stare at my phone, my finger hovering over the call button.

"Look at me, Bex," Khan demands, tipping my chin up with a thick finger. "You got this. Have them make an appointment, tell her to get their cards. You got this."

We lock gazes, and for the first time, I'm thankful for this

Neanderthal of a man. I'm sure this feeling will dissipate the next time he opens his mouth, but for now, I appreciate his assertiveness and authority.

I hit the call button and bring the phone to my ear.

"March Law Offices, Bexley March's office. How may I direct your call?"

"Marcy, I got caught up," I say in the most casual tone I can muster. "Can you please get their business cards and ask them to make an appointment?"

"Um, suuurrreee," she drags out.

"Remember to get their business cards. It's important."

"Are you in trouble?" she whispers.

"No," I blurt out. "Not at all."

"Okay."

"Thank you, Marcy. Let me know how it goes."

"You're welcome. I'll text you."

She hangs up, and Khan and I retake our seats on the bed. We both stare at the phone, waiting to see what happened.

A minute later, a text comes through.

Marcy: They wouldn't leave cards or make an appointment. They said they'll catch up with you some other time.

Me: Thanks for trying.

I tuck my phone away. "What does that mean?"

"It means they ain't cops," Khan says.

Chapter EIGHT

Khan

"Then who are they?" she asks.

"Probably hired men."

This Martin guy has most likely been planning this for years. He laid dormant, waiting to get his ducks in a row, and now that they are, he's attacking from all angles. But he wasn't expecting me or the club, and that gives us the advantage.

Bex looks wiped out. This is just another day for me, but she's not accustomed to the chaos.

"Why don't you lie down for a bit?" I suggest.

"I guess I can for a little. My head is pounding. I can't think straight."

I see the war going on behind her eyes. She's not used to the violence, but she's also not used to sitting back and letting someone else deal with her problems. She's a control freak of the likes I've never seen. This must be hard on her.

I stand and pull back the bedding, making a pocket for her to crawl into. Then I notice she's still in her uncomfortable work clothes. That won't do.

I walk over to my drawer and find a clean pair of sweatpants and a T-shirt that will swim on her but is all I have to offer. I set them on the bed and walk over to the door.

"I'm going to get you something to eat, a glass of water, and a pain pill for your head. Change and get in bed while I'm gone."

Her small nostrils flare, and I see the argument on the tip of her tongue, but she lets it go and nods.

I close the door on my way out, and seconds later, I hear the click of the lock. Good girl.

"How is she?" Duncan asks. He's sitting at the bar, sipping on a beer and no doubt gossiping with Miles, who's behind the bar.

"She'll be fine." I pull a smoke from my cut and light up. "Miles, can you grab me a sandwich or something and a glass of water?"

"Sure." He disappears into the kitchen.

I take a hefty drag of my cig, letting the smoke burn my throat and lungs on the way down. The nicotine is a balm on my frayed nerves. Every second Bex was in that apartment was torture. I want to be there for her, show her I can take care of her, even if she doesn't think she needs it, but it's impossible with this motherfucking monitor on my ankle.

"I took some pictures of her place," Duncan says, handing me his phone.

I flip through the evidence of the raid on her apartment, growing more and more pissed off with each swipe of the screen.

"The threats left in blood on the wall were a nice touch, real original," I bite out. Things like 'die, bitch' and 'cunt' are painted on every wall.

"Right? Whoever it was has been watching too many movies."

"Other than that, did it seem professional?"

"Nah. If it were, they would've made it look like no one had been there. They didn't need to destroy everything to figure out the money wasn't there."

My brows arch. "She told you?"

"A little. Not everything, I'm sure."

"You're right. These guys wanted to send a message."

"It worked. She's spooked."

Miles walks out holding a tray with a hoagie and a glass of ice water. "Here you go."

"Thanks, man." I take the tray and make a pit stop in the bathroom, where we keep bottles of aspirin. I dump two tablets on the tray and knock on my bedroom door.

Seconds later, the door opens. Seeing Bex in my oversized clothes nearly brings me to my knees. If I thought she was sexy in skirts and heels, it was nothing compared to this.

She props herself against the headboard and covers her legs with the quilt. Wordlessly, I set the tray down on her lap, hand her the white tablets, and watch as she swallows them down.

"Thank you."

"No problem. I'll be right outside, okay?"

"You can stay," she says. "I mean, I don't want to kick you out of your own room."

I'm not one to look a gift horse in the mouth, so I shrug and barrel over her, making myself comfortable on her side.

"Eat something. Your stomach will thank you when those pills kick in." I nod at the sandwich.

"Did you make it?" She lifts it up and sniffs it.

"Miles did."

She takes a small bite, testing it out for what, I don't know. Does she think we'd poison her? I take the sandwich from her hand and tear half of it off with my teeth before chewing.

"Turkey, cheese, mustard. Delicious," I say, offering it back to her, but she pushes it away.

"I don't share food."

"I'm not a stranger off the street."

"Doesn't matter."

"You're aggravating."

"So I've been told." She picks up the second half of the sandwich, her bite big enough to get the meat and cheese, then she wiggles. "This is good."

The healthy appetite I remember from our taco shop meal reappears. She devours the sandwich in less than a minute, licking mustard off her finger when she's done.

She guzzles the rest of the water and sets the tray off to the side of the bed. Her eyelids are heavy, and I can tell it won't take her long to fall asleep.

Scooting down the bed and turning on her side, she faces away from me and pulls the covers over her shoulder.

It's late afternoon, but I'm not sleepy in the least. Matter of fact, I've gotten the best sleep of my life since moving into Loki's house. And now, I'm happier than a fucking clam lying here next to her.

I wish I could see her beautiful face so I could watch her sleep, but I know that's something she won't give me willingly. Just being unconscious around me is a huge concession on her part, so I'll be patient and wait until she realizes I'm not going anywhere.

An hour later, I'm crushing candy on my phone when she bolts upright, sucking in a sharp breath.

"Hey, hey. It's okay." I toss my cell to the mattress and sit up, rubbing circles on her back.

Where there's skin and bones on other girls I've touched, Bex is soft. I can't remember why I bothered with such breakable women before now. Was it to feed my masculine need to dominate? Or to make me feel more powerful? It doesn't matter what the reason was. All I want now is to suffocate under the pressure of her thighs as I eat her out.

"What time is it?" Her voice is dry and raspy.

I need to get the fuck out of this bed before I'm forced to suffer another ego-crushing rejection.

"Dinner time. You hungry?" I climb off the mattress and grab my pack of smokes off the dresser.

"I could eat." She stands and looks down at herself. "I'll change and be right out."

"You don't gotta do that. You live here now."

She straightens and meets my gaze. "I'm only staying here until I find out what Martin is after. This isn't my home."

I crowd her space, forcing her to step backward until her calves meet the side of the bed. "I get it. Boundaries are important to you. But you spend so much time pushing people away, I doubt you even remember why."

"I do remember," she says. "The last person I let in spent his days putting men in prison for the same things he was doing to me at night. You must know I wouldn't be here if my life wasn't on the line. You're a decent man, Wes, but this fantasy in your head about us? It's not going to happen. If you'll excuse me, I need to change."

She shoves past me and throws the door open, arms folded over her chest as she waits for me to leave. She's a tough bitch, I'll give her that. But the only person she's fooling is herself.

I hold my head high, not giving her a hint of reaction, and leave the room.

As I near the main living space, I get a whiff of whatever the girls are making for dinner. Quick glance at the time tells me I have an hour and a half before I need to be back at Loki's house. Dinner better be ready before then; I'm starved.

To my left, Roch and Truly play a game of darts. Roch is

pressed into her back, showing her how to aim. Karen peeks out from under his hood and licks Truly's cheek. Thinking it was Roch doing the licking, she whips around and instead comes face to face with the tiny chihuahua.

"My sweet girl," Truly gushes, kissing the dog's nose.

Roch tucks Karen back into his hood and kisses his girl with so much passion, it has me lowering my eyes and wishing I had someone who cared that deeply about me.

When did this become something I want? Is this some biological bullshit or what?

The worst part is I can't even pick up some random chick and get my rocks off because I'm so infatuated with the bitchy lawyer in my bedroom, no one else will do.

"Khan," Loki calls from behind me, poking his head out from the Chapel. "Come here a minute."

I give him a chin lift and head that way.

"S'up, brother?" I ask.

"Shut the door and take a seat," Loki says. Next to him is Sly, laptop open.

Loki rarely pulls the Prez card and orders me around, so I know it must be serious. I do as he says, lighting up a smoke the second my ass hits the chair.

"I spoke with Sly about the security footage from the construction company. In my head, it was as easy as breaking into the evidence locker and swiping it, but that's not how things work anymore. It's all stored on some highly secure cloud, whatever the fuck that means."

Sly huffs, pinching the bridge of his nose. "Digital evidence is stored in two places. They pay for cloud-based storage, and then they have on-site digital storage."

"That's good, right? You're a hacker," I say, the first ounce of relief hitting my system.

Sly embodies his road name. He's sneaky and cunning. He's

currently on the FBI's Most Wanted List for hacking into government systems and wreaking havoc with a pseudonym they still haven't cracked. He was a prodigy as a child, focusing on computers and electronics. Now that he's an adult, he uses his genius for hacking and explosives. Nothing rattles this guy, but my dismissal of the severity of this situation does for some reason.

He shakes his head, eyes widening. "This is different. These off-site storage facilities are fortresses. I can't just sneak in."

"You're saying it can't be done?" The solace I was feeling seconds ago has vanished.

"Fuck no. That's not what I'm saying. I could do it right now if I wanted."

"Then what?"

Loki intervenes. "He's saying there's a good chance we'll be trading a prison sentence for you for a prison sentence for him, and his would be a lot longer than yours."

"Shit." I take a long drag of my cig, not even exhaling all the way before taking more smoke into my lungs.

"I need more time," Sly says. "I can figure it out. I just need more time."

"Six months isn't enough?" I ask.

"Maybe. But if Bex has a better idea, I'd feel better going that route." Sly shuts his laptop and stands. "Does she?"

"I don't know. We got sidetracked with all the shit her ex is throwing at her."

"Talk to her," Loki says. "This needs to be a top priority."

I stamp out my smoke in the overflowing ashtray. "You don't think I know that? But the bitch won't be much good to any of us if she's dead."

A gasp comes from behind me, and I look over my shoulder to see Bex's wide eyes in the barely open door. I didn't even hear her open it. Then she's gone.

"Shit." I don't bother with goodbyes as I jump to my feet and give chase. "Bex, wait. You didn't hear the entire conversation."

"Don't worry about it. We both knew this was a bad idea. I'll figure out something else," she calls out without a backward glance.

I catch up to her in my room, where I find her collecting her purse and briefcase. "I didn't mean that how it sounded."

"Really? Because to me, it sounded like you were playing me. Making me think you honestly care for me when really all you need is to keep me alive long enough to get you off on your charges." She hefts her bags onto her shoulder. "How about this instead? I'll keep my own damn self alive, and you can take your chances with a public defender. They have a heavier caseload and care about their clients less, but you'll make it work."

"Knock it the fuck off." I fold my arms and widen my stance. "You're acting like a brat. You know that's not what I meant."

"I don't give a shit what you meant, Wes." Her free hand lifts to her forehead. "I ignored my instincts, and this is what I get."

Jesus Christ, the drama with this chick. It's exhausting.

"What are you even talking about? You came in on the tail end of a conversation that wasn't even about you."

"You called me a bitch."

"You *are* a bitch."

"Damn straight. Now move so I can take my bitchy ass far away from you." She tries to push me out of the way, but it's no use. "I mean it, Wes. Move."

In one fluid movement, I shove the straps of her bags off her shoulder. Catching her off guard, she doesn't have time to react and grab them before they fall to the ground. I crowd her until she's backed up against the wall. Caging her in with my body, I block her escape.

"What are you doing?" She twists and turns, trying every angle to get free, but I'm immovable.

"We need to clear things up, me and you."

"You made things perfectly clear back there." Her fists pound into my chest, and a fire burns in her eyes.

My chest rumbles with laughter. She really thinks she can get past me.

"Why are you laughing?" she grunts, still struggling.

I grip her wrists and push them above her head, pinning her further. "You're cute when you're pissed."

She kicks my shin. That one stings a bit because her shoes could double as a deadly weapon, but I hold firm. Her lips part, and every profanity she can come up with flies out of her mouth with such ferocity, spittle hits my face. I let her get it all out, not reacting but not giving in either.

Eventually, she tires, and I'm able to loosen my grip around her wrists.

"Are you finished?" I ask.

"What do you want from me? Why won't you let me go?"

"I'm asking myself the same question. But I think it has something to do with these tits." I release one of her wrists and slide my hand down to her neck, testing her limits. When she doesn't argue, I move lower. She wets her lips, her brown eyes boring into mine. Moving lower still, I reach under her shirt and cup her lace-covered breast. I skim my thumb over her hardened nipple, watching her closely. Every signal she's throwing out tells me she wants this as much as I do. "That feel good, darlin'?"

"No," she lies.

"How about this?" I pinch her nipple, wishing more than anything I could see what color they are.

"No." *More lies.*

"Let's try this then." I lower my mouth to her shirt and bra-covered tit. Both materials are so thin, I can feel the tight nub, and I bite down gently at first. She squirms and lifts to her toes, so I clamp down harder.

A knock at the door interrupts us, and Miles shouts into the room. "Your carriage is about to turn into a pumpkin, brother. You have a half-hour to get to Loki's."

My mouth freezes in place, my breath heating the fabric of her shirt and my cock hard enough to pound nails. Bex presses a single finger to my forehead and attempts to push me away, but my teeth are still latched on to her nipple.

"Like a dog with a bone," she huffs.

I groan, releasing her and blatantly adjusting myself, showing her the effect she has on me.

"Stay here where the guys can protect you. If I hear you've left, I'll come find you and drag you back."

"Then you'll be arrested and spend the next six months in jail," she says.

"It'll be worth it to know you're safe." Because I know my request isn't enough to convince her, I add, "Please."

She appraises me for a long moment before nodding subtly. "Fine. I'll stay."

I kiss her cheek and walk out, knowing if I do any more than that, I won't have the next six months to do it over and over and over, the way I have planned.

Chapter
NINE

Bexley

Duncan tails me all the way to work, looking like a complete badass dressed head-to-toe in black from his boots to his helmet. I whip into a parking spot and step out of the car looking nothing like a badass or even a lawyer, for that matter.

Borrowing clothes from Sissy sounded like a good idea in theory, but after glancing at her closet this morning, I quickly realized how horrible it actually was. Not only are we completely different sizes, but the pleather, lace, and other revealing clothing are definitely not my style.

Without any other choice, though, I made it work by wearing Sissy's black, stretchy mini skirt, and Khan's T-shirt, shortening the length by tucking the bottom hem into my bra cups.

I open the backseat and pull out the blazer I always keep in my car. I put it on and button it up. It's the least attractive outfit I've ever worn but it'll get me through the day.

It'll have to do until I can get to the shops later today.

"Ready?" Duncan asks, hooking his helmet on the handlebars of his bike.

"You don't need to go inside with me. I'm good," I say.

"Sorry, babe. VP's orders."

"Fine. You can come and make sure the Boogie Man isn't lurking, but you can't stay." I reach back inside the car and pull out my purse and briefcase.

"About that." He gives me a sheepish smile.

"Let me guess. You're not allowed to leave?"

"VP's orders."

"Your VP is an interfering asshole," I mutter, locking my car and walking toward my building, not bothering to wait for the prospect.

"He just wants you to be safe," Duncan says, easily keeping up with my fast pace.

"Good morning, Ms. March," Renata greets from behind her desk, eyeing the biker trailing behind me.

"Good morning," I say, but don't stop to chitchat, and she doesn't expect me to.

"Mornin', darlin'," Duncan says.

"Ignore him," I call after me.

"Yes, ma'am," she says, but there's a smile in her tone.

The Royal Bastards are chick magnets, every last one of them.

Even though I got here a half-hour before the office opens, Marcy was already at her desk outside my office.

"Good morning, Ms. March." She stands to greet me.

"Morning. What does my day look like?" I ask. She glances at Duncan. "Just pretend he doesn't exist. Actually, can you show him to the break room and give him a coloring book and crayons or something?"

"Uh, sure." She opens the drawer she keeps coloring supplies in for clients who bring their children to meetings.

"She was kidding. I can keep myself entertained." He scans the hallway. "Is the break room down there?"

"Down the hall on the left," Marcy says, throwing heart eyes at the man. "I can show you if you'd like."

"That would be most helpful," Duncan flirts back.

"Stay out of trouble." I point a finger at him. "And leave my staff alone."

He salutes me and starts down the hall.

"Make sure he doesn't wander, please," I say and enter my office, thankful to find it untouched. I know my security is top-notch here, but I'm still on edge after seeing what happened to my apartment.

I spend the first two hours of the day answering emails and making phone calls. I'm completely lost in my work when my cellphone rings.

"Hello?" I answer.

"You were gone before I got to the clubhouse this morning." Wes's deep and raspy voice comes over the line.

"Most people's workday starts between eight and nine. Not noon, like you."

"I got here at ten thirty, not noon."

"Same difference. What do you need, Wes? I'm a busy woman," I say, mouthing the end of my pen.

"Just wanted to hear your voice." He exhales, telling me he's on a smoke break. I've never been a smoker, and I hate the way they smell, but I must admit—at least to myself—that I like the way the rich tobacco clings to his clothes and skin. They fit his aesthetic perfectly, an accessory to his bad-boy image I find strangely appealing.

"I'm fine. Now, if there's nothing else, I need to get back to work."

Completely ignoring my brush-off, he says, "What time are you off tonight?"

"Not sure. It depends on how much time I have to devote to clients who call me for no apparent reason."

"Goddamn, I love it when you're sassy." I hear the smile in his voice, and it has me grinning too.

"You're a masochist."

"Only for you, baby."

"Why do you want to know?" I ask, enjoying our flirty banter. I know I shouldn't, but it's been so long since a man hasn't been scared away by my pissy attitude. The last time I allowed myself to let a man in, he turned out to be the villain in my story, and I don't want to risk going through that again.

"Because I want to take you to dinner."

"You can't take me anywhere. Court orders."

"Leave that to me."

"Fine, but only so we can talk about your case," I say.

"Whatever you have to tell yourself. I'll text you the address."

"I mean it, Wes. What happened last night can't happen again."

Fire licks between my legs, remembering his mouth on my breast. I lost control, and if it weren't for his curfew, there's no telling what I would've allowed to happen between us.

Later that night, I brought myself to orgasm with his name on my lips. When the afterglow faded, though, I was left feeling disgusted with my behavior. Us having sex would be unethical and grounds for suspension of my license. Not to mention, I hate him.

Why do you keep putting yourself in these situations then?

He chuckles as though I told a joke. "Sure, darlin'. Strictly business."

The line goes dead, and I toss my phone on the desk. Why can't I tell him no? I've never had a problem turning down a man before. Usually, their egos are so bruised, they don't even argue. But Wes is a different breed. I say no, and he hears yes. I tell him to back off, and he moves closer.

And I allow it all.

I plug the address into my GPS after saying goodbye to Duncan. Apparently, Wes is allowing me to drive to wherever this is on my own. It's a Tahoe address, leaving me to believe it's Loki's house. I've never been out there, but I've heard it's beautiful, and I'm looking forward to seeing where the dark leader of the Royal Bastards goes to unwind.

I hop onto the freeway, and it's not long before the scenery changes from casinos and businesses to trees and mountains. I roll down my windows and crank my music, singing along to a breakup anthem.

I don't get many quiet moments like this, preferring to stay busy and overloaded with work. If I'm lucky, I'll get a couple hours over the weekend to indulge in a bottle of wine and veg out in front of a trashy reality show. But this drive and having dinner with Wes is something I never do.

Forty-five minutes later, I park in front of a gorgeous log cabin with a creek running through the property. The front door opens, and Wes appears, releasing three large, barking dogs. My hand freezes around the door handle. Do they think I'm an intruder?

Wes notices my hesitation, calling the dogs back and walking them to the side of the yard, where he opens the door to a kennel and herds them inside. It's only when the gate is closed that I open my door and step out.

"Not an animal lover?" he asks.

"I like dogs. Just haven't had much experience with them." For the first time, I notice he's not wearing his typical biker gear.

Gone is the vest and in its stead is a white button-down shirt I'm almost certain has been pressed. He traded in his usual grease-stained jeans for a clean pair, and his hair is pulled back in a neat bun at the base of his neck. He looks ... different. Not sure if I like it.

He holds the front door open, gesturing for me to enter. "You've been around Roch's dogs."

"Not really. They're locked up or in the backyard when I'm at the clubhouse." I look around the space in awe. I don't know why I'm shocked considering how rich Birdie's taste is, but in my head, I imagined a scaled-down version of the clubhouse. That's not what this is at all. "This place is beautiful."

"I'll tell Loki you said so." He trails behind me as I walk around, admiring every detail.

"Where are Loki and Birdie tonight?"

"They're at the clubhouse. The guys returned from their run, so there's a party going on."

"And you didn't want to be there for it?"

He grabs my hand and spins me around. "I'd rather be here with you."

I clear my throat and hold up the briefcase I brought. "I have some papers for you to sign."

He takes the bag and sets it on a chair. "It can wait. Birdie made us dinner."

"That's right. She's in culinary school, right?"

"Yep. She's going to open a restaurant someday," he says with pride, pulling a lid off a pan. "She said it was chicken picca—something or other."

Looking inside, there's browned chicken breast with lemon and capers. "Piccata."

"Yeah, that."

"It looks wonderful," I say.

"Can you cook?" He reaches into a cupboard and reaches for a couple of plates.

"I can, but I don't enjoy it. I'd rather eat out than spend my time in the kitchen." The drawer full of takeout menus in my apartment comes to mind. I've put a lot of time and effort into narrowing down the best places to order from.

Something else that was taken from me with the break-in. No more menus.

"I'm good on the grill, but that's it." He plates the noodles before topping them with some sliced chicken breast. "Let's eat outside. It's hot, but the breeze off the creek is nice."

We step outside, and once again, he's blown me away. "Wow."

"What?" He sets the plates down and pulls a chair out for me.

"Not gonna lie, I expected you to hand me a Big Mac and Bud Light."

"Are you sick of underestimating me yet?" He pops the cork on a bottle of chilled white wine and pours me a glassful before pouring himself water from a pitcher. At least he listened when I told him to stay away from the alcohol.

"I don't think I'm underestimating you." I place my napkin on my lap. "You forget I've known you for years, and you've done a good job showing me exactly what to expect. All of this isn't you. You're only making an effort because you want in my pants."

"You're a different kind of woman than I'm used to, so I adjusted my plan."

"Which is exactly why this will never happen." I sip my wine. "I'll let you in, we'll fuck, and then you'll go back to doing beer bongs, having belching contests, and sleeping with every girl who walks into the clubhouse."

"You think you know me so well." He shifts his gaze to the bubbling creek.

"Don't I?"

"No. You don't know shit. Do I like to let loose and enjoy life? Fuck yeah. Everyone should. We're all going to die, and no one's going to remember us. Might as well have fun."

"That's the problem with you. You don't concern yourself with the future. You don't take anything seriously."

"And you take things too seriously. When was the last time you had fun?" he asks.

"I have fun," I say, knowing full well it's a lie. Fun requires a certain level of comfort and relaxation. Both of which I don't allow myself.

"Riiight." He slices into his chicken and takes a bite.

"Just because I don't enjoy the same things as you, doesn't mean I don't have fun." I bring my glass to my lips and realize it's empty. Wes moves to refill it, but I cover my glass with a hand. "No, thank you. I have to drive home."

"One more won't hurt."

"See? That's what I'm talking about. You have no self-control. It's overindulgence all the time with you," I say, but remove my hand and allow him to pour more wine.

He's right; one more won't hurt.

He rolls his eyes. "Jesus Christ, woman. Is there anything about me you like?"

"Honestly, no," I lie. There's a lot about him I like and admire, but I'd never tell him that.

"Why the fuck do I bother with you?" he mutters, tossing his fork on his plate and standing up. "I think I've had enough abuse for the night. Leave the papers you want me to sign, and I'll have them at the clubhouse for you tomorrow."

Storming inside, he slams the door shut behind him, rattling the windows and making the dogs bark and growl from their nearby kennel.

I chew the inside of my mouth, shocked he has a breaking point, and I reached it. I didn't think he had one. Especially not with me. Our relationship is about demeaning and ridiculing each other, so why was this conversation any different?

Well, shit. Now I feel bad.

I bring our plates inside and set them on the kitchen counter. Not seeing Wes anywhere, I go searching. As much as it pains me, I need to apologize. He was doing something nice, and instead of being gracious, I was a raging bitch. Even if that's our normal, he was clearly trying to impress me.

The first door I open is a bathroom, simple but beautiful. I knock on the next door down. Not hearing a response, I crack it open, and my jaw drops at what I see. A gilded birdcage big enough for a person sits in the corner of the room next to a massive king-sized bed.

"What the fuck?" I whisper. I walk over, inspecting it more closely. There's a lock with a numerical keypad attached to the door. Knowing the Royal Bastards, my first thought is this is used to jail prisoners. But why is it in a bedroom, and why would they make it so pretty? Then it hits me. This isn't used for torture. It's some kind of kinky shit.

Hearing music coming from the other side of the house, I back out of the room and follow the sound to another room. The door is cracked on this one. I listen from outside, recognizing the old Eagles song playing, but it's not the version I remember from the radio. I don't have to look inside to know Wes is playing the tune on his guitar.

I walk inside and see him sitting on the corner of the bed, his shirt unbuttoned, exposing his thick patch of chest hair. His boots are off, and his bare foot taps to the beat. He's so focused on the chords, he doesn't notice me enter, and I take advantage of it, watching from the doorway.

He sings as he plays. His voice is so quiet, I can barely hear the words over the guitar, but I recognize the old song about taking it easy.

Watching him so raw, so open, has me melting the smallest amount. Okay, that's a lie. I'm a puddle of female goo at his feet, but that truth feels so pathetic and stereotypical.

He strums the wrong chord and is brought back into the moment, his eyes opening and meeting my own. His hand stops mid-strum, silence filling the room. "I can't take any more insults, darlin'. Not tonight."

I deserve that. He was vulnerable with me tonight, and I stomped all over it. "That was nice. I didn't know you played."

"I don't. Not really. I just know a few songs."

"I thought it was good." I join him on the bed, readying myself to swallow my pride. "I'm sorry about tonight. It wasn't fair to you."

Chapter

TEN

Khan

Did the stone-cold Bexley March just apologize? To me?

"Thank you," I say, setting my guitar to the side.

Tonight was supposed to prove to her I can be the man she needs and that yeah, I like to have fun and goof around, but I can be serious when I need to. She wasn't having any of it. I feel like a pussy for even trying.

I can be persistent, but everyone has a breaking point, and I've fuckin' reached mine with Bex.

"I mean it. You put a lot of effort into tonight, and I shit all over it."

I *did* put a lot of effort into tonight, and I did it all thinking she was finally going to let me in. I should've known better. It's always one step forward and two steps back with her.

"Don't matter none. You're right. None of that out there is me. Wine tastes like ass, and a bloody steak is way better than that gourmet shit Birdie made."

She shoots me a sly grin. "There's the Wes I know."

"Yep. That's me. A big dumb animal," I agree, but only to

make her leave. I need to lick my wounds a bit, and I don't need her around to see it.

"That's not what I meant."

"I know who I am to everyone. I'm the one they call when they want to have a good time or need some muscle. That's all I ever am to anyone. But with you, I thought I could open up and show you more. I was wrong. It's cool." I walk over to the dresser and open the wood box I keep my stash in, pulling out a joint and holding it to my nose.

"You can't smoke that. You could get in trouble," she reminds me unnecessarily.

"I'm not the idiot you think I am."

"I didn't say you are."

"I just like the smell. It reminds me of being a kid." I place the joint back in the box and close the lid.

"Weed reminds you of being a kid?"

"My pops smoked up in the garage every night after getting home from work. He'd sit in there for a couple hours reading the paper and tinkering on his bike."

"Was he in a motorcycle club too?" she asks.

I rejoin her on the bed, facing her. This is the only topic she could've brought up to drag me out of the pity party I was throwing for myself. Me and Pops were best friends, and most good memories I have of being a kid includes him.

"No, he just liked to ride. He owned a construction company."

She tucks her legs underneath her and tugs on the hem of the skirt so she doesn't expose herself. Hard to do with something that short. She must've raided Sissy or Tabitha's closet because her outfit screams biker bitch. It's a good look on her, though I'm sure she disagrees.

"Where is he now?"

I blow out a breath. "Dead."

"Oh my God. I'm sorry." She rests her hand on my knee comfortingly.

"It's all good. He was an alcoholic, and even after his liver failed, he refused to quit." I lift her hand from my knee and hold it in mine.

"You grew up around addiction?"

"I'm not putting any blame on that man for my choices. My addiction came from a hand injury after Pops died, and I took over his business. A buddy of mine was lowering a pallet of cinder blocks, and the chain broke. Crushed my hand in a bunch of places." I extend and contract my hand, the memory of the pain giving me flashbacks. "They reconstructed my hand and sent me on my way with a bottle of Oxy. Not only did the pills take away the pain, but I liked how they made me feel. The doctor didn't bat an eye when I asked for refills. After six months, he finally stopped it, but by then, it was too late. I was hooked."

"So you moved on to heroin?" Bexley opens my hand and studies the scars, tracing them gently with the tip of her finger.

"Yeah. I couldn't work, and I guess I was depressed, though I didn't know that's what it was at first. The heroin was better than the Oxy. There was no better feeling than when it hit my bloodstream. I was invincible. Until I wasn't. The first time I got busted and had to detox in jail, I swore I'd never do it again." A chill runs up my spine, remembering that first night locked up with no dope. "But after I got sprung, my dealer found out and came over. I thought I was strong enough to only do it sometimes. Just when I was partying, you know? And I was at first. I started my company back up and got back to work, saving the partying for the weekends. Then I started using on bad days, then every night after work, and eventually I was back to using morning and night."

"And you got busted again," she says.

I nod. "I got busted three times before I met Goblin's old

man. He was my bunkmate during my last stint in jail. Him and the Royal Bastards saved my life."

"Did you go to therapy or join NA or anything?"

I flop onto the mattress, lying on my side and propping my head on my hand. Bex shocks the shit out of me when she matches my position facing me. "Nah. That shit's not for me. I found my way on the open road and with my brothers."

All I want is for her to see I'm not a loud and obnoxious biker. Not all the time, at least.

"You should be proud of yourself. It couldn't have been easy."

"It wasn't, but also, it was. I immersed myself in the club. Kept my mind and body busy, started a new construction business that benefitted the club."

She plugs her ears. "I don't want to know."

I chuckle. "For being a defense attorney, you sure are allergic to hearing about crimes."

"I learned early on that there's such a thing as too much information. It makes things simple when my clients only tell me what's necessary."

"That all I am to you?" I reach over and tuck a strand of her long, dark hair behind her ear. "A client?"

"Who do you want to be to me?"

"Your man," I say, resting a hand on her hip.

"Do you even know how to be monogamous? Have you ever done it before?"

"Yes, Bex. I know how to keep my dick in my pants for one person. I'm a fully housebroken, obedient dog when I want to be."

She rolls onto her back, moaning in frustration and resting her arm over her eyes. "I don't trust you. And there's so much going on right now, I can't focus on making sure you're not fucking me over."

I climb on top of her, pushing her legs apart and settling

between them, not giving a shit if her skirt gets pushed up above her hips. Matter of fact, I'd prefer that. "I'm an honest man. I have a past, everyone does, and I won't apologize for it, but if you asked all those other women if I ever made promises I didn't keep, they'd tell you no."

"Those are pretty words, Wes."

"Not just words, darlin', but I get it. Trust must be earned, and that's all I'm asking of you. Let me prove I'm the man I say I am."

"Jesus Christ." Her arm falls to her side, exposing her tormented expression. She wants to give in. She wants me. But she's scared as hell. "I can't believe I'm contemplating dating my client, who is in a biker gang and an ex-con, possibly a future con."

I know I'm not the man she deserves right now, but I'm confident in myself and my brothers that we can make this all go away. I'd never pursue her if I thought I'd be locked up in six months, and if she agrees, it'll give me that much more motivation to stay on the outside.

"You think a buttoned-down business executive with a couple million in the bank and a fancy condo downtown is better than me? Because let me tell you, that kind of man is too focused on status and his bank account to love a woman like you. That kind of man is scheduling missionary sex every other Tuesday after the lights go out."

Her voice lowers, and her eyes go half-lidded. "What kind of man are you, then?"

I hook one of her legs around my waist before pinning her hands above her head. "I'm the guy who'll treat you like a whore in bed, fucking you until your pussy begs for mercy. But outside of the bedroom, you'll be my queen. I'll take you out, show you off, and make sure you know you're the only one on my mind."

I grind my hard cock against her hot center, showing her I'm ready to make this happen right now.

"Oh, God," she breathily moans. "Or we could just fuck and get it out of our systems."

"No. Absolutely not. If I slide my dick between your thighs, you're mine. All in, Bex."

"You're confusing me." She squeezes her eyes closed and swallows.

"What'll it be, darlin'? In?" I drag my length down her center. "Or out?"

I watch as her rational side battles with her emotional and sexual side. I get it; I'm not the smart choice. Bex has been relying on logic for too long. That may keep her safe, but it won't make her happy. Her body and her mind need to be satisfied, and I can tell her body hasn't been satisfied in a long ass time, if ever.

"In," she whispers.

Before she finishes speaking, my mouth is on hers. I kiss her hard and fast, wanting to take my time and learn everything about her but not having the restraint to follow through. There'll be time for all that because she's in. She's mine. And I plan on worshipping her body every chance I get.

"You taste so fucking good. These lips are so juicy." I suck her lower lip in my mouth, then bite down and drag it through my teeth. Her response is to whimper, her body squirming underneath me, desperate for more.

First things first. I push her shirt up and over her head, trapping her hands and realizing it's not a crop top like I thought it was, but a RBMC shirt she folded under and tucked into her bra.

"This my shirt you wearin'?"

"I couldn't fit in any of Sissy or Tabitha's tops. Have you seen them? They're toothpicks." She tries to shake her hand free, but I tie the sleeves around her wrists, securing them above her head.

"Shit, that's hot." Reaching behind her back, I unfasten her bra with one hand and reverently uncover the tits that I've been salivating over for too long. "Look at these. Goddamn."

I squeeze a fleshy tit, taking a rosy puckered nipple in my mouth. Circling my tongue around the tight bud, I reach over and pinch the other between my fingers. She mewls and squeezes her thighs around my waist, desperate for friction.

Soon, baby girl. Soon.

I move to the other breast, taking her nipple between my teeth and giving it a tug, watching her reaction to see how much I can get away with. Pain only makes the pleasure sweeter, and I'm not a gentle lover.

"I need you inside me, Wes."

"Not yet," I say.

"Now," she says through gritted teeth, struggling to free her hands.

Bex is a born fighter, so it doesn't surprise me she's picking a fight in bed. She'll soon realize I can back down and let her be the dominating woman she is everywhere else, but I'm in charge when we're in bed.

"Naughty girl, fighting me for control." I stand up and pull her skirt down her legs, leaving her in a lacy black thong. "So fucking sexy."

I skim my hands along her stomach, kneading the soft flesh that sits above her pussy.

"Don't do that," she complains.

"Why?" I ask, not letting go.

"I'm fat. I get it. You don't have to point it out."

"Don't put that on me." I run my hands up and down her torso and thighs. "I fucking love your body. All I see is padding so you won't get hurt when I fuck the shit out of you."

I didn't take her for an insecure woman, and there's no room for that bullshit when she's in my bed.

"Either way, you don't need to squish it."

"You're right. I don't need to, but I want to. If you're in my bed, this body belongs to me. All of it. Not just the parts you like to people to see." I unbutton my pants and push them to the ground. I don't typically wear underwear, so my cock springs free. "Look how hard you make me."

Her eyes widen, her mouth gapes, and I smirk.

She gulps. "You're pierced."

"I know."

"Twice," she deadpans.

"I know."

I have what's called a magic cross—a combination of an apadravya and ampallang. Hurt like a bitch, but it makes the ladies scream.

I crook a brow. "You can get a better look later. Right now, I'm about to eat this pussy."

My finger circles over her lace-covered clit, making her hiss and spread her legs even wider. The fabric is damp with arousal, and I can't wait any longer to see what I'm working with. I'm a visual man. I don't close my eyes when I kiss, and I don't close them when I fuck. I want to see every expression, I want to study every peak and valley, and I want to watch every second of her climax.

Hooking my fingers in her panties, I pull them down her curvy legs and set them on the bed next to us. They'll no doubt come in handy later.

"Look at this cunt," I moan, taking her in. She's waxed bare, and her puffy lips are glistening with arousal. Spreading her open, I lower my mouth onto her, licking up her seam. "Sweet like ice cream."

Her breath catches, and her hips buck. "Please, Wes."

"Gladly." I hook my arms under her thighs, pull her to the edge of the bed, and kneel. I pin her pussy lips open with my thumbs and eat my dessert—sucking, licking, and tonguing every inch of her. She's so fucking beautiful, all pink and swollen and ripe.

"I'm coming," she announces, but I already knew this by the way she's clenching down on my probing tongue.

I double my efforts, flattening my tongue and sweeping it over her clit again and again until she screams. She fists my hair, thrashing her head from side to side and screaming curses. I stay with her, giving her all I have until she settles and comes down from her high.

"What are you smiling about?" she asks when I come up for air.

"You're gorgeous when you come."

"Shut up and show me your other moves."

I scoot her back on the bed and climb onto the mattress, fisting my weeping dick. I don't want to do it, but I know it's necessary for now, so I reach into the nightstand and pull out a condom. "I'm not using these more than a couple days. Get yourself to a doctor, and I'll do the same. If you're not on birth control, take care of that shit too."

"You want to fuck me without a condom?"

"Isn't that what I said?"

"Yes, but that means you can't sleep with anyone else," she says dumbly.

I roll my eyes. "Keep up, darlin'. We already agreed to that."

"I didn't think you were serious."

"This girl," I say to the ceiling, sliding the condom down my length. "Gonna test my patience with every turn."

I lean over her and toss her tied-up hands over my head. Hugging her to me as I sit up, I put her on my lap so she's straddling me. She lifts onto her knees, giving me room to position my cock at her entrance. After the tip is secure inside, I grip her hips and slowly lower her on top of me.

"Oh my God." Her eyes nearly roll back in their sockets as I fill her. I'm not a small man, and my cock isn't any different—it's a tight fit, but this woman was made for me—and eventually, I'm buried to the hilt.

I guide her movements, circling her hips to give her clit the friction it needs. She feels so fucking good, arousal drips down my balls as she squeezes the life of out me. I kiss and suck on her neck while she works me over. I inhale her rich and floral scent that reminds me of walking through a garden in the summertime when the air is hot and thick and the flowers are at their peak.

"Feel good, darlin'?" I ask.

"So good. So fucking good, Wes." My name on her lips is like a prayer, and in this moment, I know she's the only one I'll ever crave like this for the rest of my life. There will never be enough with her. Ever.

"Fuck me, baby. I want to see these tits in action." I cup her breasts, teasing over her sensitive nipples.

She lifts higher onto her knees and uses her thick thighs to bounce up and down on my dick. I release her breasts and watch as they move to the beat she sets right in front of my face.

"Mmm, that's it," I encourage. "Just like that."

I lean back onto my hands and watch her like a movie as she does her best. I'm thankful for all the years of practice I had to build up my stamina because otherwise, I would have blown my load right here and now. She's beautiful and ripe with desire, intoxicating me more than any liquor could.

When I'm certain she can't keep the pace any longer, I release her hands from their binding, push her down on her back, and take over, pressing her knees into her chest to give me room to work. From this angle, I can go even deeper. I wish I didn't have to wear a condom so I could feel inside her. I hope she knows I'm serious about the doctor. I don't want anything between us, ever.

"Harder. I need it harder," she whines, her breasts jiggling with each thrust.

"I know what you need."

"If you did, then you'd be doin' it."

I bend over and kiss her mouth to shut her up, reaching for her discarded panties. I smile against her lips and pull away, quickly shoving the black lace into her mouth. Her complaints are muffled, and her eyes burn with anger.

Just the way I like her.

Chapter
ELEVEN

Bexley

What in the actual hell? I taste my arousal through the fabric and shout obscenities at the caveman, whose only response is a wicked laugh. I lower my hands to remove it, but he stops me and forces my hands over my head once again.

With no other choice and not wanting to waste a perfectly good orgasm, I shove my anger away. If I'm honest, it kind of turns me on. Most men I've slept with are kittens in bed, asking me what I like and don't like while hesitantly trying to deliver and failing.

Not Wes, though. He's a goddamn sexual magician. He fills me up so completely, and his hardware rubs me in all the right places. I've never been with a pierced man before, but I'm not going back now that I have. Those little balls send me into another dimension.

"If you try to remove your panties again, I'll duct tape your mouth shut. Got it?"

I really don't want that, so I nod. He releases my hands

and, keeping himself buried inside me, throws both my legs to one side.

My body stiffens.

All I can think about is how many dimples he can see or if he's turned off by the silver stretch marks that run like roadmaps on my hips, ass, and thighs. I'm not normally self-conscious, but I'm also not normally with a man like Khan, who is chiseled from stone, hard everywhere.

"I lost you," he says, slowing his punishing thrusts. "Am I hurting you?"

I shake my head. I must be quite the vision. Mouth full of lace, hands partially bound by even more lace, body twisted into a position that has my belly folding in unflattering places, and my big ass in full view.

"Do you want me to stop?" he asks, concern on his handsome face. I shake my head again. He grabs my panties and pulls them from my mouth. "Where are you? Because you're not here with me."

"I'm fine. Keep going." I circle my hips, encouraging him to get back to his masterful fucking.

"Not until you tell me what's wrong."

"It's nothing. It's just this position isn't the most flattering one."

He sits back on his haunches, eating me up with his eyes. If he sees something he doesn't like, I'd never know, judging by his expression.

"You wanna know what I see?" he asks, palming my breast.

"Not really." I know what he sees—every one of my flaws.

"Too bad. I'm gonna tell you anyway." He leans over and runs a thumb along my bottom lip. "Your lips are swollen from my kisses." He bends down and gives me a peck. "Your hair is wild and sexy." He brushes the stray hairs from my forehead. "Your tits are red and swollen from being sucked on." He flutters his tongue over a sensitive nipple. "The way your body is twisted gives me perfect access to this ripe cunt." He grips my hip and pushes his cock inside. "This gives me something to hold on to while I fuck you." He slaps my butt. "And this gives me something delicious to look at while I do it."

"Oh," is all I manage to say.

He smiles. "Are you done worrying about this shit? Because I'm ready to get back to it."

I nod, and he bites his lip as he does just that. With a hand digging into my hip and his eyes focused on the place we're joined, he pistons into me, rolling his hips to drive his cock into my G-spot. I lose myself to the sensation, feeling another orgasm coming on.

My pussy throbs, and my nipples tighten as I listen to the wet slapping sound of our bodies. Every muscle in his body is taut and damp with sweat. He's beautiful in the most masculine way. He doesn't shave or manscape; every inch of him is raw and manly.

"Mine, Bex. You're mine. I don't care how far you run, I'll find you," he grunts.

"Wes," I start, but he cuts me off by slowing down, keeping me from reaching my peak.

"Say it. You're mine."

His cock is barely moving, and even when I pulse around him to encourage movement, he remains still. He's not going to let me come unless I tell him. What does it even mean to be his? That there'll be more of this? I can handle that.

"I'm yours," I whisper.

He pulls out and thrusts back in with force, making me gasp and desperate for so much more of that.

"Louder," he says, giving me another punishing thrust that feels so goddamn good.

"I'm yours, Wes," I say, using my voice this time. The second the words hit his ears, he's grinding into me, hitting me in all the right spots. It's heaven.

"Oh, shit," I call out as my body shudders and goosebumps climb over my skin. He tugs on my nipple, giving me a bite of pain that I had no idea I'd love so much. I clench down, making the orgasm even more intense. "Wes, oh my God. Yes."

"Goddamn, you're fucking beautiful." He pulls out and flips me over, pulling on my hips to lift me to my knees. Then he's back inside of me, stretching me. Now that my needs are sated, and he's not worried about making me feel good, he shows me what he likes, skin slapping and rough, breath-catching thrusts.

I bury my face into the pillow, my teeth clattering with each drive forward. He slaps my ass so hard the sting has my eyes burning. But I fucking love it. All of it.

"Gonna fuck this ass one day." If I was shocked by the slap, it's nothing compared to what I feel when a finger prods my asshole. I squeeze, rejecting the intrusion, causing him to chuckle devilishly. "That won't keep me out, darlin'."

I've never had anal sex, never even considered it. But as his finger breaches that tight ring of muscle up to his first knuckle, I know I'll let him. It's wrong and forbidden, yet strangely exciting.

I'm not in shape, so my muscles burn and ache as he continues, moaning and whispering things I don't understand. But they're dirty, judging by his gruff tone that sounds like it's coming directly from his chest.

I can't go on much longer. Soon my body will give out and collapse.

"Come, Khan. Please come," I beg.

He pulls out, and I hear the snap of the condom coming off.

"I'm gonna paint this ass with my cum." His voice is deep and husky.

I lift onto my hands and peer over my shoulder, wanting to see the moment it happens. He braces himself with a hand on my ass, the other gliding up and down his rigid length furiously. He lets out an animalistic roar, tipping his head back as hot semen sprays from his tip, landing on my back and ass. His strokes slow, squeezing his tip to milk every drop of cum, then he falls to my side, and I collapse onto the mattress.

Our heavy breaths are the only sound in the room as I process what just happened and what I agreed to. Surely he knows the reason I said what I did was because I was horny, right? He can't expect me to really be *his*, right?

"I'll be right back." Wes hops off the bed.

"Where are you going?"

He palms my ass. "To get a washcloth. Gotta take care of my woman."

Okay, so maybe he did take me seriously.

"Good Lord," I murmur to myself, my eyes zeroed in on his firm, round behind. He may be an oaf, but the man is sexy. As I scan down his muscular legs, I catch the small black box around his ankle.

Oh, no ... I slept with a criminal who is my client. What was I thinking?

I wasn't thinking. I was too busy experiencing the most erotic sex of my life.

"Goddamn, look at you," he says when he returns. "All loosey-goosey from sex and painted in my cum."

"Listen, Wes, what I said—"

"No." He gently wipes me clean.

"No, what?"

"Whatever you're about to say, it's gonna be some bullshit, and I'm not down with it." He tosses the rag into a basket in the corner and flops down next to me. Despite struggling to put distance between us, I'm no match for the muscular arm that pulls me to him.

"Wes, come on. I should go."

"Not going anywhere, babe." His eyes flutter shut, and his voice is drowsy. He's seconds from sleep.

Good. Maybe then I can sneak out.

"I still have to swing by the mall for some work clothes."

"Not tonight, you ain't. Prospects aren't around to take you, and it's not safe."

Right. I'm currently in hiding. Wes's dick made me forget I'm currently in hiding. Considering Martin hasn't left my mind since I heard his ominous voicemail, that's saying a lot.

Except now I am, and a chill runs up my spine.

"Maybe I should call his office. Set up an appointment with him and find out what he wants and what it'll take to get him to disappear from my life."

The relaxed muscles in his face tighten and his jaw ticks. When his eyes open, they're burning with an intensity I only see when he's angry. "Fuck no. If anyone meets up with him, it's me. Matter of fact, I got a lotta shit to say to that motherfucker."

"That will only make it worse."

"This happens when you turn a blind eye to everything except what you need to know for my case, darlin'. You have no idea what I'm capable of. You want him gone, and I have the means to do it. No one will fuck with you ever again."

"Don't even joke about that. Your freedom is already on the line. One small misstep, and you're gone. That prison cell you hate so much will be your permanent address." The day I picked him up from jail still haunts my memories. He was so sad, so emotional. I don't want him to feel like that ever again.

Motherfucker. I'm catching feelings.

A smug smile spreads across his kiss and wind-chapped lips. "I don't get caught."

"Really? Because your impending trial begs to differ."

"That couldn't be helped. But trust this, if I weren't good at what I do, I'd be locked up with the key destroyed by now for the things I've done. Hell, I might be on death row."

If simply hearing words could give a person whiplash, I'd have it right now. Does he not hear how insane this sounds? He's telling me he's a killer and expecting me to what? Praise him? Congratulate him? No. Fuck that. I scramble away from him, but before I get too far, he's dragging me back into his arms and positioning himself on top of me.

"Let go, Wes." I shove away from his chest and throw myself to the left. It's a move he was expecting, and his hips pin me in place. We're still naked, and his semi-hard dick slips between my legs.

"No. Not until you tell me what you're thinking."

"I'm thinking I have the worst taste in men ever. I'm thinking I got out of bed with a crooked judge and got into one with a homicidal maniac." Struggling gets me nowhere, so I move to begging. "Please, let me go."

"Nah, because you're not understanding. Your husband was taking bribes and letting white-collar criminals off the hook to keep doing what they were doing. Everything I've done has been for the greater good. Each soul I've sent to Hades deserved that shit, and I've never laid hands on a female or a child." He slaps his palm to his chest, his eyes burning with conviction. "That motherfucker and I are not the same kind of criminal, Bex. The world is better for the things I've done."

"You are not God, judge, or jury. You don't get to decide things like that."

He genuinely believes everything he's saying, but this isn't me or the life I want for myself. I spent so many years looking over my shoulder after I left Martin. It wasn't until recently I relaxed enough to enjoy the things I worked so hard for. Being with Wes will bring back all my paranoia and force me to live in fear once again.

Wes's an amazing fuck, but I won't share his sins or his enemies.

"You think some ancient book is going to tell me what's right or wrong? Hell no. My brothers and I live by our own code that protects the ones we love and keeps us alive. Some people are happy to have a boring ass normal existence, but I'm not. I live the fuck out of my life, and I won't apologize for it. I ain't scared of Hades."

"I live." It sounds like a lie, even to myself.

His eyes widen as though this was the most shocking thing I could say. "Babe. You ain't living. You're surviving."

"No, I'm not." Indignation burns in my belly. He has no idea what I've done to get to where I'm at now.

"You've spent years hiding and looking over your shoulder. You should be the person someone else is hiding from and looking over their shoulder to make sure you're not after them." He brushes his thumb over my cheek. "Do me a favor and close your eyes." Out of sheer curiosity, I do as he says. "Think of yourself as a queen on a throne. There are guards all around you and people cowering at your feet because they know what you say goes. You're the one calling the shots, and you have an entire army backing you up. How does that make you feel?"

It's a stupid exercise, but the imagery in my head has me feeling calm and powerful. It would be such a relief to not carry the weight of my past.

"Feels good, right?" he asks.

"Yeah, but that's not real life."

"Yes, it motherfucking is." He presses his lips gently to mine and whispers, "You're a queen. Make that motherfucker pay for pushing you off your pedestal. And that army you see around you? That's the Royal Bastards. You became my old lady tonight, and that means no one touches you, and no one hurts you, ever again."

Goddamn. This man.

His words hit home and become truth in my head. I'm his reluctant queen. It's not smart, and I know there will consequences, but right now, I don't care. I want this fairytale more than I've wanted anything else in my life. I wrap my arms around his neck and crash my lips against his, kissing him with everything I have in me.

Chapter
TWELVE

Khan

"You look . . . weird," Loki says, handing me a bottle of water.

"Weird?" I toss the bottle cap on the ground and chug the water. I've been working on the basement all damn day, and I'm fucking exhausted.

"Happy or something. I don't know. Just . . . weird. Your girl finally giving you some lovin'?" he asks, smirking.

"I ain't kissing and telling."

He punches my arm, laughing. "I owe Sly fifty bucks."

"You bet against me?" I toss the empty bottle into the trash pile.

"That bitch is hardcore. I didn't think you had it in you."

"Nah, she's a pussycat. You just don't know her yet." I lift a sheet of drywall. "Give me a hand."

He holds the sheet in place while I screw it to the wall. "Yet? Does that mean she's not a one and done?"

"Nah, brother. I got that shit locked down."

"No shit?"

"No shit. She's it for me."

Last night was touch and go. It's not easy for people to understand what we're about, and I saw the indecision warring behind her eyes, but I had faith, and I was right. My girl's a badass, and by the end of the night, she was on my level.

"Happy for you, brother." He pounds me on the back. "Don't want to pop your bubble, but I had something I wanted to talk to you about."

"Oh yeah? What's that?" I point to another sheet of sheetrock. "Grab that, would ya?"

"Sure." He lifts the sheetrock into place, and I drive some screws through it. The basement is the same size as the entire upstairs, minus our kill room that's already sectioned off and hidden behind a shelving unit. That'll stay how it is, but the rest will soon be four bedrooms and a massive party room complete with a bar. "Will this thing between you two become a conflict of interest?"

"What are you talking about?"

"Maybe we should find you another lawyer until this thing with her ex gets cleared up. The last thing you need is for him to go after her and have it affect your case. If shit goes bad, you don't want it to touch you."

"It's not going to go bad. I've got a plan." I tap my temple.

"What's that?"

"Let's ride." I brush the dust off my white t-shirt and jeans before heading upstairs. "Sly? Moto? Goblin? You guys want to take a ride with us?"

They both look up from where they were bullshitting over a beer on the couch. "Sure thing."

As we mount our bikes, I nod over to them. "Leave the cuts here."

"It's that kind of ride, huh?" Sly removes his leather and stuffs it in his saddlebag. Moto, Goblin, and Loki do the same.

"Yup." The engine of my Harley roars to life, and I steer my way out of the parking lot.

I thought about the best way to handle this all night, and the only thing I could come up with was scaring the pissant into submission.

Martin's office is next door to the courthouse, which is one of the few places I can go without getting into trouble. Coming here is risky, but it's all I got.

I park on the street to give us quick access out of here and climb off my bike.

"You sure about this?" Loki asks.

"I don't see any other way." I stare up at the glass and steel building.

Goblin sighs. "Not how I thought my afternoon was going to go."

I chuckle. "Losing some of your steam, old man?"

"Fuck no." He cracks his knuckles. "Let's do this."

The five of us enter the gaudy building. Right when we walk in, there's a security guard behind a podium. Her eyes widen and her hand goes to the radio clipped to her collar.

I storm over and cover her hand with mine, stopping her from alerting anyone of our presence. "You wouldn't want to ruin our surprise, would you?"

She shakes her head vigorously, her eyes watering in fear.

"Is Judge Alexander in?" I ask.

She clicks a few keys on her computer and nods.

"I'll stay here and chat with our new friend," Goblin says, strolling around the podium and taking a seat on her stool.

"Be nice," Loki warns.

Goblin holds a hand up in defense. "I'm a pussycat. Right"—he picks up her lanyard and squints to read the name—"Leona?"

The woman nods in response.

I shake my head and walk over to the elevator, pressing the call button. "What level is he on?"

"F-five," Leona stutters. "Top floor."

"Of course."

As the doors close around us, Loki asks, "So what's the plan?"

"Fear of God." I crack my neck.

"Got it."

The doors open to a lobby just as over the top as the bottom floor. Only this time, there's no one behind the front desk. Good, then I won't have to leave another babysitter behind. We go down the only hallway, reading the names on the doors as we pass. Of course, Martin has the corner office.

I place my ear to the door and hear a man's voice. "I think he's alone and on the phone." I turn the knob but pause before pushing it open. "Ready?"

My brothers nod, and we step inside to see exactly what I was expecting. An old, white dude in an expensive suit with an earpiece in his ear. His spine stiffens when our eyes meet, and his jaw hangs open. I walk casually over and remove the headset from his ear. Lifting it to my lips, I say, "He'll call you back." And toss it onto the mahogany desk.

Martin clears his throat, and to not look like a pussy, he says, "Can I help you, gentleman?"

"Sure can." I plop down into a chair opposite him, hearing the wood crack below me, and look around. The far wall is a floor-to-ceiling window, giving him a bird's-eye view of the street below. Behind him sits a bookcase lined with boring-looking books and generic knick-knacks that probably cost a fortune but hold no meaning. Like a crystal swan. *What the fuck?* "I'm here on behalf of a mutual friend."

He huffs. "I seriously doubt we run in the same circle."

"Why's that?" Loki crosses his arms over his chest.

"Come on. It's obvious." He lets out a humorous laugh that quickly dies when a growl rumbles in my chest.

"You might not want to make the big one angry," Moto says, propping himself up against the window.

I'm all too happy to play the "big dumb animal" role right now. I know what people assume based on my size, and most of the time, it works out in our favor.

"Okay, I'll bite. Who is this friend we share?" he leans back in his executive chair.

"Bexley March," I say.

"You mean my wife?" he asks with smug irritation.

"*Sienna* was your wife," I correct, resting my forearms on his desk and leaning forward. "*Bexley* is protected by us, and that means she's untouchable by you or any of your associates trying to intimidate her."

Martin laughs humorously, scratching at his brow. "She fooled you too, huh?"

"Excuse me?" Sly grumbles.

"Don't feel bad. She tricked me, too. That's why I'm here, to make things right between her and me and to make sure she gets the help she needs." Martin stands and buttons his suit coat. "Sienna suffers from a few mental health disorders. She is a master manipulator and a compulsive liar. She does and says whatever she has to to get what she wants."

I jump to my feet and drill a finger in his direction. "You're the fucking liar."

Loki places a hand on my shoulder. I'm sure it's meant to calm me down, but it only pisses me off more. "Easy, brother. Let's hear what he has to say."

"Fine, but I can't guarantee I won't murder this asshole if he doesn't watch his tone," I growl.

"Fair." Loki's hand drops to his side.

"I didn't mean to offend you. I get it, she's beautiful, smart, and that body . . ." He blows out a breath. "It's easy to lose yourself."

"Mention her body again, motherfucker. I dare you." My fists ball at my sides, itching to pound this guy's face in.

He visibly swallows. "All I'm saying is, don't trust the bi—"

"Seriously, man. Do you want to die?" Sly asks.

Eyeing me, Martin continues, but this time he watches his mouth. "She lured me in, said all the right words, did all the right things until I fell in love with her. Then, out of nowhere, she up and left me, taking my money and humiliating me."

"That's not the same story she tells," I say.

"Of course it isn't. I'm sure she made up a bunch of bullshit just to get you to feel sorry for her."

"Not exactly." I stalk slowly over to him. "I heard you liked to keep your woman submissive and quiet. And when she wasn't that way, you laid hands on her."

Martin's eyes dart between the four of us. "Come on, now. You know how it is. I bought her everything she could ever want, including a multi-million-dollar condo in downtown New York. None of that made her happy. So yeah, I smacked her around a little to put her in her place when she'd mouth off. It was no big deal."

My chest heaves, and burning hot fury spreads through me. People like to stereotype bikers and put us in a category full of blind abuse and violence. Yet every biker I know would kill or die for their family.

I crowd his space, bending over until our faces are inches apart. "We're not the same. I don't give a fuck if a woman has a gun to my head. I still ain't putting a hand on her. Only weak men do that."

With his voice lowered to almost a whisper, Martin says, "Good thing she isn't mine anymore."

"That's a real good fuckin' thing. But we still have the problem of you destroying her apartment and threatening her."

The door bursts open, and we all turn to look. Goblin barges in, breathing hard and looking a little nervous. "Time's up. Cops are on their way up."

I whip around to face Martin. "If you even think of doing anything else to my woman, I'll be back. But next time it won't be in a public place. It'll be when you're least expecting it, and trust when I say I don't touch women, but I have no problem taking care of trash like you."

"If you'll excuse me. I have meetings to get to." He motions toward the door that my brothers are already on the other side of.

With one final stare down, I leave.

"We need to take the stairs. Cops took the elevator," Goblin says.

Our boots hitting the ground echo in the sterile-looking stairwell as we rush down to the lobby. Leona stands as we jog past her desk. She holds her hand up in the universal motion for "call me" toward Goblin. He throws her a wink, and I shake my head, grinning. He turned a hostage situation into a first date.

We hop on our bikes and peel out, not even pausing to put our domes on. I'm not sure if the cops saw our bikes, but we need to get out of here as quick as possible, just in case. Slowly we break apart, all going in separate directions to not gain attention.

I ride around the block a couple of times and, not hearing any sirens, park in Bexley's office's parking lot. She isn't going to like what I have to tell her, but it's better to get ahead of the situation instead of hiding it from her.

She's been our attorney for a long time, but I've never been to her office, so I'm stunned when I see how classy the joint is. If she said she spent the entirety of what she stole from Martin on this place alone, I wouldn't be surprised. It's as fancy as the place we were just in but trendier and sexier. Just like Bex is.

A woman greets me just past the front door from behind her desk. "Good afternoon. Do you have an appointment?"

"Here to see Ms. March."

"Who can I tell her is here to see her?"

"Khan."

"Oh, Mr. Khan. You can go right up. Top-level, Marcy will show you Ms. March's office."

I nod and take the elevator up. A girl who must be Marcy is waiting when the doors open. "Mr. Khan, right this way."

"Just Khan, darlin'. I ain't no mister."

"Of course."

Even the experience between Martin's office and this one is different. Bexley's a defense attorney, and everyone around here is used to seeing people like me walk through the door. Still, I appreciate not being treated like a criminal by strangers.

Marcy opens a door and motions for me to enter. "Do you need anything? Coffee? Water?"

I wink. "Nah, I'm good. Thanks."

She blushes and shuts the door behind me.

"What're you doing here?" Bex asks from behind her desk. She looks drop-dead gorgeous. Her hair is pinned up off her long, delicate neck, and the teal-colored button-down she's wearing is undone just enough to show off some black lace underneath.

"Fuck me, you're beautiful." I grab ahold of her ponytail and yank it to tip her head back.

"Wes," she breathes out.

I lower my mouth to hers, getting my first taste of the day. It was hard to let her leave last night, but I didn't push to make her stay since she'd already given me everything I wanted—herself. I sweep my tongue across her bottom lip, asking for entry, and am pleased when she lets me in. My girl is so fuckin' sweet. Tastes like candy canes and coffee.

"Mmm," I moan against her lips. "Want to bend you over this desk and fuck you."

She pulls away, laughing. "Down boy, I have a client appointment in ten minutes."

"I can be fast."

"Save that big dick energy for later, okay?"

"Fine." I sit down on her desk and spread my legs wide, then pull her to her feet and against me. "Need to be close then."

"I can handle that."

"Where's Miles hiding?"

"He's not hiding. He's in the breakroom down the hall." She grins. "Why are you here?"

I wrap my arms around her, rubbing up and down her back before settling my palms on her ass. "Before you react, I want you to hear me out, okay?"

Her face falls, and guilt hits me in the chest. She's gonna be pissed. "What did you do?"

"The guys and I went and had a chat with your ex." Goddamn if she's not always trying to get away, shoving against my chest to put distance between us, but I'm not having it and tighten my grip around her. "Stop struggling because I ain't letting go."

"I told you to stay clear of him. You're only making things worse."

I wish I could deny her accusation, but I never got a clear answer from Martin about whether he'd leave her alone.

"I didn't make it worse, baby. I only warned him off you. It wasn't a big deal." I grip the back of her neck and stroke my thumb down her cheek, trying to calm the wild banshee. "Swear to God. Everything's fine. Not into keeping secrets from you, so I thought better than to hide it."

"Thank you for that, but seriously, Wes. That was the dumbest thing you've ever done. Why would you do something like that?" Her muddy brown eyes peer into mine, full of concern.

All that worry is because of Martin, and I fight the urge to ride back to his office and put him in the ground.

"I get it, you've never belonged to a biker before, so you don't know how this works. When you agreed to be mine, that made me responsible for your safety. I see a threat, I'm going to take care of it, and I won't ask for your permission or forgiveness. Just the way it is."

"Oh yeah? And what happens if he finds out who you are and you get put behind bars again? You won't be around to protect me, and he'll be even more pissed off." She reaches up and twists a strand of my long hair around her finger.

"I'm not there for you, darlin', my brothers will be. We protect old ladies like they're our own."

"I'm not an old lady," she argues.

I chuckle and collect a handful of her ass. "Just what we call our women. No matter how young and sexy as fuck they are."

She gives me a chaste kiss, then asks, "So what did he say?"

"He said you're a liar and a manipulator who tricked me into protecting you."

Her lips part, and her gaze shifts to the floor. "Do you believe him?"

I cradle her cheeks in my stained and calloused hands, tipping her head up so she can see the truth in my eyes. "Fuck no."

Breaks my heart when I see relief cross her face. She whispers, "I never told anyone what was happening because he was so good at making people believe his lies."

"That's reasonable. You didn't have someone you could trust before now. But darlin', there ain't nothing he could tell me about you I'd believe."

"Thank you."

"Now come here and give me some more sugar."

She kisses me hard and fast for a long minute and rubs her tits against my chest, bringing my dick to life. It's not until I try to snake a hand under her skirt that she stops.

"Client meeting," she says in explanation.

I groan. "Fine, but you're sleeping over at Loki's tonight."

"I can't. That's so weird." Her little nose screws up.

"It's not weird. Birdie told me she wants you there. She's happy for us."

"Fine. I'll bring dinner."

I set her back in her chair and walk over to the door. "My girl taking care of me, making sure I eat dinner. A man could get used to that."

She rolls her eyes. "It's Chinese, not a home-cooked dinner."

"Don't matter. Still like it."

Chapter
THIRTEEN

Bexley

My eyes open to a beautiful sight. Wes is facing me, eyes closed and face lax. His bushy beard is messy, matching the caramel brown hair that is sticking up in every direction.

He's naked, though the sheet is covering his lower half. His chest is covered in curls, but they're sparse enough to show off the plethora of tattoos scattered all over his torso, which are dark both in color and theme. There's a snarling evil skull with sharp teeth on one pec, and the other has the same skull, only this one has a sinister smile and crown on his head. Above both are the words "Full Throttle" in a regal font.

All the Royal Bastards have their RBMC logo tattooed somewhere on them, and even though I can't see it from this position, I know Wes's covers his entire back.

His whole body tells a story that's dark and bloody. All except one. I lightly trail my finger down the tattoo on his shoulder so I don't wake him up. It's the only one he has that isn't black and gray, so it stands out against the others. The style is original, too, this one being a realistic portrait of a woman I don't know. She's on a swing, legs straight out in front of her and golden hair trailing behind her as she leans back, a big smile on her pretty face.

"It's my mom," Wes says, his voice sleep-rough and sexy.

"She's beautiful." I prop myself up on an elbow to get a better look. "Where is she?"

"Lives in Vegas last I checked."

"You don't know for sure?"

"Nah. She left when I was seven, fell in love with my little league coach. She divorced Pops and moved in with him. For about a year, I got tossed back and forth. When her new husband got a job in Vegas, I guess he became more important to her than I was." His tone is so matter of fact, he could be reading an article from a paper.

"You never saw her after that?" I ask.

"I flew to Vegas for the weekend a few times. But it was clear to everyone that I didn't fit in with her new family. My coach was a widower with two small kids who were total opposites of me. They didn't want to play in the mud or take things apart to see how they worked. They were content reading books and doing art projects. Eventually, my mom phased herself out of my life completely." He reaches over and pulls the sheet down to expose my breasts. His hungry gaze fixates on them while his fingertip circles my nipple slowly.

I ignore my tingling pussy because I'm not done with this conversation. "Have you thought about reaching out to her now that you're an adult?"

His finger continues to circle teasingly, moving back and forth between my heavy breasts. "No. The memories I have before she left are good ones. Like my tattoo. That day she'd taken me to the park. We swung on the swing set for hours and hours. Pops even came for a while, which is how I got the picture for this. It'll be devastating if I contact her and find out she's anything but the person in that picture. I'd rather remember her like this." He slaps a beefy hand over the tattoo before returning to cup my breast.

"I guess I just... mmm." My thought gets caught off by the feeling of his warm, wet mouth on my neck. He sucks and bites his way down to my collarbone, where he licks a path down to my breast. I guess this conversation is over.

"Gotta say, love when you sleep over," he says, latching onto my nipple and sucking hard.

This is the fourth night in two weeks that I've stayed at Birdie and Loki's place. Despite them telling me they don't mind having me here, it makes me feel like I'm a teenager sneaking into my boyfriend's house. I don't like it.

I don't particularly like staying at the clubhouse either, but at least I have my own space, and the guys mostly leave me alone. My apartment was cleaned, but it's empty, and I don't feel safe there anymore.

He releases my nipple with a *pop* and moves to the other. My breasts have always been sensitive to the point where I can orgasm from stimulation alone. Wes figured this out real quick, and now most times we have sex, my first orgasm comes from his mouth on my breasts.

"Fucking hell, these tits drive me crazy." He throws the sheets and blanket off the bed, exposing both of our naked bodies. "Lie back. Picked something up the other day."

I fall back, curious about what and how he picked something up, considering he has that monitor on his ankle. "*You* picked something up?"

"I'm not stupid. Had a prospect do it." He reaches over me, opening a nightstand and coming back with a black velvet bag.

"You had a prospect pick up a sex toy? That's not embarrassing."

"Maybe for him because now every time he sees you, he'll be thinking about your tight buds pinched between these." He pulls out two metal clamps held together by a chain. They look like industrial tweezers with a black silicone tip.

I cover my breasts. I thought he meant an edible bra or lube. "Those look painful."

His lips curl ever-so-slightly. "You're a pain slut. You just don't know it."

"I am not," I say with conviction.

He puts the clamps back in the pouch before setting it on the bed. Pushing my hands away, he says, "Tell me you don't cream all over my cock when I slap your ass hard enough to bruise it."

He's right. I love the sting, and the marks he leaves turn me on. But a clamp? On my nipples? That seems aggressive. "That's different."

"Mind if I test my theory?"

Wanting to know if he's right, I say, "Do your worst."

With a hand on one side of my right tit, holding it in place, his other rears back before slapping it hard. I gasp and feel moisture building between my legs.

Oh, my God. I'm a pain slut.

"Tell me you aren't dripping wet right now." He slaps my breast again, harder, and in a way that catches my nipple. "Spread your legs for me, darlin.'"

When I don't react quick enough, he smacks the soft skin of my inner thigh to get me moving faster. It works, and my thighs spread for him.

He presses a finger inside me and groans. "See? You're soaked for me. Can we try the clamps?"

Another finger joins the first, filling me deliciously. He strokes me from the inside, causing my body to light up from head to toe. I'd agree to anything if it meant he kept playing my body like an instrument. "Okay, I'll try."

He removes his fingers and licks them clean. I've never met a man who loves to eat pussy as much as Wes. I'm not complaining; his tongue is magic, and the sounds he makes while he does it make me feel like the sexiest woman in the world.

"I should shower if you're going to do any more of that," I say. I showered yesterday after he fucked me twice, but I sweat in my sleep, especially with a bear of a man holding me to him all night. There's no way I'm fresh down there.

"You fucking crazy? Can't taste you after a shower." He picks up the pouch and pulls out the clamp again.

"You're weird."

He shrugs. "Like the way you taste. Especially after a long day of work when the flavor has time to develop."

My face twists in disgust, but the expression dies when Wes places a clamp on my nipple and tightens it to the first notch.

"This okay?" he asks, and I nod. "How about this?"

He tightens it to the second notch. Instantly, the tip of my nipple pinks up and swells out of the clamp. It stings like a bitch, but it's a pain that only adds to my arousal.

I like my dry lips and say, "I like it."

"Knew you would, darlin'. I'm gonna leave it there for now." He pulls out the other clamp and repeats the process, going slow and checking in with me.

When he moves away, the chain connecting the clamps falls and tugs on my nipples enough to make me gasp. I squeeze my eyes shut, trying to ignore the constant sting, but Jesus Christ, this hurts. Then his hand is between my legs again, two fingers stroking slowly and his palm grinding against my clit.

My eyes pop open to see a behemoth of a man raised up to his knees, his pierced cock hard and the tip glistening with pre-cum. It turns him on to see me like this. He finger fucks me until my toes curl and an orgasm claims my body. I cover my mouth to stop the moan from escaping as I writhe in pleasure with Wes's gaze devouring my every move.

"Luckiest man in the goddamn world," he says, his voice thick with lust.

"Come here, and you'll get even luckier." I take his cock in hand and stroke him as he straddles my torso, careful not to put pressure on my achy breasts.

"Open wide, darlin.'"

I wrap my lips around his tip, twirling my tongue around each steel ball before lowering down his hard length and sucking. His pre-cum is salty and heady, a small taste of what's to come. His thrusts are slow and drawn out. He wants this to last, and goddamn it, I do too.

I flatten my tongue and open my throat to accommodate his size, relaxing into it despite my nipples being on fire. No matter how careful he is, every time his heavy balls drag against the chain, a current of pain shoots through my chest.

"Sexy as hell with my dick in your mouth, darlin'. Be even sexier with my dick between these tits." He pulls out, his cock wet and dripping with saliva, leaving a trail down my body as he moves lower and positions his dick between my breasts. "Might hurt some, but I know you can handle it."

He squeezes my breasts around himself, using my spit as lube. My nipples scream at me, but the sight of his veiny cock completely wrapped up by triple Ds turns me on. On a forward thrust, I tilt my head up and lick his head, needing more of his taste on my tongue.

"Shit, you'll make me come if you keep that up. And I have other plans for you." His hands move away, and my breasts fall to the side. "I don't want to spill my seed anywhere but inside you now that there're no barriers."

We both got tested and are completely healthy. I was a little surprised by Wes's results. I know his history with women, and although he told me he always used protection, it's hard to believe. Last night was the first night without, and all I have to say about that is I'm glad I'm on birth control because he would've knocked me up.

He kisses his way down my body, stopping to flick my nipples with his tongue. I groan and twist away, though they're mostly numb from the lack of blood flow.

"Next time, I'll clamp your clit," he says, pinching the very bundle of nerves he's talking about.

"We'll see."

"You don't think I can talk you into it?" One eyebrow raises in challenge.

"I can say no to you."

"Oh yeah?"

"You don't own my body."

"Oh yeah?"

"Just fuck me already," I say. I'm so aroused, I can't take it. Every inch of me feels antsy, creating a sense of urgency.

"Yes, ma'am." He spreads my thighs and positions himself at my opening. "You're so wet, darlin'. It's dripping down to your pretty little asshole."

He pushes into me with one solid thrust, my body stretching to accommodate him. A rush of air leaves his lungs as he presses even further in. I squeeze my internal muscles, loving the way it feels to be this full. He rolls his hips with each thrust, his thumb rubbing circles on my clit and his other hand pulling on the chain connecting the clamps.

"Baby, oh my God. That feels so good." I reach above my head, gripping the headboard as he picks up the pace, drilling me into the mattress. I tilt my hips, meeting him thrust for thrust.

"Best pussy I've ever had. Never gonna give you up. Not ever," he swears.

I know it's something people say in the moment, but I hold on to those words. It should terrify me. After all, I currently have a man out there who won't let me go, even though I don't want anything to do with him. But Wes is different. He's kind and respectful yet turns into a filthy animal in bed, so I don't mind when he says I'm his. I know if that ever changed for either of us, he'd let me go.

I've been so skeptical of him and so hesitant to trust him, but he proves his integrity every day. I didn't want this. I had plans that didn't involve a man, especially a client and a criminal, but here I am, falling for this man.

"Need you to come, darlin'. Can you do that for me?" His movements become erratic and urgent. He's on the brink but, like a true gentleman, denies himself until he gets me off.

He pinches my clit and tugs. Like detonating a bomb, I explode around him.

"Yes. Yes. Yes," I call out, not caring if Birdie and Loki can hear me.

"Fuck. My girl milks me so good." The muscles on his face tense and his jaw clenches. He grips onto my knees for purchase, his hard cock hitting the spot inside that drives me crazy.

He thrusts harder and harder, drawing my orgasm out until my vision tunnels, and I'm worried I'll pass out. It'll be worth it to keep feeling like this a while longer.

My entire body spasms, and I have no idea what's up or down. The only thing I know is I've never felt this incredible in my life. Warmth gushes inside me, telling me Wes is right there with me. We ride it out until we're nothing but loose limbs, and he collapses at my side.

"Give me a minute, and I'll get those things off you," he says. Beads of sweat have collected on his hairline and in his chest hair. He worked hard for that one.

"I don't know if I want you to. Something tells me it's going to hurt." I glance down at my puffy nipples.

"Part of the fun." He sits up and carefully removes the one on the right.

"Holy shit," I curse. It hurts so much worse than I imagined it would, but it also wakes my overstimulated clit up. My whole life, I never realized what I'd been missing.

Wes gently kisses my abused flesh, running his tongue along my areola. I wince, not because it hurts, but because it's turning me on. He unclamps my left breast and gives it the same treatment. He moves to pull away, but I'm too lost. I tangle my fingers in his hair, keeping him in place.

"Gotta say, babe. Love that your tits are so sensitive," he mumbles before getting back to work.

He flutters his tongue along my stiff peaks while kneading my breasts before sucking each one into his warm and wet mouth. He switches from gentle and soft touches to tugging, pulling, twisting, and biting until a second orgasm racks through my body. It's not nearly as intense as the first, but I'm not complaining.

I relax into the mattress, smiling and feeling light. Wes brings me to his chest, snaking an arm under my head and clamping his hand on my bare hip.

"Never knew what I was missing," he says.

"What were you missing?" I ask, lifting my head to look into his whiskey eyes.

"You."

Chapter
FOURTEEN

Khan

I kick up my feet on the cinderblock surrounding the fire pit outside of the clubhouse and light a cig, ready to watch the show that's about to go down.

Bex has been bugging us to teach her some self-defense, and somehow, she talked Roch into doing some training with her today. He's ex-Army and has combat training, so he's a good resource, but the kid doesn't talk much—been through some trauma he doesn't like to talk about—and he's not the most outgoing person. Yet somehow, my woman talked him into it.

Truly steps out of the casita she and Roch live in, looking a bit green. She plops down in the chair next to me and sighs.

"What's going on with you?" I ask.

"Morning sickness. Our little peanut is trying to kill me." She rests her hand on her small bump.

"Sorry about that. The baby doing well otherwise?"

"Yep. Growing like a weed." She beams at me, but it's a tired smile.

"That's good. Hasn't been a Royal Bastard baby born in a long ass time. I can't wait."

Our chapter started with Loki and Goblin's old men. We've always been on the smaller side, keeping under the radar to not become a target of law enforcement. The old-timers all had kids, but the only ones who stuck around to become legacies are Loki and Goblin. We're now at eight patched members and three prospects. We've had too many losses the last few years and are only now building our numbers back up.

"How do you think this is going to go?" Truly nods toward where Roch and Bexley are standing in the middle of the lawn, cuddling up with a few of Roch's rescue pit bulls. The man has never said no to taking in a dog who would otherwise be euthanized.

"Not sure."

Truly cups her hands around her mouth and shouts, "Show her some moves."

Roch stands, and instead of voicing a fighting stance, he physically positions her. If it were anyone other than my brother handling Bex like that, he'd be dead before he could ever even look at her again. But I know my brother only has eyes for his much younger, pregnant girlfriend, so I tamp down the possessiveness.

Truly and I watch as Roch tries to show her some power moves and how to get out of holds. Bex's determination only adds to her sex appeal. Even after she nails a move, she makes Roch repeat it over and over with her until she's confident.

"Bexley's pretty awesome," Truly says.

"I'm a lucky bastard." I take in my woman, dressed in black shorts that appear to be painted onto her body and a low-cut tank top showing off her ample cleavage. Today her hair is pulled up into a high ponytail. It's my favorite way she wears it, though it doesn't happen often. She prefers it down, but I like it when she exposes her long and delicate neck. Gives me something to wrap around my fist while I'm fucking her from behind.

"She's lucky too, you know? When I first started coming around, I didn't think I would fit in. But you took me under your wing and showed me how to loosen up and have a good time."

"Got bitched out by your grumpy-ass man a lot in those early days." I scratch my chin through my beard, remembering how pissed Roch was when he was out of town, and I taught Truly how to walk on hot coals.

Truly laughs. "I miss being able to participate in all your shenanigans. Now that I'm knocked up, Roch won't so much as let me walk to the mailbox alone."

"Don't blame him. The second I knock up that woman out there, I'll have her in bubble wrap with a prospect trailing her wherever she goes."

Truly stills and glances over at me. "You're thinking about babies?"

"Wasn't until now."

"That's a big step. It's only been a few weeks."

I get what it must look like to her. Before I went to jail, I was fucking every woman I came across. Then I get released, and I'm talking babies.

"Been a long time comin'."

"I honestly thought you two hated each other. You fight like cats and dogs whenever you're in the same room."

I smirk. "That's called foreplay, darlin'."

She presses her lips together and nods. "I guess that makes sense."

"When did you know Roch was the one for you?" I ask.

"First day I saw him." She bites her smile. "I was a little girl, so of course it was a stupid crush, but deep down, I just knew. There was this magic between us I couldn't deny."

I ponder that for a minute. I wouldn't say I knew I was

gonna lock Bex down the first time I saw her. I thought she was hot, but I knew she was out of my league, so I brushed it off. Or tried to, at least. She wasn't my type in the least, but I think that's because I wasn't ready for a forever kind of girl.

After spending time in lock-up, I realized I wanted more for my life. The second that hit me, there was no question about who I wanted the *more* with. It's always been her. I was just too stupid to act on it.

"Never seen my brother so happy. Glad he found you," I say.

"Shit. Y'okay?" Roch asks. I look over to see Bex on the ground and Roch standing over her.

Truly and I are on our feet, rushing over to the lawn in seconds. Bex's eyes are pinched shut, and she's rubbing the back of her head.

"Back up," I growl, crouching down and looking Bex up and down for injuries.

Roch moves to stand next to Truly.

"I'm okay. Just missed my cue and hit my head on the ground." Her eyes open, and she sits up. "Won't make that mistake again."

"What the fuck, Roch? She's new to this." I look up at my brother, who turns sheepish.

"Sorry."

"It's not his fault," Bex scolds. "This was on me."

"Still. He should've been more careful." I brush a strand of hair that had worked itself out of her ponytail from her forehead.

Before I can react, Bex sweeps a leg under me, throwing me off balance. I land on my back, the wind leaving my lungs. Then she's on top of me, pinning me to the ground.

"Listen, caveman. I got this." She grins proudly.

"Can't breathe," I groan, clutching my chest.

"Don't be a baby. You're fine." She leans over and kisses me full on the mouth.

"I think they've got it from here," Truly says, grabbing Roch's hand and dragging him back to their casita.

"Thanks, Roch!" Bex calls out.

"Pretty damn smug, aren't you?" I ask.

"Just a little." She grips my wrists and pins them to the grass. "I think I like being in charge. Better watch out, or I'll make you my bitch."

I let her go on, thinking she's in control for another minute before rolling us both. In seconds, we've switched positions. She struggles from under me, twisting and turning, her face turning red and working harder than she was with Roch. I admit, she learned a few things today, but it's not enough to overpower a man as big as I am.

"What were you saying?" I ask.

"Asshole," she grits out, all her smugness wiped away, and what's left is a spittin' mad, adorable kitten. Though I'm sure if I called her that, she'd cut my balls off while I sleep.

"I think it's my turn to train with you," I say, standing and holding out a hand to help her up, which she ignores.

"You got moves?" She gets up and dusts herself off.

I hook an arm around her waist and pull her to me. "You know I do."

"I'm not looking for those kinds of moves, perv. I need to know how to protect myself. This is serious."

"All right. Calm down and come here. I have something for you."

She follows me into the clubhouse and down the hall to my old bedroom that she's now taken over. I hardly recognize the place anymore. Anything that was mine has been tucked away somewhere, replaced by tons of girly shit.

"Been doing some shopping?" I ask, walking the perimeter of the room and taking in all the recent additions.

A jewelry stand now lives on the dresser, along with a variety of makeup and perfume. There's a plant stand in the corner with some kind of large-leafed species in it. On the nightstand sits a laptop and phone charger. The bedding's been swapped too. The black and white checkers are gone and in its place is a silky purple comforter with matching pillows.

"A little. Miles makes an awesome shopping partner." She sits down on the bed.

A jealous spark ignites in my gut. I fucking hate that I can't take her out and have her on my arm. Instead, a motherfucking prospect gets the honor.

"What's wrong?" she asks, noticing the shift in my mood.

"Wish I didn't have this fucking tracker." I lift my pant leg.

"You don't like shopping," she reminds me.

"No, but if it meant spending time with you and making you happy, I'd do it."

She laughs. "Enjoy your time outside of the mall then, big man, because once you're clear, I'll be dragging you all over this town. I have an entire wardrobe to replace. That takes time. Did you say you have a present for me?"

"Right." I walk over to the closet and pull a wooden box from the top shelf. "You been snooping around in here?"

"No. Should I?"

I shrug. "Don't care if you do. Got nothing to hide."

I sit down next to her and open the box, revealing my knife collection. Before I got locked up, I always had one or two of these knives on me. Can't do that now in case the cops show up, or I get pulled over. I miss my life.

"Roch's good with hand-to-hand combat, which'll get you out of certain situations. But you need a backup plan, and that's where my specialties come in." I pull out my push dagger and remove it from the leather sheath. It's a two-inch, serrated-edge blade with a polymer handle that fits nicely gripped in a fist between the pointer and middle fingers. Perfect for self-defense. "If you get in a bad situation, you won't have time to unfold a knife. This one is a fixed blade and can be stored in this sheath when you're not using it. You can tuck it in your bra or wear it around your neck."

"I'm not wearing a knife as jewelry."

"Until this shit with Martin gets fixed, you sure as shit will."

"I don't even know how to use that thing."

"It's not hard." I position it in my hand, making a fist to hold it in place. "One side is serrated and will shred your target's flesh. The other side is sharp enough to slice. And the tip can pierce through leather, so you can stab or slash, whatever feels right in the situation."

"I can't believe this is my life." Bex rubs her forehead.

"I'm doing my damnedest to make sure you never need to use it, but you should be prepared." I hand it over and show her the correct positioning and hold.

She stands, moving to the center of the room, and punches through the air, getting a feel for the weight and movement. I lay back on the bed, smiling and propping myself up with an elbow to watch the show.

"Take that." She slashes the knife to the right and left. "Oh, you weren't expecting this"—she thrusts it forward—"now were you?"

"You're sexy when you get all violent."

"I look stupid."

"Nah. My woman armed and ready to take someone out? That's sexy as fuck."

"Oh yeah?" She faces me, her eyes going half-lidded and her lips parting. I sit up as she walks over to me and lightly drags the blade from my jaw down to the base of my throat. "Is that sexy?"

"Fuuuuuuuck," I groan, slightly nervous but mostly aroused.

With one hand, she grabs the neckline of my T-shirt, and with the other, she glides the blade through the fabric. Cool air hits my now exposed chest.

She shoves me onto my back and straddles me. "Does this turn you on?" I gulp, and her pretty face pinches in concentration as she trails the blade down my torso until she reaches my belt, leaving a scratch behind.

"Didn't take long for the power to go to your head," I say.

"It's heady knowing I could take a life." She swirls the tip of the blade across my lower abdomen.

"You wanna kill me, darlin'?" In one swift motion, I grip her wrist—the one holding the knife—and roll us over, pinning her wrist above her head and squeezing. She squeals in pain, trying not to drop the blade, but eventually, it falls to the mattress. "You're gonna need some training."

"Ow!" She cradles her wrist to her chest.

I take off my ruined shirt and pick up the knife. "What about you? Does this turn you on?"

Unlike her cautious moves, mine are practiced and swift. I slice down the center of her black sports bra, and her tits spring free. Her delicious rosy nipples are pulled tight, giving me my answer.

"Better hold still. Wouldn't want to cut you," I say as I take the tip of the blade and drag it across her neck, then circle it around each full breast, pressing hard enough for her to feel the bite but not hard enough to break the skin.

"Wes," she breathes out, her chest rising and falling.

"Tell me to stop and I will." I bring the blade to her nipple and push lightly. "These nipples would look so pretty pierced. Would you do that for me, darlin'? Would you pierce these pretty nipples for me?"

She nods, her hips lifting and grinding against the steel rod in my pants. Goddamn, this woman is perfect for me. I push a little harder, barely piercing her skin. She gasps when a drop of blood appears. I pull away, watching the bright red collect on her puckered skin.

"Beautiful," I murmur, taking her nipple into my mouth and sucking it clean. The metallic taste bursts on my tongue as I suck and nip. "Now you're part of me."

I release her nipple with a *pop* and pick the blade back up. The blood ignited my inner demon, and there's no stopping me now. I need her naked and under me. I need to fuck.

I slice down the front of her tiny black booty shorts, pleased to find she's not wearing panties. A few more cuts and I'm able to strip her free of the fabric. The entire time she watches me with lustful excitement twinkling in her eyes. I don't think she's ever felt what it means to be free. She's been in fight-or-flight mode her whole life, never allowing the twisted and perverse in.

She has me now, and in my world, nothing is off-limits. We chase what makes us feel alive, grabbing ahold of it and using it for our own pleasure. I'm about to show her what it feels like to be me.

"Look at this pussy, all wet and swollen for me. I think she likes the danger too." I take the blade and carefully run it up her slit, gathering moisture. With our gazes locked, I bring it to my mouth and lick her juices off it. "Mmm. You taste like heaven. Men like me don't deserve heaven, but you're taking me there anyway. Spread those legs wider. Show me what's mine."

Her knees drop to either side, pussy lips parting and sweet little clit peeking out. I gaze down at my woman, eating up the vision in front of me. Her fat tits, soft belly, and thick thighs do something to me that no woman has ever done before.

"What now?" she asks, placing a finger on her pouty lip.

"Now we play."

Chapter
FIFTEEN

Bexley

The person I've forced myself to be for more than half my life wants to jump off the bed and run. I seriously allowed him to puncture my nipple and lick the blood. And instead of being disgusted, I encouraged it. I embraced it. I got turned on by it.

I don't recognize who I am when I'm with Wes. I've been called cold-hearted and detached, but it never bothered me because I was doing what was necessary. Things like love and sex were luxuries I couldn't afford. No one could know who I really was and what I did.

Then Wes happened. I don't know how he snuck in, but he's here and my defenses are gone. He knows everything and still stands by me. I don't have to hide. I'm stripped bare for him, physically and emotionally, open to whatever he wants.

It's scary and thrilling.

He kneels before me, removes my socks and shoes, and lifts my left leg onto his shoulder. He hums as he kisses the sole of my foot and sucks my toe into his warm mouth. I don't have a foot fetish, but I'm finding I'm into a lot of things I didn't even know existed.

With Wes, nothing is off-limits, and it's so fucking sexy.

Pulling back out the sinister-looking blade, he runs it down the underside of my foot, making me giggle. His brow lifts in response, and he presses harder, cutting off all my laughter. I don't know why I trust him not to hurt me more than I can handle, but I do. I crave the way he takes control and how he makes me feel.

"Look at how pretty your skin looks with my marks all over it." He drags the knife down my calf and up my inner thigh, leaving an angry red line behind. I glance down my body and see similar marks around my breasts. "Someday, I'll take you to my tattoo artist and have 'property of Khan' inked on your ass."

"I don't like tattoos," I say, then amend, "On me, I mean. They look fine on you." I wince, but he moves on.

"Doesn't matter. You'll do it because you know it'll make me happy." He traces the blade around my pussy lips. It's so sharp that one slip could be tragic. The thrill only arouses me more.

"We'll see," I say as the blade slips between my lips, finding my clit where he digs in just a little more. I fight the instincts telling me to move away from the intrusion. The sting of the blunt tip on my sensitive bundle of nerves makes my pussy drip with arousal.

What the fuck is wrong with me?

He sets my leg down, moves the blade to my belly button, and slowly drags the knife from my naval to the top of my pussy, only this time he breaks the skin, causing me to hiss. "You're so pretty when you bleed."

This is so fucked up, but I'm too far gone, too entranced in the sensations of pain and pleasure. With the palm of his hand, he smears the small amount of blood across my stomach, his eyes wild with animalistic lust.

"You with me, darlin'?" he asks.

"Yes. God, yes." My pussy aches for him, my nipples tingle with desire for him. Only him.

"Tell me what you want."

"You. I want you," I plead.

"Be specific. Need to hear the words."

I've never been a talker in bed. I've never even been much of a participant. It was all so mechanical before, like a chore list: undress, put penis in vagina, man orgasms, kick him out, and then use my vibrator to do what he couldn't. Even when I was with my husband, sex was for his pleasure only.

Such a stark contrast to what is happening now.

"Your cock, Wes. I need your cock."

He tosses the knife onto the mattress and undoes his belt buckle before letting his pants drop to the floor. My mouth waters at the sight of his engorged dick pointing in my direction and weeping with pre-cum.

"You want it? Come get it." He folds his arms, challenging me.

Like a wanton hussy, I sink to my knees in front of him and take his hard length in hand. Wrapping my lips around the tip, I glide my palms up and down, feeling every pulsing vein. I moan when his pre-cum hits my tongue. Pride fills me knowing I did this to him. He's hard because of me.

"Not in the mood for your sweetness," he says, tipping my chin up. "Wanna fuck your face. You good with that?"

"I don't know." He must know by now that before him, my sex life was stale.

"I do something that makes you uncomfortable, and you can't use your words because your mouth is too full of my cock, smack my thigh. Got it?"

"O-okay."

"Now open wide and stick your tongue out," he orders.

I do as he says, shaking from nerves. I've seen porn, I know what this is, but does the woman enjoy it? Because it doesn't seem like fun to me.

He slaps his dick on my tongue once, twice, three times before inching it into my mouth. I remain frozen, unsure if there's something I'm supposed to do. It's a wasted worry, though, because Wes takes over by wrapping my ponytail around his fist and holding me in place while he pumps in and out.

The thrusts are slow and teasing at first, but he soon quickens the pace and the depth. He bumps the back of my throat. The metal balls of his piercing are unforgiving, and I fight the intrusion, gagging and pushing against his thighs to get away. What I don't do is slap his leg. That's all it would take to make him stop, yet I can't do it. I *want* him to keep going.

"Relax. Let it happen," he coos, pulling out of my mouth. I get ahold of myself, taking a deep breath and nodding up at him to continue. "What do you do if you need me to stop?"

I slap a hand on his thigh, proving I remember.

"Good girl. Now open up." He grips the base of his cock and feeds it to me. This time, I breathe through my nose and open my throat. He pushes all the way in until his balls are pressed against my chin. "Fuck yes."

He repeats this over and over before returning to his punching, fast-paced thrusts, careful not to pull out too far to save my teeth from his piercings. Drool and pre-cum drip down my chin and onto my breasts. The small voice in my head tells me this is debasing, but instead of it turning me off the way it would with any other man, I embrace it.

Yes, it's demeaning, but I fucking love every second.

"Reach down and play with that dripping pussy," he growls out.

I skim my hand down my body and settle it between my legs. Wes is right. I'm so wet I'm leaking onto the floor. I moan around his cock as I rub my swollen clit, my senses going into overdrive. The wet, slurping sounds of Wes's dick working in and out of my mouth, his leather and cigarette scent invading my nostrils, his intense stare focused on me, and the feeling of my finger slipping around in my own arousal is too much, and an orgasm hits me like a ton of bricks.

I cry out, the sound muffled with my mouth full of him. My body's shaking, and my weak legs want to give out, but I stay strong, clinging to his thighs as I start to come down from my high.

Wes pulls out and lifts me to my feet before bending me over the bed. He drops to his knees and, with his big palms, spreads my ass wide. He buries his face between my cheeks and licks me clean. I squirm when his tongue probes my back entrance, but his hold is solid.

His hot breath on my most private area, along with his magical tongue hitting all the right places, forces another, more powerful orgasm to hit me. Everything I've ever thought about sex has been turned upside down by this man.

"Oh my God. Oh my God. Yes!" I cry out, aware that the entire clubhouse can probably hear but not caring even a little. He stays with me, flicking my clit with his tongue through my release, only pulling away when I become over-sensitized and squeeze my legs together.

He stands up and slaps my ass hard enough to leave a stinging handprint. "Gonna fuck your pussy now, baby. Hang on."

The next thing I feel is his huge cock slamming into me. I blow out a breath. My walls are engorged, making it a tighter fit—especially with the steel balls circling his tip—but holy hell, does it feel good. He slaps a palm across the other cheek, causing me to jump. Then he does it again and again until I'm not sure I can take anymore. But I take it because I love it, and

I want my ass to be bruised by him. I want to remember this moment every time I go to sit, and the ache is there, throbbing.

He curls his body around me, still rutting into me, and reaches underneath to palm my breasts. His fingers find my nipples, and he tugs on them roughly. He said he wanted me to get them pierced. Never in my wildest dreams would I even consider it, but now, all I can think about is making the appointment when we're done here.

If he doesn't kill me.

"Mine. You hear me, darlin'? Mine." He chants over and over until even I believe it.

A powerful gush of warmth fills me as he bites down on my earlobe and tugs. His movements slow, and on his final thrust, he holds himself deep inside me.

I squeeze around him with all my might, eliciting a full-body shudder from him.

We're both panting as the sexual frenzy around us slows. Along with that, my rational brain decides to finally show up, making me realize what we just did. Shame, like I've never felt, hits me, and I move out of his hold to scour the floor for my clothes.

Wes, like the arrogant bastard he is, flops onto the bed like he hasn't a care in the world. He rolls to his side and props his head up with a hand, watching my freak-out with a devious smile on his lips.

"What are you looking at?" I ask, giving up on finding my top and instead pull his oversized T-shirt over my head.

"Knew you were going to freak," he says.

"I'm not 'freaking.'"

"Darlin', you are."

"Why am I gathering my things? This is my room. You should be the one to leave." I toss his jeans at him. "Put those on."

"Nope." He lies back and stretches. "I got another hour, and

I'm gonna spend it cuddling with your crazy ass. Now come here."

I whisper shout, "Do you know what we just did? It has to be illegal in all fifty states." I lift my shirt up to expose my bloodstained stomach. "I'm bleeding."

"Eh, it's just a scratch. Gotta say, it's hot as hell you bled for me. Shows me how much you trust me, and darlin', I love that too."

"Did you do this with all your other women?" I hate myself for asking. It sounds so insecure and not who I am. This man is making me insane.

"First of all, I don't have other women. If you're asking about past *relationships*, no. Can't say I've ever done anything like that. Dreamed of it, wished I could find someone who let me be as wild as I want. Now that I found you, I don't plan on ever letting you go."

I've spent a lot of time talking myself out of giving into Khan. I made all the reasons why into mantras I'd repeat to myself whenever I knew I'd see him. Mantras that mostly involved other women. It's hard for me to turn that voice in my head off. But hearing those words calms my rapid heartbeat and reminds me we're not in that place anymore.

I drop his pants to the ground, pull his T-shirt off, and climb into bed, resting my cheek on his chest and tangling my legs with his.

"There she is." He smooths down my hair. "Knew I'd get my woman back, just gotta let her throw a tantrum now and then."

"You say that like I'm a child."

He reaches under my arm and grins, my breast in his palm. "Not a child. Just a woman who doesn't know what it means to have a man."

"I've been in relationships," I defend.

"Not with a man like me." He tips my chin so our gazes meet. "I think we need some rules."

"You have rules?"

"Not yet, but they'll come to me." He thinks for a minute, a devious grin on his lips. "Rule number one, as long as we're both into it, we do it. No judgment and no feeling guilty afterward, because darlin', I don't regret one second of what we just did."

"I don't either," I realize aloud.

"Rule number two, no more freaking out and trying to escape after we fuck. Just had you dirty, now I want you sweet." He wraps his arms all the way around me and plants a kiss on my forehead. "And rule number three, your problems are my problems. None of this handling shit on your own anymore. I'm your man, and I don't take that shit lightly. You got issues, you tell me about them. Got it?"

His brown eyes pierce my own, holding so much truth, it hurts to see. "Got it."

"Good. Now rub those titties on me, so I have something to look forward to when I'm sleepin' all alone at Loki's."

I laugh but climb on top of him and kiss him while I move my breasts up and down his chest. We make out like high school kids for an entire hour before there's a knock at the door.

"Time to go, VP," Miles yells.

"On it," Wes calls back before turning his attention back to me. "You could always come to Tahoe with me so we can continue this."

"Not tonight. I have a client meeting early tomorrow morning, and I need some sleep." I peel myself off him and pull the sheets over my naked body.

"You can sleep over there," he argues. I pin him with a knowing look. "Yeah, you're right. Fine, but tomorrow night, yeah?"

"Sure, Wes. Tomorrow."

He climbs out of bed, quickly dressing before bending down and kissing my temple. "Good luck tomorrow. Call me."

"Goodnight."

"Night."

The door softly clicks shut after him, and I get out of bed, first to lock the door and then to start the shower. The pipes are old, and it takes a good five minutes before the hot water reaches this end of the house. While I wait, I trace the scratches and cuts down my body. I don't understand why it turns me on to see them there, but all I can think about is next time, next time, next time.

I need there to be a next time.

Chapter SIXTEEN

Khan

"Wes?" Bex's voice carries down the stairs at the clubhouse where I'm working.

"Down here," I holler back.

She reaches the bottom of the staircase and looks around. "Wow. It looks amazing down here already."

"What do I have to do to get you to call me Khan?" I ask.

"Um, nothing because it's not going to happen." Bex flips her hair off her shoulder.

I remove my safety goggles and stalk toward her. "Can we negotiate?"

"I'm not calling you by some stupid nickname."

"It's not a nickname, and it ain't stupid. It means something to me and this club," I say. Bex has a lot to learn about club life and what it means to be part of our family.

"Fine. What's the compromise?"

"When we're at the clubhouse or with my brothers, you call me Khan." I rest my hand on the base of her throat, smiling when her lips part and her breath catches. "When we're out in public but not with my brothers, you call me Wes." I tighten my grip and lean down until our faces are inches from each other. "And when we're in bed, you call me God."

I give her a quick peck and back away before she kicks me in the balls. Gotta stay on my toes with this one.

She snaps out of her fog, shaking her head. "Why don't I call you 'jackass' all the time instead?"

"That's not part of the deal." I put the goggles back on and sand the mud I used to fill the drywall joints. "Stay there unless you want to be covered in dust."

Today she's wearing a long-sleeve pinstriped shirt that wraps around her middle, emphasizing her glorious tits, and a pair of gray trousers that hug her ass then fall loosely down her legs. When my gaze reaches her feet, I notice she's wearing a pair of brick red high heels.

Need to fuck her in those shoes one day.

"Gladly."

"So, what's up?" I ask.

"I received a voicemail." She holds up her phone with a shaky hand.

"Oh yeah? Who from?"

"Martin," she chokes out.

I toss the sandpaper and rush back over to her. It's been a quiet few weeks with no contact. I thought my intimidation efforts worked, but I should've known better. Men like Martin have more money than sense.

"Gimme that." I take the phone from her and press the play button.

"Good morning, wife," he snarls. *"Sending the Royal Bastards after me was a nice touch. I see you've surrounded yourself with an unsavory clientele. It's a smart move, I'll say that much. But I'd think twice about doing that again. You don't seem to grasp the situation. I could call the disciplinary board right now and tell them*

who you really are. I could also tell them you're sleeping with your clients. I'm sure they'd be interested in both pieces of information.

"I think the voicemail is about to cut off, so let me get to the point. I want to schedule a meeting with you to discuss what you can do for me to keep your secrets buried. Tomorrow night. My office, say around six. Come alone. If I even hear a motorcycle engine, the meeting will be over, and I'll report you to the board. Don't try me, Bexley. You know what happens when I get mad. Speaking of, how's your arm? Last time I saw you, wasn't it broken in two places? See you then."

I'm so pissed, I hurl the phone at the wall I just built, denting it and probably breaking the phone in the process. Who the hell does this guy think he is? No one is above the Royal Bastard's wrath. He has no idea the war he just started.

"Wes! That's my work phone." She picks it up off the ground and holds up the broken screen.

"Fuck the phone and fuck that motherfucker. Swear to God, he's a dead man walking, babe." I pace around the room, fighting the urge to put holes in all the walls I just finished erecting. "Sly has a whole closet of new phones. Have him give you a new one."

"That's not the point and you need to calm down. I spent the morning thinking about it, and I've decided I'm going to do it. I'll meet with him, find out what he wants from me, and then at least I can formulate a plan to get him out of my life." She covers her forehead with a hand and blinks away tears.

"Absolutely not. It's not safe, and we can't keep eyes on you. The bastard has tucked himself into the top corner office of that building. We can't get in without someone noticing." There is no way in hell I'll let her do this. I'll chain her up in this basement if I must. Or maybe lock her in a cage like Loki does to Birdie.

"I'll be fine. You've been teaching me some moves, and if he tries anything, I'll be prepared." She stands straighter, her confidence returning, remembering she's been learning a lot of self-defense techniques lately. She knows how to fight back.

She works hard every day with both me and Roch. She's a fast learner and is stronger than she looks. I'm proud of how determined she is, but practicing techniques and putting them to use in a real-world situation are two different things.

I stand firm. "This conversation is over. I said no. We'll figure something else out."

She tilts her head and narrows her eyes. Whatever thoughts are brewing in her head aren't good, and I almost back down. I put up a good front, but that's all it is, a front. This woman has my balls safely tucked away in her purse.

"With or without you," she bites out.

"What?"

"I'm doing this with or without you. So get on board or keep doing"—she motions around the room—"whatever it is you're doing."

"Not if I handcuff you to my bed, you won't. Don't think I won't do it either. I'll do whatever it takes to keep you safe."

"Want to make a bet?" She turns on her heels and stomps up the stairs.

"Goddamn it," I curse, tossing my face mask and goggles. I quickly brush the dust from my shirt and pants, knowing Sissy and Tabs will have my ass if I mess up their floors. Only thing worse than having one woman pissed at you, is having three women pissed at you.

I rush up the stairs and find Bex sitting at a table with Sly, talking in a hushed tone.

"What are you doing?" I demand.

"Sly is helping me come up with a plan," Bex says proudly.

"No, the fuck he ain't."

"Sorry, brother. Thought you were on board." Sly scoots his chair a few inches away from Bex. Smart man.

"Not on board," I clarify. "Not taking chances."

"Actually, of all the places he could've asked for her to meet him, his office isn't the best one if he has bad intentions. There're only two exits to that place, and they're both monitored twenty-four hours a day by a third-party security company. Those guys don't make enough money to overlook a body being carried out." Sly turns his laptop to show me what he's discovered. "And they don't make enough money to reject a bribe."

I sit down and light up a cig. "They'll give you access to their feed? Is there a camera in his office?"

"No, only in the hallway. And yes, I'm positive I can talk at least one of them into it. As for getting a camera in the office, I already took care of that when we paid him a visit. Asshole was so distracted by you, I slipped a cam in his bookcase. There's no audio, but at least we'll have a visual." Sly's grin is smug and proud.

"Have you been watching him this whole time?" I ask, pleased he had the forethought.

"Nah. It was more a 'just in case' situation. Wasn't sure we'd need it or not, but it looks like we will."

"Still not feeling good about sending her in there."

"You guys can watch from the street. If anything goes wrong, you'll be right there," Bex says.

"That's the problem. I can't wait on the street. Got lucky I didn't get picked up last time I paid him a visit. Can't risk it again. It'd kill me to be locked up, knowing that psycho is still after you." I flick my cig into the ashtray before taking another long drag.

"You trust your brothers, right?" she asks, knowing I do and also knowing that's how she'll get her way.

Gonna beat that ass red later for going around me. I shoot her a look that says as much, but she doesn't back down. Probably because spanking her makes that pussy gush.

"Yeah, I do," I concede.

"Perfect. Now I just have to talk to Loki," she says.

"I'll do it." I stamp my cig out and stand. "He doesn't like outsiders talking about club business."

"Except this isn't club business, and Loki and I have a good rapport." She stands and brushes a hand down her clothes.

"You're a difficult woman," I grumble.

"All the good ones are." She brushes her hair off her shoulder and walks into the Chapel where Loki's doing whatever the hell he does.

I follow her to the doorway, where I lean against the jamb.

"Do you have a minute?" Bex asks him.

Loki looks from me to her, confused. "Sure," he draws out.

Bex turns around and swings the door closed. I jump back to avoid getting slammed in the face by the heavy oak door.

I'm going to clamp her nipples extra tight tonight.

I pace up and down the main room, anxious for the door to open. Ten minutes later, it does. Bex walks out smiling, but Loki looks pissed.

"Khan, you got a minute?"

"Shit," I curse under my breath.

I shut the door behind me and take a seat across from him. "What's up?"

"Don't like being ambushed by your woman. The only reason I'm not pulling rank and giving you a disgusting chore list as penance is because she's our lawyer, and I don't want to piss her off." He pulls out a smoke and offers me the pack, but I decline.

"Understood."

"Next time your woman has a problem, I expect you to solve it," he says.

"She's been the club's lawyer long enough for you to know that's not going to happen."

He chuckles. "Guess you're right. But I'd still like to hear shit from you whenever possible."

"I'll let her know." I smirk and move to leave.

"We got her back, brother. Hand to God, this won't go south."

"Appreciate that." I give him a nod and set out to find my naughty girl.

I find her in our room, on the bed, laptop perched on her lap.

"Not now," she says. "I have a million emails to answer."

I kick the door shut and flip the lock before walking over to her and picking up the laptop.

"Wes, I told you. Not now."

Setting the laptop on the dresser, I say, "Don't like getting my ass chewed out by my prez."

"I'm sorry, but he was very accommodating. Along with him, Sly, Moto, and Goblin are coming. They'll take the cage, or whatever you call it, and watch from the street. If anything happens, they can be there in minutes."

"The way I see it, you have three strikes against you. First, going behind my back with Sly. Second, talking to Loki after I said no, and third, you see nothing wrong with any of this." I remove my belt slowly. Her brown eyes watch with interest and maybe a little fear.

She licks her lips. "What are you going to do? Spank me?"

"You'd enjoy that too much." I weave my belt together in a way that creates two holes. "Hands."

"What if I don't want to?"

"You say no, and this is over. You know that."

She rolls her eyes and offers up her hands. She can sass me and argue all she wants, but I know the truth. I place her hands through the two holes in the belt and pull it tight, making her gasp in surprise. I lift her by the leather until her hands are above her head, securing one of the belt loops over a hook I installed on the back of my headboard.

"You come prepared," she says, her voice already breathy and lust-filled.

"Regular boy scout." I salute her, then move to her shirt. When I pull on the tie at her waist, the shirt falls open, revealing a plain, black cotton bra. It's so unlike her to not have on something lacy.

"Sorry, I went for comfort today."

"You think I don't find this as sexy as lingerie? If anything, I'm even more turned on. You're giving me all-girl college vibes. Innocent and naïve." I trail a finger down the cup of her bra. She winces, and I pull back. "What's wrong?"

"I might've done something else behind your back." Her sheepish grin intrigues me. I reach behind her back with one hand and undo her bra like a fuckin' professional. Learned that trick at thirteen, and to this day, it's the most useful thing my friends ever taught me.

I carefully lift on the cups of her bra, revealing her newly pierced nipples. Bex chose titanium straight barbells that have a beveled diamond on each end. They catch the light and sparkle.

"Holy fuck, you did it." I stare at her tits, wishing more than anything they were healed enough to play. "When can I touch them?"

"Six months," she replies.

"Hell no."

"Sorry, big boy. They're officially on the 'look, but don't touch' list."

"Is there anything we can do to speed it along? Hyperbaric chamber or something?"

She laughs, making her tits bounce and my dick even harder. "I can just imagine the look on the doctor's face."

"I'm serious. Six months is unacceptable." I cover her tits back up. Looking at them is a painful reminder I can't smother myself in her cleavage or twist her nipples until she screams and her pussy gushes.

"You're the one who told me to get them pierced."

"That was before I knew the healing time. My dick took three months, and that about killed me."

"Think of it as a challenge. Now you have to find new ways to get me off."

I take a seat on the edge of the bed and rub her inner thigh. "Did it turn you on to get them pierced?"

She flushes and looks away. "I orgasmed while she was piercing me. I tried to hide it, but I'm certain she knew."

"Fuck, that turns me on. Wish I would've been there." It only takes me a second to realize why she didn't ask me. I lift my ankle. "Stupid fucking tracker."

A commotion sounds from the other side of the door, and I jump to my feet. Someone knocks, and I flip the lock before opening the door a crack.

"Need you," Goblin says, eyes wide.

"Okay, gimme a second."

He nods, and I shut the door. "Got some club shit to deal with."

"Okay."

"Be back soon." I move to leave, but she stops me.

"Wes, my hands." Her arms are still strung up above her head, her shirt open, and her bra barely covering her tits.

"Sorry, darlin'. I know you enough to know no matter what I say, you'll leave this room, and this is one of those situations you need to stay out of."

I know by the look on Goblin's face, whatever they need me for will absolutely be illegal and possibly bloody.

"I won't, I swear." She yanks on her makeshift cuffs.

"This is for your own good." I slip out the door, shutting it behind me, muffling Bex's shouting threats.

I'm gonna be paying for this for a long time.

Chapter
SEVENTEEN

Bexley

Who the hell does he think he is, leaving me tied up like this? I let my head fall back, hoping to see what I'm hooked on, but I can't tell.

"Motherfucker," I scream, hoping to get someone's attention, but knowing none of the Royal Bastards will go against their brother and rescue me. "I'm going to murder you, Wes!"

The doorknob turns, and Tabitha pops her head in. "You good, Bex?"

"Do I look like I'm good?" I bite out, and she winces. "I'm sorry. It's not you I'm mad at. Come on in."

She reluctantly enters, closing the door behind her before taking me in. "Got yourself into a pickle, huh?"

"Can you see what I'm caught up on?"

She approaches the bed and bends over the headboard to get a look. "There's a hook through the belt loop." She reaches behind the headboard and lifts the belt off the hook. "There."

"Can you help me out of these, please?" I hold my wrists up to her.

"Normally I'd say no, given the deep shit it'll put me in. But I like you. Just promise you'll stay here until they're done handling their situation."

"Yeah, sure," I say with zero conviction.

"I mean it. You're better off not knowing." She releases me from the belt and sets it aside.

"Do you know what's going on?" I ask.

"No clue. The nomad, Coyote, brought a man in. Don't know why, but the dude was fucked up. Blood dripping everywhere." She sighs. "Ruined the floors. Gonna have to clean that up later."

"Are they fixing him up or finishing the job?" My stomach does a flip-flop thinking about the latter.

"Not sure. Could go either way."

I fasten my bra back in place and retie my shirt. "Does this happen a lot?"

It's been over a month since I moved in, and nothing like this has happened in that time. Now that it has, I realize I need to move out. Like yesterday.

The guys cleaned up my apartment weeks ago, but the image of what was done to it is still burned in my memory, stealing any sense of security I had living there. I could've found a new place by now and gotten it outfitted with top-of-the-line security by Sly, but to be honest, I like sleeping in Wes's room. I like knowing that I'm in his bed. And I'm really enjoying getting to know the guys. I've even had a few conversations with Petra.

"I wouldn't say a lot, but definitely more than a few times. It's fine, though. Sis and I hide away in our room and watch romcoms. Wanna join us?" She perks up.

I haven't been mean to Tabitha and Sissy, but I haven't been friendly either. I know they've *been* with Wes. He's admitted as much. It's not their fault; they did nothing wrong. The logical side of my brain knows this, but the catty side of my brain wants to hate them. More than that, I want to claw their eyes out.

"No, thank you. I have work to do." I motion to my laptop.

"Okay, no worries. If you finish up, you know where we'll be." She leaves me with a genuine smile that both endears me to her and makes me want to murder her in her sleep.

I get up for my laptop and then get comfy back in bed, returning to my emails. I respond to three before my mind wanders back to what they're doing with the bloody man. Surely Coyote wouldn't drag a man back here if he planned on killing him. He would've just done it on sight wherever he found the guy. Right?

I close my laptop and chew on the inside of my mouth. If I'm going to be with Wes, I need to see all of his sides. The good, the bad, and the murderous. If I can handle him at his worst, then maybe this thing can work between us. If I can't, then at least I'll know now before things get too serious.

It's already serious, dumbass. He's claimed you.

Nope. Not thinking about that. I creep down the hall, scared to my bones about what I might find.

I don't know where they are, but the main floor is eerily silent and empty. It looks like a ghost town, frozen in time. Half-drunk beers line the bar, the crusts from a sandwich sit on an abandoned plate, and the pool balls are scattered on the table, mid-game.

If they're not up here, that leaves two places: in Roch's casita or downstairs. I look to my left where the stairs are and see the trail of blood going from the front door to the stairwell.

Downstairs it is.

I take a calming breath, shake out my limbs, and clear my throat, ramping myself up. Taking one step at a time, keeping my weight on the balls of my feet so my heels don't clack against the wood as I go, I stop when I hear something, or rather, someone.

"You have two choices. Don't tell us where she is, and I'll make this as slow and painful as possible. Or you can tell us what we want to know, and I promise, you won't feel a thing." The voice is familiar but also not. I recognize the throaty rumbling. It's close to what I hear when Wes is buried inside me and on the verge of coming, grunting "mine" over and over. This isn't Wes, though. No, the person behind this voice is distinctly Khan.

He wonders why I won't call him by his road name, and this is why. When he's with me, he's Wes, the oaf of a man who makes me laugh and gives me more orgasms than I can count. But right now, he's Khan, Vice President of the Royal Bastards.

I know better than to continue into the basement, but my feet carry me there anyway. Behind a shelf that houses heavy-looking boxes is a secret room I didn't know existed. The door is propped open by the nomad who goes by Coyote. His body blocks me from seeing what's happening in that room.

Coyote is an enigma to me. He's a beautiful man with dark skin and darker eyes. The lower half of his head is shaved, the top covered in shoulder length dreadlocks that are pulled up into a ponytail, and like most of the RBMC, he's covered in tattoos. But unlike most of the other members, who are loud and obnoxious, Coyote has a Zen-like way about him. His energy is inviting and calming. I often catch him doing yoga in the yard next to the tent he sleeps in.

For such a muscular man, he sure is bendy.

"So it's gonna be the hard way, huh?" Khan says before inhaling deeply. I picture him circling a bloody man with a cigarette hanging from his lips.

Suddenly, a blood-curdling scream echoes through the basement. I stumble backward, tripping over the bottom stair and landing on my ass. Coyote hears me over the ear-piercing wailing and spins around, a hand moving to his hip where the black metal of a gun rests. He relaxes when he sees it's just me.

"You okay?" he asks, moving toward me, leaving the doorway, and giving me a visual of the inside.

A man bleeding from what seems like every orifice is hanging from chains attached to the ceiling, his feet unable to touch the ground. He's shirtless, showing off the beginnings of large bruises down his ribs, and his head is hanging, snot, saliva, and blood oozing from his mouth as he continues to cry out.

He spins on the chain, and that's when I see it. Khan has carved RBMC into his back. The cuts are deep, and flaps of his flesh hang over the crude carving. Blood oozes from the wounds and follows the path of least resistance down his body.

It's the most grotesque thing I've ever seen in my life. My stomach turns, and I retch onto the stairs.

"Time for you to go, sister." Coyote lifts me up by my armpits.

"Don't touch me," I spit out.

He immediately drops me to my feet. On wobbly legs, I push forward into the secret room. Khan circles around the room, flipping his bloody knife into the air and catching it by the handle expertly each time.

"Just tell us where she is, and this will all be over," he says, still unaware I'm watching the whole thing.

"She inherited a couple acres in the Saddlehorn neighborhood." The man's voice is tired and his words are slurred.

Khan grabs the man by his hair and jerks his head back. "That wasn't so hard, now was it? Loki, hold him."

Next thing I know, Khan raises the long blade above his head and, with all his might, thrusts it into the man's forehead. Loki lets go of his hold on the corpse, sending him swinging through the air.

I fall to the ground, screaming until my ears sting from the high-pitched sound. I try to close my eyes so I don't have to look at the horror in front of me, but I'm frozen. My body shakes uncontrollably, and fear like I've never felt before rushes through me.

Khan's face crumples as the realization that I witnessed the whole disgusting scene seeps in. I scream louder when he crouches and reaches over to touch me.

"You're covered in blood, brother," Loki says.

He looks down at himself, seeing how horrific his appearance is. In an outright panic, he rips his shirt and pants off, leaving him completely naked.

I'll bet he wishes he wore underwear now.

Coyote tries to silence me by sitting next to me and whispering things I can't hear. I tear at my hair, my head bowed, and the screaming, Jesus Christ, the screaming. I'm not even sure I'm breathing. Dizziness sets in, and blackness fills my periphery. I'm going to pass out, and I'd welcome it with open arms, but it never comes.

Khan rushes over to a sink in the corner and scrubs his hands clean before ripping off a paper towel and drying them. Then he's kneeling in front of me, pulling me off the floor and lifting me into his arms. He takes me back up the stairs.

He lays me down on his bed, where my body curls into a ball, shaking violently.

This is all too much. Too much. Too much. Too damn much.

"Goddamn it, Bex. I told you to stay here. I told you there's a part of me you don't want to see. Why the fuck don't you listen?" Khan rants while he digs through his drawers, looking for the clothes he left behind.

I want to tell him I folded all his clean laundry and put it in a bin in the closet, but I can't stop crying. No matter, because his next stop is the closet. He digs around until he finds the bin pushed back on the top shelf. He searches for a minute until he finds what he was looking for, a pair of black boxers.

He disappears for a moment before returning to retrieve

me. The sound of water fills my ears, and the next thing I know, I'm being carried to the bathroom. He stands me up and all but rips the clothes off my body, all while I'm still howling out a pained cry I can't control.

Khan wraps me in a hug, shushing me. But I can't stop. In my head, the scene plays over and over.

The blood.

The helpless expression on that man's face.

The protruding veins on Khan's neck as he—

"That's enough, Bex." He grips my biceps and holds me at arm's length. "You hear me? Knock it off."

The way Loki and Coyote stood there watching as though they were watching a basketball game.

The vacant eyes on the man after Khan—

"Sorry about this," he says right before smacking me across the face.

I'm stunned silent. I place a hand over my stinging cheek and look up at the man I thought I knew so well.

"Shit." Khan runs a hand through his hair. "This is so fucked up, I know it. But I promise this'll make you feel better." He carries me into the shower.

Cold water hits my skin, and suddenly I'm shivering for a whole new reason. Khan sets me down directly under the icy spray.

We've been in this shower multiple times, all for one reason—to wash our sins away after copious amounts of sex. I wish that was why we're here right now, but it's not. No matter how hard I try to pretend.

I don't know this man. Not even a little. He's a monster, just like Martin.

I did this to myself again. What the fuck is wrong with me?

"Shh, baby, it's okay. It's okay," Wes coos, running his hands up and down my arms. He's back to being my sweet Wes.

But how can he be two different people? It's not possible. The man from the basement five minutes ago is the same man who was between my legs last night.

"Who are you?" I ask through a choking sob, shoving his hands off me.

"Same man I always been. Never hid nothin' from you." He holds up his hands in defense. "I get knowing what I do and seeing it are two different things, but you gotta know, I'm the same man who was in your bed this morning when you woke up."

I glare at him. "No, you're not. That man is kind and considerate. That man brought me breakfast in bed and kissed my nose. The man I see in front of me right now is a murderer."

The cold water sets into my bones, making my teeth chatter and goosebumps prickle along my skin. Wes notices and turns the dial to warm. While he's careful to keep his distance, there's only so much room in this small shower stall.

"Got an angel and a devil living inside me. Tonight, you met the devil, but I swear on my life, it'll be the last time. You'll never have to see it again." He stands a foot away, completely naked, his dick flaccid and hanging between his legs. I've never seen him like this, and it almost makes him human.

But he's not. He's a monster.

"Please leave," I whisper.

"Can't do that until I'm certain you're okay. You had some sort of attack down there. Scared the shit out of me." He reaches over to caress my cheek, but I turn my head before he makes contact. His face falls and his hand drops.

"I'm fine, but I'd like some privacy now."

"Don't push me out, Bex. Talk to me. Tell me what you're thinking," he pleads.

My throat constricts, and my eyes burn hot. "You don't want to know what I'm thinking."

"Come on, darlin'. Don't do this. Please," he begs, daring to take a step closer and pull me into his arms. I allow it only because I know he has the power to do it whether or not I want it, but I don't reciprocate. I remain stick-straight, my arms wrapped around myself. "I'll give you some time, but this isn't over. We will talk about this. Bet on that." He kisses the top of my head and releases me.

Then he's gone.

I drop to the tiled floor and curl up, wrapping my arms around my legs, allowing myself to cry and wallow, not caring about time. Wes is right. I know who the Royal Bastards are, and I've heard the rumors of bodies gone missing. I know they transport weapons, delivering illegal guns to the highest bidder while laundering the money through Wes' construction business.

I ignored it all, and instead, I basked in the attention Wes gave me. I was drunk on dick. It's the only explanation. Why else would a woman like me go for a man like him?

No, that's wrong. Because I'm no better than him. I fantasized about killing Martin. I wanted to do all the things to him that he did to me. Then I wanted to shoot him between the eyes and watch his body fall to the ground. I wanted it so badly I could taste it.

That's why I ran. I was worried about what I'd do if I stayed.

I guess that's the difference between Wes and me. I stopped myself before I turned into a murderer while he embraced it.

After I don't know how long, the water runs cold, so I turn it off and crawl out of the shower, pulling a towel off the rack to cover myself. I stare out the glazed window on the far wall as I lie on the unforgiving floor.

Nothing has ever hurt this much. I'm torn between the man I'm falling in love with and the man I saw in that cement room. It just so happens they're the same person.

I don't know how long I lie there, but it's long enough for

the sunlight to disappear, drowning me in darkness. I haven't been this crippled from anxiety since—

I sit up. This isn't me. I'm not Sienna anymore. Standing up, I move to the bathroom sink and wash my face. My eyes are swollen and red and my hair's a tangled mess. I brush it out before moving to the bedroom to dress.

Without a plan, I pack up my clothes and toiletries. I don't care where I'll go, but I can't stay here. Not anymore. Not knowing what's going on one floor below me.

Are they butchering his body to make it easier to carry him out? Are they soaking him in acid like I've seen in movies? Are they dragging him out the front door in a plastic bag like trash?

All the questions I don't want to know the answers to, and I worry if I stick around for much longer, I'll find them out.

Sly. He's the answer. He'll help me even if it means angering his brother. I don't know his story, but he has a soft spot for women in need.

And I'm in need of a new home.

Chapter
EIGHTEEN

Khan

I want to bring that asshole back to life just so I can kill him again. I'm pissed at everyone and everything. I don't get a lot of good in my life so when I do, I hold on to it. It's how I feel about the club, and it's for damn sure how I feel about Bex.

My chest aches, and my limbs are antsy. I can't even stay to make sure she's okay because if I don't get my ass to Loki's in the next half hour, the cops will be at my door to take me to jail. Then there'd be no way for me to undo the damage I've done.

Something claws at my leg, and I look down. Roch's chihuahua, Karen, is trying to climb my leg like a spider monkey. I lift her into my arms, and she settles herself into my chest. I run my hands down her soft fur, feeling my heart rate slow.

No wonder he keeps her in his hoodie all the time.

I glance up to see Roch watching the interaction.

"You send her to me?" I ask, and he nods. "Thank you."

"Take her," he mumbles.

"I don't want to be responsible for her, bro. I know she's special to you." Even as I say it, I find myself tucking her into the hoodie I borrowed from Goblin. After Bex kicked me out of the shower, I grabbed my boxers and left the room, locking it behind me so I wouldn't be tempted to return. My brothers took pity on me and tossed mismatched clothes into my lap.

"Take her," he repeats.

"Thanks, man. I'll bring her back tomorrow."

He nods and ducks out the back door. I'm not a crying man, but seeing my brother hand over his best friend to make me feel better almost has me choking up.

"Let's get out of here," I tell the dog.

I hop on my bike and tighten the strings of my hoodie to prevent Karen from falling out. It's not the safest method, but I've seen Roch do it a million times. Even after being run off the road and crashing his bike, Karen was safe in his hood.

I push my dome onto my head and take off toward Tahoe. If it were any other day, I'd enjoy the ride. But my head is a mess, and my world is upside down. Until I can talk to Bex—make her understand—I won't be okay.

I love her. I think I always have. From the first time I saw her glide into the clubhouse, dressed in one of those tight skirts she loves so much, I've been obsessed with her. Maybe it's why I only fucked women who were her opposite. Maybe I didn't want to be reminded of something I couldn't have.

Except I did have her. And it was fucking heaven.

Now I'm back to where I started, pining after a woman I don't deserve. And to top it all off, I still have no idea why Coyote needed to know where his mystery girl is so bad that he'd kill for the information. But he's my brother, so when he needed an interrogator, of course I had to help.

I have a knack for drawing information out of people. I don't normally do the killing—we save that for Roch so he can let his demons out—but I got caught up. It's the first time I felt a part of the club since I got released from jail. I needed to be a

Royal Bastard again, even if it meant killing a man I'm not sure deserved it.

I pull into Loki's driveway and park my bike. After checking on Karen—who's peacefully sleeping—I go inside, heading straight for my room. I don't want to talk. Especially not to Loki.

As I storm through the living room, I spot him lazing on the couch with a movie playing. Thankfully, he must see I'm not in the mood to shoot the shit, and he lets me pass without saying a word.

I'm almost in the clear until I enter the bedroom and find Birdie sitting on my bed.

"Not now," I growl.

"Rough night?" she asks, not taking the hint.

I empty my pockets into the bowl on the dresser and kick off my boots. "Love you, Birdie, but I'm begging you to leave me be."

"I love you too. That's why I'm not going to leave. I'm going to force you to have a conversation."

"I told her it was a bad idea," Loki calls out from the living room.

"Ain't nothing to talk about. She can't handle what I do. We were doomed from the beginning." I fold my arms across my chest.

"Before the break-in at my dad's house, the most amount of blood I'd seen was from my period. Then my dad got shot and"—her eyes water, and she sniffles—"it changed me. At first, I was in shock. I was irrational and wouldn't talk to anyone. Then a switch flipped when I realized the world I thought I knew wasn't real at all. Give her time for the switch to flip."

"You don't know what the hell you're talking about. Bex isn't anything like you," I say, instantly regretting it when Birdie's beautiful face pinches. "I'm sorry. I just mean she's seen some shit in her life. She wasn't a naïve princess lounging in her castle."

Birdie stands, her head held high. "I'm going to let all of that slide because I know you're hurting. But hear me when I say I'm not the bad guy. I'm on your side, and you might need a few people on your side right now."

"I'm sorry. You're right," I say just before she reaches the threshold.

"I know I am." Birdie closes the door after her, leaving me alone with my thoughts and Karen.

"Where did she go?" I roar at my brothers, who are sitting around drinking coffee like nothing is amiss.

"Chill, bro. She's safe," Sly says from where's he's sitting at a corner table.

"I didn't ask if she was safe. I asked where she was."

"Can't tell you that." He lifts a mug to his lips and blows before taking a sip of his morning joe.

My boots clomp against the wooden floors until I'm at his side. I shove him in the chest so hard, he falls backward, landing with a *thud*.

"I'll give you this one free pass. Any more of this bullshit, and I'll fight back." Sly's on the thinner side, but while I'm nothing but brute force, he's fast and accurate.

"Tell me where she is," I demand.

"Khan, you're my brother. I'd do anything for you." He stands and holds a hand over his heart. "I'd fucking die for you. And you might not see it right now, but by not telling you where your woman is at, I'm keeping you safe. You aren't thinking straight. That device on your ankle is the one thing standing between being here with us and being locked up."

"I think I lost her, bro," I croak.

Sly shakes his head. "I know you're hurting and all you want to do is fix the shit going on, but no chick is worth getting locked up for the next five months until your trial."

"She is," I say and move to leave.

"I have something that might cheer you up," he calls out, stopping me in my tracks. "The surveillance footage is gone."

My head hangs, and the weight of those words sinks in. "No trail?"

"Nope. Got in and out. Free and clear."

Now I feel like an even bigger piece of shit for attacking him. The video evidence of me stealing that work van is gone. Once the prosecutors find out, the charges will most likely be dropped. But how will I know if my lawyer isn't talking to me right now? Will she fire me? Fire the club? Loki will be pissed if that happens.

"That's good. Thank you," I mumble and drag my feet down the hallway.

Stepping inside my room, I find it clean and empty. No lacy panties on the floor. None of her uptight lawyer clothes hang in the closet. She even changed the sheets and took her silky bedding.

I sink down onto the bare mattress. It's like she was never here. Is that what she wants? For me to forget she was ever mine?

My gaze catches on the little trashcan in the corner. It's overflowing with paper. Maybe there's a clue about where she went in there. I carry it to the open space next to the bed and dump it on the ground. For the next hour, I carefully sift through bills, receipts, and scratch paper, none of it giving me the information I need.

I toss the wire bin across the room, denting the closet door.

She won't answer a text, but I get my phone out anyway.

Me: Where are you?

I stare at the screen for long minutes, willing a message to pop up, but nothing comes.

How is it so easy for her to walk away? When I told her she was mine, I fucking meant that shit. Ride or die. Through life and death. A woman like her is heaven-bound, but she won't get that far because I'm dragging her to down Hades with me so we can rule the underworld together.

That's what I fucking meant when I said "mine."

Guess I didn't make that clear enough for her.

I leave the mess and storm out of the clubhouse. Hopping on my bike, I secure my helmet and take off toward downtown. It's almost noon, so she should be at her office, which is on my list of places I can go. A criminal needs to visit his lawyer now and then, right?

The ride is quick, and I find a parking spot easily. The chick at the front tries to stop me, but I ignore her and press the call button for the elevator. Within seconds, I'm on her floor. The chick outside her office is a little more persistent about announcing me, but she and I both know all she has are words.

Not many people can physically stop me from doing something I want to do.

I swing open the door and find her at her desk, a man and teenager in the chairs across from her.

Her eyes widen, and her sweet lips purse. She's pissed. Well, good. Because so am I.

"Wes, it's not a good time," she says.

"Don't care." I plant my hands on my hips.

The man stands. "We can reschedule if—"

"No. It's fine. I'm so sorry for the interruption." She crosses the room and pushes me toward the door. "Can you give me five minutes to handle this?"

"No problem."

Bex shoves me down the hall until we reach another door. I take the hint and open it to find an employee lounge. When we're both inside, she locks the door before facing me. She glares at me, her face and neck turning an angry shade of red.

"What the fuck?"

"You didn't answer my text," I say.

"I'm working," she grits out.

"You moved out," I accuse.

Her shoulders fall, and I get the first glimpse of how torn apart she is. That's good. It means she's warring with her decisions, and I still have a chance to convince her to stay.

"I can't do this with you. I'm barely hanging on right now." Her hand goes to her forehead the way it does whenever she's stressed.

"Then when?" I ask.

Her mind turns as she debates her answer. "Give me a week."

"Fuck no." A week is too long. It gives her enough time to forget what we had and focus on what she saw.

"I need time," she says.

"Tomorrow."

"That's not enough."

"A week, and you let me kiss you right now." I need to remind her. I need the last thing she remembers about us to be our chemistry.

"Wes—"

I don't wait for the no. I grip the base of her throat, roughly back her against the wall, and press my lips to hers. At first, everything about her is stiff. Her body, her lips, her demeanor—all unyielding.

I don't let it deter me. I devour her, thrusting my tongue into her mouth without permission.

Whether she gives in, knowing I won't stop until she does, or she remembers how good everything is when we're together, I don't know, and I don't give a fuck. She melts into me, her soft body relaxing and her lips moving with mine.

I fucking love the way her skin tastes, and I tell her as much while my lips move to her neck. The hand that isn't around her throat goes to her ass. I dig my fingers in and squeeze, pulling her hips to mine so she can feel how hard I am for her. Her soft hands go under my shirt and rub up and down my abs. I flex, giving her the ripples I know she loves so much.

"Wes," she breathes out.

"I know," I say, hiking up her skirt to reveal a pink silk thong. I drop to my knees and bury my nose in her cunt, inhaling like it's my oxygen.

"I have a client in the other room." She pushes at the fabric, but I hold it in place.

"I'll make it fast," I assure her.

I ignore her weak objections and rub circles against her clit, feeling her arousal seeping through. If I have to walk away from her for a week, I'll make damn sure to blow her mind before I do.

I pull her panties to the side and spread her lips open, revealing her pretty pink cunt that's practically dripping for me. I swipe my tongue up her slit, gathering her juices on my tongue. I'm addicted to her unique flavor.

Giving up drugs was hard. Giving up her pussy would be impossible.

I latch onto her clit and suck until it's swollen and throbbing. She's on the verge already. My hands itch to reach up and grab her tit, but when I remember they aren't healed, I'm pissed off all over again.

"Hurry," she says, thrusting her pelvis at me. "Eat me, baby. Please."

Goddamn. My woman can dirty talk. I insert one finger into her tight channel, and she moans softly. After a few thrusts, I step it up to two fingers. Her responding whimper is less than quiet as I fuck her with my fingers and lap at her clit with my expert tongue.

Her hands go to my head, where she grabs two handfuls and shoves my face deeper into her pussy.

Hell yeah. Suffocate me, darlin'.

Within seconds, she's coming apart. Her arousal drips down my hand, her internal muscles squeeze the life out of my fingers, and her clit pulses against my tongue. I keep at it until her body sags and she releases my hair.

"Oh my God," she says, and I can't tell if she realizes what she did at her place of business or if she's thanking the heavens for orgasms.

I place a soft kiss on her mound before adjusting her panties back in place. She shoves her skirt down and pushes off the wall, darting around me.

Can't get away that easy.

I stand and find her facing away, that damn hand on her forehead again. I wrap my arms around her from behind and push her hair off her shoulders so I can kiss the sweet skin of her neck.

"Love you, darlin'. I'll respect your wishes and leave you be for a week. But that's it."

Her head shakes dismissively. "You don't love me."

"Unfortunately, that's not somethin' you can control," I growl into her ear.

She cranes her neck so she meets my eyes. "What if I decide I'm not cut out for club life?"

"You won't," I say with conviction.

"Wes. What I saw . . ." she trails off.

"It's my fault. Should've never happened. You were thrown into the deep end without knowing how to swim. It wasn't fair. But darlin', that's as worse as it gets."

"It was pretty bad."

"I know. But that shit happens once in a long while. Most of the time, it's what you see every other day. Family, fun, and loyalty."

She nods and tips her chin in offering. I kiss her like my life depends on it. Because it does.

Chapter
NINETEEN

Bexley

I pull away from our kiss and separate my body from his. "I need to get back."

I should be ashamed I allowed him to give me oral sex in my breakroom, but he's not Khan right now. He's Wes. My dirty-talking, giant teddy bear and the man I'm falling in love with.

"Okay." He tucks his hands in his back pockets. It's painful to see him so distraught. His visit was a manipulation tactic, and a successful one at that. Prior to him barging in, my mind was firmly made up. Something changed during him burying his face between my legs, and now, I'm not so sure. "Will you tell me where you're livin'?"

I think about that for a second. I instructed the guys not to say anything. Not because I was in fear of Wes, but because I knew he'd come looking for me, and I don't want him to get into trouble.

"Promise you won't show up?" I ask.

He traces an X with his finger over his heart. "Swear it."

"I'm at the Haskell Row building."

He lets out a whistle. "Nice place. Sly check for security?"

"Yes. I'm sure he's installing a doorbell cam and cameras in the hallways as we speak."

"Good. You still going to confront Martin?"

"Yes. I know you don't agree, but it will be okay," I say. "But I called him to delay it until next week, given all the everything going on. He wasn't pleased."

He lowers his head and nods. My heart aches to see him like this. It makes me want to run into his arms and forget about everything that happened last night. But then the memories return, and I hold fast.

"I'll call you," I promise and reluctantly walk out, leaving him in the break room.

My steps down the hall are weary and not from the incredible orgasm he gave me. I'm exhausted after the shock from yesterday and moving last night.

It wasn't easy to find an apartment on such short notice, especially one that met my security requirements, but with Sly's help, I managed.

Despite it being late, he got the complex's manager on the phone. I used my deep pockets to persuade her to cut through some red tape and secure me a one-bedroom, one-and-a-half-bath apartment on the second floor. Sly was gracious enough to put it under his name to keep things less obvious.

I knew Wes would get to the clubhouse first thing in the morning, so I made sure to be gone by then.

Miles took all my things in the cage and helped me unload. By eight, I was sweaty from the move, and my hair air had dried into a frizzy mess. I barely had time for a shower before I had to be to work.

The last almost twenty-four hours have been a whirlwind that I still feel caught up in, spinning in circles and not knowing which way is up.

At least now I have a week to decide where I want to land.

I smooth down my hair and clear my throat before stepping back into my office.

The days fly by when you have a major decision to make, and before I know it, it's the seventh day.

I kick off my heels and strip out of my clothes before flopping on my bed after a long day at work. Pulling out my phone, I see a text from Wes. He's been good about leaving me alone except for one text every night.

On day one, it was, "I love that you're a ball buster. You don't put up with my shit and I need that in my life."

The second day, he got sexual with, "I want to be the one who gets to play with your pierced titties after they've healed. Drives me crazy to think someone else might get the honor."

After that, he turned sentimental. "Miss you, darlin'. I'm not a man who begs, but for you, I'm on my knees. Come back to me."

By day four, his frustration came out. "Maybe I never spelled out what kind of men we are, but you're a smart girl. You can't tell me you were surprised."

After reading that one, I spent all night thinking about my relationship with the Royal Bastards. It was mutually advantageous for us to partner up. They needed someone who didn't ask questions and had no problem looking for loopholes to keep them out of jail. I needed clients who were so reliant on me, it'd be in their best interest to keep me alive. Just in case Martin came back for me.

But I didn't put all my eggs in one basket with the RBMC. I also took on dirty politicians and rich businessmen with questionable practices. I went from being a nobody to the lawyer every rich scumbag kept on retainer. I didn't worry about my reputation; I worried about my safety.

Getting involved with Wes wasn't planned. It was a stupid decision. One made from either loneliness or love. I don't know which.

On day five, he made me laugh. "Thinking about the time you left me in the parking lot of Roberto's. Never had a chick ditch me before and gotta say, darlin', never been so turned on by rejection before either."

I almost responded to this one. I had it all typed out and everything. But I deleted it. I couldn't get sucked in. I still needed that time to think.

Day six I could practically hear the fear in his words. "Wish I knew where your head was at. Don't like knowing that kiss in the break room might be our last."

Honestly, that thought gutted me too.

I click on today's text, expecting something heartfelt and convincing. But all it says is, "Tick tock."

What the fuck does that mean?

I toss my phone onto the nightstand and sit up.

It's decision day, and although I know what I must do, it doesn't make it any easier.

Especially since Wes managed to sneak his way into my heart. I love him, and he makes it blindingly obvious he loves me too. It's an unexpected complication to my plans, but it doesn't change anything.

I only hope he's able to forgive me someday.

My phone alerts me that there's movement in the hall. It's most likely my neighbors. It usually is, but I reach for my phone and bring up the feed because I'm still on high alert after Martin.

It's not my neighbors, and it's not Martin or his hired men. It's Miles. I throw on a robe and dash to the door.

"What are you doing here?" I ask, motioning him inside.

"Came to pick you up." He looks me up and down. "Might want to change."

I tighten the silk sash around my waist. "Where am I going?"

"VP sent me." He strolls through my living room and plops down on my brand-new sofa. It took me a couple of days to arrange deliveries for all my furniture. I slept on the hardwood floors for two nights before my four-poster, king-size bed was delivered. Highly worth the wait; that bed is like sleeping on clouds.

"That doesn't answer my question."

"Told me to take you to Loki's."

Guess my time is up. I need to think fast . . . or stall. "You don't need to escort me. I need to shower and get dressed. It's better if I drive myself."

"Not gonna happen. VP gives me a job, I complete the job."

I place a hand on my forehead. "Okay. Make yourself comfortable, I guess."

He kicks his feet up on the coffee table and picks up the remote to the flat screen delivered and installed yesterday. "I will."

I roll my eyes and head into my room, closing the door behind me. I drop my robe, pin my hair up, and strip out of my bra and panties before climbing into the shower.

My best thinking happens in the shower, so as I'm exfoliating, shaving, and cleansing, I let my mind wander. There's so much to think about, it hurts my brain. While I should be more concerned about my meeting with Martin tomorrow night, it gets pushed to the side by thoughts of what I'll do about Wes.

My priorities are fucked. Looking Martin in the eyes terrifies me, but not as much as walking away from Wes does.

Way too quickly, I run out of things to do in the shower, and I'm forced to dry off and get dressed. I scan my closet for the perfect outfit, but I have no idea what to wear for such a life-changing moment.

Ultimately, I decide on a pair of high-waisted, mineral-washed black jeggings that have distressing on the pockets and the knees. I pair it with a spaghetti strap white tank that doesn't allow for a bra but is tight enough to hold me in place and show off the imprint of my nipple piercings.

For my shoes, I go for a pair of Pedro Garcia gold metallic platform sandals. While I choose them because I know Wes has a thing for my feet, I'll never admit it to myself, let alone him.

I go light on my makeup—just covering the dark circles under my eyes—adding some bronzer to my cheeks and running mascara through my lashes. For a final touch, I let down my long brown hair.

"You can do this," I say to my reflection.

The only thing is, I don't know what *this* is.

The drive takes forty-seven minutes. I know because my eyes were glued to the clock on the dashboard the whole time. Miles tried to make conversation, but when it became clear I wasn't up for talking, he cranked the radio instead.

He puts the van in park. "Time to face the music."

"Will you wait for me?" I'm only now realizing that by not driving myself, I'll be stranded. It was probably an intentional move on Wes's part.

"That wasn't part of the deal."

"Please?" I beg.

He blows out a breath. "Yeah, I've got the night off, so I'll hang around for a while."

"Thank you."

"No problem. If the VP asks, tell him the van broke down, would ya?"

"Sure thing." I step out of the van and walk toward the

house with the same enthusiasm I'd have if I were walking the plank.

The door opens before I have the chance to knock. Wes stands before me, looking as irresistible as ever and pissing me off in the process. How am I supposed to have a serious conversation when all I want to do is climb him like a tree and hump him like a dog?

His long hair is pulled back into a bun, his beard is tame for once, and if I'm not mistaken, he ran the beard oil I bought him through it. At the time, he called it "preppy boy shit" and tossed it in his closet. His heather gray shirt is pulled tight across his chest and stretched wide around his bulging biceps. God, how I wish I could feel those arms around me right now.

He looks distraught, with his hands tucked into his jeans and his shoulders hunched forward. It's an apprehensive stance that breaks my heart until I see the sexy veins on his forearms on display. Then I'm back to the tree and dog fantasy.

The jeans must be new because they lack the usual holes and are a darker wash. That's not what catches my eye though, it's the way he fills them. Tight across his hips and thighs before dropping straight down his legs. God, I miss the way those powerful thighs felt between my legs as he thrust into me over and over.

I blink, snapping myself out of a lusty fog. That's not why I'm here.

He takes me in the same way I do to him, and I don't miss the way his eyes linger at my breasts. The lack of bra puts the outline of my nipple jewelry on display.

"Babe," he says as though he's in pain.

"Can I come in?" I ask.

"Yeah. Of course." Like a gentleman, he stands to the side and motions for me to enter.

I expect to see Loki and Birdie inside, but they're nowhere to be seen. "Where is everyone?"

"They fucked off for the night. They're thinking of having their wedding at a resort on the lake and wanted to stay the night at the resort they're considering. Or some shit like that. I don't know."

"That's nice. I'm happy for them."

Silence spreads between us. I know he's waiting for me to say something. I made my decision between minutes twenty-seven and thirty on the ride over. I just don't know how to start.

"Gotta be honest, darlin'. I'm fucking freaked out right now. Need you to start talking." He takes me by the hand and pulls me to the overstuffed sofa. We sit side by side as I try to gather my words.

My stomach cramps, my heart beats out of my chest, and there's a ball in my throat I can't swallow down. I know what I must do, but it's not going to be easy for either of us.

"I'm sorry, Wes. I knew this was a bad idea from the start." A tear falls down my cheek, and I swipe it away, pissed I'm breaking down.

"Wrong answer, babe." His brows furrow, and his jaw ticks.

"I know you think that, but in time you'll see I'm right." I clear the emotion from my throat and straighten my posture.

"You're fucking crazy if you think I'm letting you go." His gentle tone is a harsh juxtaposition to his threat.

I tug on an invisible thread on my pants. "That's not really up to you to decide."

He jumps to his feet and moves to one of the floor-to-ceiling windows. During the day, they display the thick forest and soothing creek right outside. Now, at night, they show a dark abyss. "You want to what? Walk away and pretend this never happened? Pretend you didn't and don't still feel something for me? Pretend I barely have to look at you, and you come apart for me? That's your plan?"

"Of course, it will be challenging at first—"

He scoffs. "Challenging? Is that really how you feel? Because you're shredding my heart to pieces and ripping my soul in half. It's a little more than challenging."

"You feel that way now, but—"

"But nothing, Bex. I've spent the last few years thinking I'd never find a high like the one I got with heroin. Do you know how depressing that is? To know there's something out there that makes you feel like you're the king of the world and you can't have it?" He turns to face me and what I see devastates me. This bigger-than-life man has tears in his eyes. "Then I met you, and you're better than anything I could shoot up my arm. I'd choose the high I feel when we're together over any drug in existence. Now it turns out you're just another drug I can't have."

"You don't mean that. I'm nobody special. I'm just a messed-up girl who keeps putting herself in bad situations."

"So now I'm a bad situation?"

"Not you. Your lifestyle. It's a stress I don't need." I know I sound cold, but if I let my facade slip, I won't leave him.

"That's such bullshit. You didn't learn anything new about me after what you saw last week. Maybe you chose not to think about it or pretend I was someone I'm not, but you *knew*," he spits out.

It's true. I can't argue that point. I looked the other way when it came to the illegal activities they participated in, and I said nothing when he told me he's killed. But again, knowing and seeing are two very different things.

"I hope we can still be friends since we'll see each other from time to time. And, of course, I'll still represent you. Sly told me the video somehow disappeared, so I'm hoping to hear from the prosecution soon. I'd call them, but I don't want them to know that I know it's gone. That would look suspicious." Maybe by mentioning this, it'll soften the blow.

It doesn't.

He walks over and sinks to his knees in front of me, his hands going to my knees. "You think I give a fuck about that? I'm fucking dead inside either way."

"That's not true. You're an incredible person I was lucky enough to get to know very well. I can say, with certainty, that you have so much to offer. You're loyal, kind, and funny. Don't let this ruin your life." I scoot to the side and stand, making his hands fall to his lap. I'm losing it, and I can't be here when it happens. "I need to go."

"Goddamn it, Bex. Please." He balls his fists from where they rest on his thighs. "Let's talk this out."

I lean down and kiss him on the temple. "Thank you for everything. You're my favorite mistake."

His body sags in defeat, and his eyes squeeze shut, teardrops springing free.

"Bye, Wes," I say and walk out, biting down on the inside of my mouth until I taste blood.

Thankfully, Miles is still outside, and I hop into the back seat, telling him to leave before the sliding door even latches.

We don't make it to the end of the road before I break down in pathetic sobs.

Chapter TWENTY

Khan

A knock sounds on the door. I ignore it.

"Come on, brother. Time to go," Loki calls, cracking the door open.

"Not going in today," I mumble from under the blankets.

His boots clunk against the wood floors as he moves further into the room. "Yeah, you are. Today's the day Bex meets up with her asshole ex. We need you."

"For fucking what? I can't be there. Best I can do is sit on my ass at the clubhouse. I can do that from here." I chuck the nearest thing to me, which happens to be my phone, in his direction.

I miss, judging by the sound of it hitting the wall.

"Jesus Christ. What the fuck happened last night?"

How do I explain how my soul was ripped from my body without sounding like a pussy?

"I don't want to talk about. Go the fuck away."

"Fine." His steps get quieter as he moves to the door. "But you won't be able to live with yourself if shit goes south and you're not there to ride."

I can't live with myself right now anyway. What's the difference?

The bedroom door slams shut, and I tighten my hold on the comforter. Part of me feels jumpy thinking about what's going down today, but the other part of me remembers what a cold bitch Bex was last night, and I don't give a fuck what happens.

That's not true. I trust my brothers. They'll take care of her, there's no doubt in my mind.

I feel both antsy and exhausted. I'm so fucking pissed off. When I left Bex's office after giving her an earth-shattering orgasm, I was feeling confident. Then, over a week with no contact, that confidence slipped, but I really thought she'd choose me.

It's not the first time a woman I love didn't choose me. My own mother walked away from me when I was just a child. Maybe I'm meant to live a life of solitude.

I poke my head out and stare out the window. The scenery is peaceful, but I can't enjoy it. Then my gaze catches on a splitting maul buried in a hunk of wood.

That's exactly what I fucking need.

I climb out of bed and push my feet into my boots, not bothering to put on clothes. Loki's place is remote, so I'm unconcerned anyone will see me.

I step outside and walk over to the woodpile, letting the crisp morning air fill my lungs.

I tug the maul out of the stump and grab a log from the stack behind me. Resting it on the stump, I heft the maul above my head and bring it down with a force driven by my anger. The wood breaks apart, flying in either direction.

It's a dangerous job to do naked, but self-preservation has taken a backseat.

I build a rhythm, and in no time, I'm sweating like a pig, glistening from the morning sun beating down on me and burning off my frustrated energy. It's not a cure to the devastation Bex put my heart through, but at least I'll be able to sleep without my legs itching to run and my fists craving something to punch.

In less than an hour, the entire cord is split. I stack it all up on the covered rack against the house and go back inside for a shower. The hot water beats on my back as I rest my forehead against the cold tiles.

How could I be so wrong about Bexley? What I feel for her is so strong, I thought there was no way it wouldn't be the same for her. When I pressed inside of her for the first time without a condom, I swear I found heaven in her body. After lusting after someone for so long, I finally had her. She said she was mine.

But it was all a fucking lie, wasn't it?

I don't bother with a towel when I step out of the shower and crawl into bed.

Fuck this day. I close my eyes and easily slip into a dream that feels more like a memory.

"You're too young to understand, but moms and dads are people just like you. They make mistakes, and sometimes to fix those mistakes, you have to walk away." Mom's crouched in front of me, holding my hands in hers. "But I want you to know, I'm not walking away from you. We'll see each other all the time."

I stare over her shoulder at the suitcases she filled with all her clothes and bathroom shit. Pops gets pissed when I swear, but if I don't say it out loud, he can't get mad. "You aren't going to live with me?"

"No. You'll stay here with Pops, and I'll live across town with Owen. You remember Owen, don't you?"

"My coach? Why are you movin' in with him?" I ask. Owen is nice and all, but his breath smells like onions, and he says stupid shit like 'atta boy.'

Mom glances over at Pops before focusing back on me. "You can't help who you fall in love with."

"You love him?" My nose screws up in disgust.

"Yes. I know grown-up stuff is hard to understand."

"I don't want you to go." My nose runs, and I wipe it on the back of my hand.

Mom's nose runs, too, and tears escape from her eyes. But she doesn't wipe the mess away. "It'll be a change, but think of it as an adventure. Pops and I will take turns with you. One week here and one week at Owen's house."

"Will I have my own room?"

"Even better. You get to share a room with his two boys. At least until we find a new house."

"But they're babies," I whine.

A car pulls up, and Coach Owen steps out. Pops growls at him, and I know right away this isn't something he wants. It's Mom's fault. She's leaving me and Pops to be a mommy to Owen's babies. Why? Does she love them more than me?

I pull my hands away and rush to Pops' side. I adopt his positioning, widening my stance and balling my fists.

"Really? This is what you want to teach your son?" Mom stands and places her hands on her hips.

"You wanted to get gone, so do it," Pops says through clenched teeth.

"Fine. I'll pick up Wes next Sunday." She rushes over to me and kisses the top of my head. I growl at her, and she rolls her eyes. "Hopefully, Owen's good influence will override whatever bad habits you teach him."

"That asshole has five seconds to get off my property before I'm grabbing my shotgun."

"Pathetic," she mutters as she walks away.

Owen and Mom carry her suitcases to his car in two trips. It takes longer than five seconds.

"Want me to go get your shotgun, Pops?" I ask.

He pats me on the head. "Sure, kid."

I run into the house and through the living room until I reach the kitchen. Pops keeps his guns on racks that are high out of my reach, so I push a chair to the wall and climb onto it. I grab the prettiest gun he owns. It has carved wood on it, and it's real shiny.

I run back to his side and hand him the gun. "Here you go."

Pops chuckles and takes it from me. "You're a good kid."

He positions the gun with the wood part pressed to his shoulder. I pay close attention so someday when I'm bigger, I'll know how to use it.

Pops aims the gun at Owen, who's sliding behind the steering wheel. He presses the trigger, and I whirl around, expecting Owen's head to be blown clean off. But it's not. At the last second, Pops must've lifted the gun because it's a branch on Mrs. Whittaker's tree that explodes, not Owen's head.

Owen's tires make a squealing sound as he speeds away.

"Come on, kid. Us McMillen men are meant to be alone."

I wake up with all the emotions I felt as a boy bubbling to the surface. I was too young to understand any of it. All I knew was Pops was my hero, and he was mad at Mom, so that meant I was as well.

Truth be told, though, I don't know what happened; it haunts me to this day. I don't blame her for putting space between us. I was a little shit to her and her new family because Pops told me to be.

That was who he was. No matter how big or small the transgression, anyone who crossed him was booted from his life. It's why, even as a boy, I knew not to cross him.

I promised myself I wouldn't turn into him. That no matter what, I'd fight for the ones I love. Yet here I am, sulking like a pathetic asshole instead of proving to Bex that she can count on me and that I'm not going anywhere.

It may take a while, but I'll win her back.

I jump out of bed and throw on some clothes. After pulling

on my boots, I run outside and hop on my bike. The engine roars to life like it always does. I peel out and speed down the road.

Half hour later, I'm pulling into the compound. Stepping inside, I see the clubhouse is mostly empty.

"Khan, brother, where you been?" Goblin calls out, waving me over.

"What's up?" I ask, taking a seat at the bar.

"Sly gave us a direct feed to that lawyer's office so we can watch. She should show up any minute." He points to the laptop.

The screen shows the back of Martin's head. He's typing something on his laptop I can't read while bobbing his head to a tune we can't hear.

"What's with the no sound bullshit on this feed? Does Sly need some more money in his tech budget?" I ask.

"He has cams with audio but they're being used for other reasons." Goblin jerks his head toward the hallway.

"Petra?"

Goblin nods.

"Jesus, fuck. That's creepy." I shake my head and return my attention to the screen.

Seconds later, his hands freeze, and he looks up at the door that's slowly opening. Bexley steps into the frame with all the hesitation in the world.

My pulse pounds seeing her look the opposite of the tigress she usually is. Instead, she looks like a frightened kitten. The only confident thing about her is the stuffy lawyer suit she has on.

Her hair is a curtain around her face, and she's hunched over, making herself as small as possible. This isn't the woman I know, and it makes me want to feed Martin his cock and balls.

He motions for her to sit. I wish I could hear what he's saying. Though maybe it's a blessing since one wrong word and I'd be on my bike.

Like a servant, she scurries in and sits down across from him, her hands wringing together in her lap.

I light up a cig, hoping the nicotine can control my anger. I want a beer so bad, I'm salivating for it, but I hear Bex's voice in my head telling me no. For some stupid reason, I can't go against it.

He says something while reclining in his chair, like he has all the confidence in the world.

I can barely make out Bex's lips moving when she replies. He says something else, gesturing with his hands, and her brows furrow in question.

He laughs, but there's no humor on his face.

Then Bex's spine goes ramrod straight, and she tucks her hair behind her ears.

There she is.

She crosses her legs, and when this time she speaks, her lips move plainly and purposefully.

He stands and strolls over to the window, pretending to admire the view. I fucking hate everything about this dip shit.

Bex nods slowly in response to whatever he said.

My frustration level increases the longer this goes on. He gestures to her; she gestures to him. He gets angry, then she does. Meanwhile, Goblin, Roch, and I watch with rapt attention.

Then Martin crosses the room and sits on the edge of his desk, facing her.

She scoots back in her chair, not liking his proximity.

He says something while leaning in and brushing her hair off her shoulder. I'm going to break each finger that dared to touch her.

She slaps a hand over her neck, and I realize he's pointing out the mark I left on her well over a week ago. Good, it's still there. He should know she has someone.

They're arguing now. The gesturing is bigger, and their

expressions are fierce. Then he says something that shuts her up. My jaw ticks, wondering what vile thing he spewed at her.

He draws a circle on her knee, and I jump off the stool. She may not be my woman anymore, but she's not fucking his either. He has no right to touch her.

"Chill, brother. Loki will step in if it gets too far." Goblin slaps a hand on my shoulder and pushes me back onto the stool. My eyes immediately go back to the screen.

Bex stands and takes a few steps back. He shakes his head, still seated on the edge of the desk. Her chest heaves when she opens her mouth to say her next words. Whatever it is, it pisses him the hell off.

He pushes off the desk and stomps over to her. His hand rears back, and before she can react, he slaps her across her cheek.

I only make it two steps toward the door when Goblin groans and curses. I turn back to see what happened. Martin is doubled over, clutching his balls.

"She kneed him in the fucking balls! Holy shit." Goblin pounds his fist into the bar.

Roch, who was silently watching next to Goblin, smirks. "Taught her that."

I chuckle.

With her fists balled at her side, she shouts something at him. Martin slowly stands upright and walks with his legs spread over to his desk. He pulls a small black rectangle from his drawer and tosses it at Bex. She catches it mid-air.

She says her parting words before tucking the rectangle into her bra and hiking her purse onto her shoulder. Then she turns on her heels and walks out of the office.

I blow out a breath and run a hand through my hair.

"That was intense. Was that a USB he handed her?" Goblin asks.

"Honestly, I don't know. Sure as shit looked like it," I reply.

"You two work things out yet?"

"She decided club life is too much for her."

Goblin shakes his head. "Sorry about that, brother. I know you were into her."

I want to correct him. I'm not just *into* her. I'm in love with her. I gave her my heart and soul, and she stomped all over it. But I don't. Instead, I head downstairs and get back to work.

Soon after, Loki comes down to talk to me, with Bex nowhere to be found.

"She didn't want to come tell me to my face what happened?" I ask.

"She said she had shit to do." He shrugs and takes a seat on the old futon I've yet to throw in the trash.

"What did she say?" I take a seat on a stool across from him.

"Martin had a feeling the evidence against you might go missing, so he used his credentials to get into the system and download his own copy a few weeks ago. Apparently, he's pretty interested in seeing you go away for a while."

"Of course he is. He obviously wants her back. He's too fucking stupid to know I'm not what's keeping them apart. He did that all on his own." I stand back up and pace. "He'll resubmit the evidence, and I'll be locked up, unable to protect her."

"We wouldn't let that happen," he says.

"You can't watch her twenty-four hours a day," I argue.

After I get sent away, it'll take him less than a week to get ahold of her. Then what? He'll lock her up and spend the rest of his miserable life hurting her? No way. Fuck that.

"Let's not worry about that yet. Bex didn't say she had a plan, but her mind was racing. I saw it. She's the best lawyer this club has seen. Let her work it out." His tone is placating, and with my temper already flaring, it has me wanting to punch him in the fucking throat.

He's your Prez. Calm down.

"Why did he give her a thumb drive?" I ask.

"It's a copy of the footage from the night we stole the van." He rubs at the back of his neck. I know he battles with guilt over both of us being there that night, but only me getting caught. There's nothing he can do about it, though. "He can't resubmit it, or he'll get in trouble for tampering with evidence."

"He wants her to do it?"

"Yeah."

"Is she going to?" I can't imagine she would. Unless he's holding something against her. Like maybe outing her real identity. "Fuck!"

"What?"

"Martin is the only other one who knows who she really is. If he told people, she could have her license taken, or worse, be sent to prison herself."

"Jesus." Loki runs a hand down his scruff.

"I need to talk to her." I pull out my phone and open my text messages.

Me: Need a meeting with you.

Bex: Can you come to my office tomorrow?

Me: Not tomorrow. Now.

Bex: I'm busy.

Me: Bexley.

Bex: Tomorrow at ten. I'll see you then.

Me: Where are you?

That last message goes unanswered.

Chapter
TWENTY-ONE

Bexley

I fiddle with my desk, putting everything in its place. I have ten minutes to kill before Wes gets here, and my stomach is in knots. Actually, it's been in knots since yesterday before I met up with Martin.

I was glad the Royal Bastards couldn't hear everything he was saying. It's important they know nothing about what's going on. Ignorance is never bliss, except for right now. If they knew, people would die, and my plan would fall apart.

Looking for something to do, I dig my makeup bag out of my purse and step into my private bathroom. I brush away the mascara flakes that have settled on my cheeks and reapply my brick red lipstick.

Did I choose this color because I know it's Wes's favorite? Maybe. But I'd never admit to it.

I reach into the top of my gray and white bandage dress and pull my tits up higher, creating an almost obscene amount of cleavage. I know I'm the one that broke things off, but that doesn't mean I want to look ugly around him. When the girls are nice and high, I move onto my hair, fingering the curls at the end.

A knock sounds at the door, and I walk over to answer it.

My breath leaves my lungs when Wes strolls through the door, looking much better than the last time I saw him. He was kneeling on the floor in anguish then. An image I wish I could wipe clean from my memory.

"You're early," I say.

"You got something better to do?" His tone has fangs.

My tone, however, is sickly sweet. "No. I was just catching up on your case."

As if he's just now noticing what I'm wearing, he looks me up and down. "That dress new?"

I smooth my hands down the fabric. "Yes."

"It looks . . ." His gaze settles on my breasts, and I'm certain the words 'fuck hot' or 'sexy' will come out of his mouth, but he finishes with, "nice."

Nice? This dress deserves way more than nice. I didn't spend five hundred dollars for a dress to look 'nice.'

"Thanks. You look nice as well." Lies. He looks mouthwatering. Normally I like his hair down but slicked back in a bun at the base of his head gives him an edge that has my nipples drawing up tight. "Why don't you have a seat?"

"You gonna hand over that thumb drive?" he asks, plopping down in a chair and kicking his feet up on my desk.

I take a deep breath. He's hurting, and just like a man, is expressing that by being a dick. I cross the room and sit opposite him.

"Don't worry about the thumb drive. I have it covered."

He narrows his eyes on me. "What does that mean? That you destroyed it?"

I glance away. "Yes."

"How?"

"Excuse me?" I croak. I'm a terrible liar. Always have been.

"How. Did. You. Destroy. It?" He punctuates each word. When I don't answer, he continues, "Did you crush it? Burn it? Stomp on it with your six-inch heels?"

"I burned it."

"Where?"

"In my fireplace."

"What did you do with the melted plastic?"

I suddenly feel like I'm the one on trial. "I threw it away. It's all good."

He studies me for a minute. He knows I'm lying but doesn't call me on it, and I'm not sure why.

"Okay then. Good. Thank you." He puts his feet on the ground and stands. "It's over then? When can I get this thing off my ankle?"

"The prosecutors haven't dropped the charges, so it stays on for now. The trial is still set for October twelfth," I say in the most professional voice I can muster.

"Why wouldn't they drop them? That makes no sense. They don't have any evidence."

"I'm not sure. Maybe they think they'll be able to find something between now and then."

His jaw ticks. "Isn't it your job to know?"

"As we get closer, I'll know more."

"Fine. Are we done?"

"We are. Thanks for stopping by."

He stands. "No problem."

Before he reaches the door, I can't help but call out, "Wes, wait."

He looks over his shoulder. "What?"

"Are you okay?"

His head sags forward as he considers. The look on his

face when his gaze returns to mine punches me in the gut. "I'm fine, darlin'. Just fine."

Then he's gone, and I'm alone.

My heels nearly slip on the gravel as I walk across the dark parking lot of the clubhouse. I don't want to be here, but it's Loki and Birdie's engagement party, and when I tried to decline, Birdie wouldn't hear any of it.

Music blares and cheerful voices sound from the backyard. I walk around the side of the house and enter through the gate, feeling more than a little out of place. Then I see how casual the event is, and I feel even more out of place.

To me, an engagement party is a dressy event. It's why I chose this sage green plunge-neck dress with cutouts on the side. The gauzy fabric moves with my body and makes me feel pretty. However, I'm the only one who didn't get the memo about the dress code.

Birdie rushes over to me. She has on a pair of tight, high-waisted jeans and a floral crop top with bell sleeves. She looks gorgeous but ten notches lower than me on the formality scale.

"I'm so glad you could make it. Do you like what we did to the place?" She motions to the backyard.

I hadn't even noticed. On top of the engagement party invitation, a wedding invitation for October thirty-first came two weeks later. Yep. They're getting married on Halloween, and the backyard reflects that. It's a gorgeous mix of traditional Halloween and Birdie's very feminine style.

A long table spans the length of the house. A black, gothic candle-lit chandelier hangs from the pergola, and pale pink and white floral arrangements are on the underside. Candelabras, in the same style as the chandelier, are spaced down the center of the table. On a side table sits a single-layer chocolate cake with individual cupcakes surrounding it. But the kicker is the fondant hands reaching out of the top of the pastries like they're zombies reaching out of their graves.

"It's gorgeous," I say, my eyes wide as I take in all the other details.

"Thank you. Let me show you around. Truly has zero interest in things like this, so I've been dying for you to show up."

Her excitement is contagious, and I soon find myself immersed in our conversation. That doesn't mean I don't keep an eye out for Wes.

I didn't sleep last night, my nerves making me antsy. It's been a month since I saw him at my office and I'm unsure how this will go. Will he try to prove he's over me by having patch pussy hanging all over him? Will he pretend like we don't even know each other? So many predictions ran through my head, I couldn't relax.

She shows me the cocktail table, where martini glasses full of a black drink sit.

"What's in this?" I ask, lifting a glass up and inspecting it.

"It's a black martini. So, vodka, Blue Curacao liqueur, black raspberry liqueur, and a lemon twist." She brings her glass to her lips and takes a sip. "So good. These are dangerous."

I take my own sip and moan. "Oh, my God. Don't let me have more than two."

Birdie giggles. "As long as you don't let me."

"Deal," I say, taking another sip. I glance around, still not spotting Wes but catching sight of something else interesting. "What is that?"

Sitting next to a table covered in chafing dishes is a four-foot black decorative birdcage. Inside is a blond doll, frozen in midair on a trapeze swing.

Birdie blushes. "It's my engagement present. It's an inside joke of sorts."

"I see. Well, it's beautiful."

"I'm going to put it next to our fireplace."

"That'll look gorgeous," I say.

My eyes wander, still wondering where the hell he is. Maybe he's inside playing pool? I see nearly all the other guys. Loki and Goblin have beers in hand, chatting. Roch and Truly are playing with the dogs further out in the yard. Moto and Sly are missing, but so is Petra, so that makes sense. Ford, Duncan, Bullet, and Miles have a beer bong out and are taking turns with it. There is even a scattering of people I don't know.

Yet no Wes.

"He's on the other side of the house. We made him move his smoker and grill, so we didn't all end up smelling like meat," Birdie says.

"Who?" I ask nonchalantly.

"Don't play dumb." She elbows me. "Can I ask what happened between you two? Because he's tight-lipped about it."

"I saw something I shouldn't have, and it scared me. This life you guys lead is incredible, but it's also risky. I love the family you've created, but—"

"It's not for you?" she guesses.

"Exactly. My entire career is built upon the law. It's all I know. I can't ignore that part of me when I walk through the doors of the clubhouse."

She nods, taking another sip of her drink. She has something to say; I know it.

"What?" I bite out.

"You love him."

That's all it takes for my eyes to sting, and I have to blink back tears.

"Yeah." The word comes out choked.

"Oh, God. Don't cry. Please." Birdie digs a tissue out of her pocket. "I put them there just in case. Loki isn't a very romantic guy, but sometimes he surprises me, so I keep tissues handy. I was a blubbering mess an hour ago when he gave me the birdcage."

I accept the tissue and dab at the inner corners of my eyes. "I'm sorry."

"Don't apologize. It's clear you're both still hung up on each other. Maybe there's still hope." Her doe eyes are so sweet and innocent. I adore her.

"Some problems can't be fixed."

"Well, think fast because he's coming this way." Birdie flitters away, leaving me alone.

I pretend to be very caught up in the beer bong boys and not having a panic attack. I don't see him approach, but I feel it. The chemistry between us is a palpable thing. I can feel it in the air anytime he's close by.

"Didn't expect to see you here," he says.

"I was invited," I blurt out. *Facepalm.*

He chuckles. "I figured."

"This is quite the event." I swig the last of my drink and set it down before reaching for another.

"It's all right. Not what I want my engagement party to look like."

"Are you getting engaged?" I ask, hoping some chick didn't swoop in over the last month. Though that's a selfish thought because no matter what, it'll never be me.

"Not yet," he says cryptically.

"Narrowing down your options?"

"Nah. My options are already narrowed," he whispers into my ear before walking away.

Goosebumps spread across my skin, and like a starving

woman who just got her first taste of food in a long time, I crave more of him.

This is going to be a long night.

Then I remember his curfew. I glance at my phone, noting he only has forty-five minutes before he must leave. Surely I can make it through forty-five minutes. I shake off the tension and walk over to where Loki and Goblin are.

"Congrats," I say, giving him a quick hug.

"Thanks. I'm a lucky guy."

"You are," I agree.

Goblin wraps an arm around me and squeezes me to his side. "How are you, Lawsuit?"

"Lawsuit?" I ask.

"That's your road name, I've decided."

"Hmm. Not sure I like it." I hate it.

"I don't know. I think it fits," Loki says, grinning.

"Aren't road names like sacred or something? You can't go around giving everyone you meet one."

Goblin lets out a hearty laugh. "Woman knows her stuff. I'm just teasing ya. Your glass is empty. Let's go change that."

I didn't even realize I all but chugged my last drink, but I'm not feeling tipsy, so one more can't hurt. Goblin and I walk back over to the martini station, and I take another of the sweet drinks.

"Oh, shit." Goblin points to the yard that's illuminated by these large, round balls of light.

My jaw drops when I see Miles strung up, spread eagle, on a large spinning wheel. Tabitha gives him a good spin, and round and round he goes.

"What the hell are they doing?"

"Wheel of death." He nods to Wes, who stands across the yard, holding a large, double-edged knife.

"He's not," I say, leaving Goblin to get a better look.

In a quick, fluid motion, Wes hurls the knife at Miles. It lands between his legs, way too close for comfort, yet I know it landed exactly where Wes wanted it to.

"You fucker," Miles yells. "You promised not to go after my junk."

Wes laughs. "I wouldn't have tried if you hadn't made such a stink about it."

"Get me off this thing. I'm going to barf." Miles's cheeks blow out wide, and I'm sure he's seconds from spewing all over the lawn.

Tabitha slows the wheel until it finally stops. She undoes the leather cuffs, and he stumbles away, looking green.

"Who's next?" Wes calls out, Coyote chuckling at his side.

I gulp my drink, praying he doesn't look my way. I should've known better.

"Lawsuit?" he shouts in my direction.

Great. The nickname has already caught on.

"I'm good." I hold my drink up.

Then the chanting begins. "Lawsuit, Lawsuit, Lawsuit." Fists bang on every available surface, and Goblin, along with Ford, ushers me across the lawn. Tabitha encourages me over to the wheel, but Wes stops her.

"Let me," he says. "You trust me, Lawsuit?"

"I hate that nickname."

"That's the thing about nicknames. You don't get to choose them. Tabs, take her drink, will ya?"

I chug the rest of the black liquid before handing over the glass.

"You didn't answer me." He grips my wrist. It's such a simple touch, yet it has my pussy throbbing in need. He lifts it up, pins it against the wheel, and buckles it into the leather cuff. "Do you trust me?"

I gulp. "You know I do."

After everything we've done behind closed doors, trust is not an issue.

His fingers trail down the underside of my arm and skim across my belly before reaching my other wrist. He raises it above my head and cuffs it as well, our eyes locked the entire time.

"I'm wearing a dress. Everyone will see my panties," I say, finally feeling the effects of the alcohol I consumed.

"Girl, I got you. I have a pair of biker shorts under this dress since I'm usually the one spinning around on that thing." Tabitha unceremoniously yanks down a pair of stretchy black shorts, probably mooning everyone behind her but not caring in the least.

Wes takes the shorts from her and holds them out so I can step into them. He pulls them up my legs—careful not to expose any skin—until he has them up to my waist. My breath hitches when his fingers skim my bare stomach. I'm desperate for his touch.

"Better?" he says.

"No," falls from my lips, and I look away.

He chuckles lightly and crouches, putting his face right in line with my center. I think I hear him inhale and my eyes flutter closed as I try to regain composure. God, I want him so badly. I shouldn't be here. It's too tempting.

He helps me out of my heels and sets my foot on a peg. "Keep your feet on the pegs and hang onto the ones by your hand."

I bend my wrists until I feel the cold metal, then I grip onto it like my life depends on it. If it weren't for the drinks, I might freak out.

He gently tightens the cuffs around both my ankles and stands. "You good?"

"Yeah, I'm good."

He stands so close I get a whiff of his intoxicating scent. Last week, I went to six candle stores looking for anything that resembled nicotine and leather. Nothing compared to the real thing.

"Any last words?" he asks.

"No. Do I need last words?"

One corner of his lips tips up. "I think you'll live."

He walks backward until he reaches the far end of the yard. Nodding at Tabitha, he takes his knife in hand, face pinched in concentration.

"Ready?" Tabitha asks.

"As I'll ever be."

She gives me a good spin, and I close my eyes as I go upside down and right side up, over and over. My stomach turns, and I don't know how much longer I can do this.

"Open your eyes and focus on one object," Wes shouts.

I obey, picking him as my object to focus on. It works. Until I see him pull the knife back over his shoulder. A rush of adrenaline hits my bloodstream. With no other place for the sudden surge of energy to go, I burst out in laughter. That is until his arm swings forward and the knife soars at me.

A very unladylike scream leaves my mouth before I hear a distinct *thunk* on the wheel. I freeze, mentally going down my body to search for pain. Nothing registers, and then Tabitha has me stopped. I'm too dizzy to find the knife, so I close my eyes and rest my head against the wheel, waiting to be set free.

"How was it?" a deep and throaty voice asks. It's a voice I know well.

I open my eyes, and Wes is there, unbuckling the cuffs. "That was a rush."

"Did you see where the knife landed?"

"Not yet."

He reached under my arm, his hand skimming the side of

my breast. Then he yanks the knife from the wooden wheel. "I think I ruined your dress. Sorry about that."

I pull my hands free from the loosened cuffs and attempt to see the part of my dress he knifed, but I can't see over my tits. I feel around, and yep, there it is. I tear in the fabric.

"This was new," I pout.

"We just paid your bill this month. You can afford it," he teases, lowering to his knees and undoing the cuffs.

I step down onto the cool grass and seek out my shoes, finding them to the right of the wheel. I push my feet into them and turn back around, expecting to find Wes still there, but he's gone.

"You can return my shorts next time I see you," Tabitha says, still loitering around.

"Where did Wes go?" I ask.

"Khan? Oh, he had to get back to Tahoe."

"He left?"

"Yeah. Damn shame about his ankle monitor, am I right?"

I nod politely but, on the inside, I'm dying. Why didn't he say goodbye?

Chapter
TWENTY-TWO

Khan

I want to gag at how pussified the basement looks. I don't even know what's going on with this club. Pink and blue are everywhere I look. Even the damn stripper pole I installed is covered in pink and blue flowers.

What the fuck?

I finished the basement a couple weeks ago. After Bexley broke up with me, I had nothing but time and could bang it out in five weeks. I installed a beautiful, reclaimed wood bar. Bought leather couches and even had a second pool table delivered. The ultimate man cave.

Now my leather sofas have stuffed animals for throw pillows. My four-thousand-dollar pool table has a tablecloth over it and is being used to hold snack foods. *Tiny* snack food. All with a baby theme. Rice crispy treats in the shape of baby bottles, pigs in a blanket wrapped to look like a swaddled baby, and deviled eggs. The egg is carved out in the shape of a cradle, and the yolk mixture settled inside looks like a baby with black eyes piped on.

I thought Loki and Roch nabbing themselves some old ladies meant we were maturing and growing the fuck up. Not a sign our balls are shrinking. I wonder what Miguel, our gun supplier, would say if he saw this. He'd probably fire us on the spot.

"Do you love it?" Truly asks. She has on a white dress with a blue and pink sash tied just above her bump.

"Suuuurrreee," I drawl out.

She laughs, holding a glass under a beverage dispenser labeled *Mamatini*. "I know. It's a bit much."

"No, it's great. This is exactly what I envisioned when I secured that stripper pole into the ceiling."

"The house is coming along nicely," she compliments.

After finishing the basement, I started work on her and Roch's house out near Loki's. With a baby on the way, they're gonna need more space.

"Yeah. It's coming together. How much longer do we have before this one is born?" I nod at her belly.

She rests a hand on her bump. "Three months. Is that enough time?"

"All the permits are in place, so should be." We have a relationship with the building official. A few years back, he ran into a bad situation with a bad man. We took care of the man, and now we never have to wait to get a permit issued.

"Good." She winces and presses a hand on the side of her belly.

"Everything okay?"

"Baby gymnastics. Do you want to feel?" She reaches for my hand and, without waiting for my answer, places it on her bump.

We wait for a second, and then I feel it. A kick right into the center of my palm.

"Holy shit," I curse and then add, "Sorry for swearing."

That was incredible. There's a life in there. One she created with Roch. An image of what Bexley would look like pregnant flashes through my mind. Fuck if I don't like that idea.

Truly laughs. "I don't think they'll repeat that for a while."

Roch appears, glaring at my hand placement. I jerk it away, and he tugs her to his side. His possessive instincts have been heightened since he knocked Truly up.

"Need you," he says.

"For what?"

He pins her with a look that says he needs to fuck her because another man had his hand on her.

"Guests will be arriving soon," she complains, but it's no use. He ushers her up the stairs and out of sight.

I scan the room, seeing women everywhere. Truly's mom is busy hanging a "Pin the Baby on the Stroller" game or some shit, Tabitha and Sissy are fussing over the cake, and a few of Truly's friends from school are spiking their Mamatinis with a flask they pulled from their purses.

I don't blame them. I accidentally catch their gazes, and they look me up and down. Oh, hell no. I turn around to head to the backyard, where the men are gathered.

"Hello?" The voice that haunts me in my sleep calls down the stairs.

I haven't laid eyes on Bexley in a month, and I wasn't expecting to see her today, though I should've expected it. This friendship she's developed with Birdie and Truly is really fucking me up. She's now around for every gathering we have. It's annoying. I can't possibly get over a woman who's constantly around. It's bad enough I have to keep checking in with her about my case.

Bexley appears, and I'm reminded why she's so fucking hard to forget. Her top is a taupe-colored spaghetti strap flowy number that ends just below her breasts. A sliver of stomach shows before the matching pants begin. They're flowy, too, the bottoms hiding the top of her high heels.

Fuuuuuuuuck.

"Wes," she says, surprise in her tone.

"Not expecting to see me?" I ask.

"I ran into Birdie upstairs, and she said the guys were in the back." She takes me in shamelessly. "Did you trim your beard?"

I run my fingers through my facial hair. "A bit. It was getting a little unruly."

"It looks good." She blushes, and oh, how I wish that color on her cheeks was there for a different reason.

"Thanks. With the trial coming up, I'm thinking of ways to look more trustworthy."

At the mention of the trial, she glances away. I'm not a fucking idiot. I know something's going on that she's not telling me. I could get it out of her, but despite everything that's happened, I trust her. Or at least I'm trying. She let me throw a knife at her, after all.

"Well, you're doing a good job. I'd trust you," she says quietly, even though we both know she doesn't. If she did, she'd tell me what the fuck was going on with my case.

More guests arrive, and I make my excuses to go hang out with the guys. In the backyard, Roch looks a little more relaxed than he did a half-hour ago, but he must still be uncomfortable from the attention because Karen, the chihuahua, is held firmly in his arms.

The guys are their usual loud selves, growing louder the more the beer flows. I haven't been asked for a piss test once, but I still refrain from drinking, just in case.

I try to join in, to get caught up in the happiness of Roch bringing a baby into the club. But I'm not feeling it. I slink back into the house and head down the hallway to my empty room. I've got a hundred good memories of this room. All of them involving one woman. The rest are blurs in my vision that I don't recall anymore.

I flop down onto the bed and stare at the ceiling. The closer the trial gets, the more I don't feel like myself. Ever since I patched in, I've had a strong sense of security. I knew that no matter what, the guys would have my back. But being arrested makes me feel like I'm on an island, alone.

They'll show up for me, and the club'll pay for all my legal fees, but it's not their asses on the line. It's mine. They won't be in the jail cell with me if things go bad.

The doorknob turns, and Bexley pops her head in. "What are you doing in here?"

"Thinkin'."

"Mind if I join you?"

I scoot over. "Come on in."

She closes the door behind her and lies down next to me, mimicking my position with her hands under her head.

"What are we thinking about?" she asks after a few quiet minutes.

"Life."

"That's deep." She knocks my elbow with hers. "What specifically about life are we thinking about?"

I blow out a breath. "You want the truth?"

"Always."

Since I've held all this in with my brothers, it would feel good to talk to her about it. But it also feels too personal for the place we're in. She's my lawyer. That's it. She made it abundantly clear she wants nothing else to do with me. If I can pretend it's three months ago, though, I might be able to get it out.

"I have a real bad feeling about this trial. Can't fuckin' shake it. Every day that passes feels like I'm inching closer and closer to a prison cell."

She rolls onto her side and props her head on her hand. "I wouldn't let that happen."

"Do you control the courts? A jury?" I turn my head to the side to meet her brown eyes.

"No, but I'm damn good at what I do. You need to trust me." Something about the way she says it is off. Like she's sending me a subliminal message I don't understand. Maybe I'm reading too much into it.

"You'd tell me if there's something I needed to know?"

"Yes," she says vehemently.

"Okay." I return to staring at the ceiling. With her this close, it's too tempting to reach over and kiss her pink lips.

I feel her eyes on me for a long time before she asks, "Where do you see yourself in five years?"

"Assuming I'm not in prison?"

She giggles. "Yes. Assuming that."

"Here, with my brothers. Maybe I'll build a house out in the woods, or maybe I'll stay in this room. Either way, I'll still be VP and still be a Royal Bastard."

"But what else?"

"What do you mean?" I ask.

"Don't you want something for yourself? Maybe build up your construction business? Take on actual jobs? I've seen your work. You're amazing with your hands."

"That an innuendo, darlin'?"

"God. It always comes back to sex with you." She returns to her back, and now it's me on my side, facing her.

"Since my hand injury, I can't take on the jobs I once could. Too much time with a hammer or drill, and my joints freeze up," I explain.

"Is it painful?" She reaches over and grabs my hand to study the scars. She's done this a hundred times, but each time she inspects it like she might find the cause of my pain and be able to fix it.

"Yeah. Feels almost like a pinch coming from deep inside

that radiates down my fingers." I make a fist, then extend my hand.

"I could kiss it better," she offers.

"Think that'll work?"

"I could try. You never know."

The air thickens, and the energy around us buzzes to life.

"You do have a magical mouth," I say.

She lifts my hand to her lips and kisses up and down each scar, leaving a wet trail behind her. Each time I feel her kiss, my cock grows harder and harder, and the urge to climb on top of her and fuck her into the mattress grows.

"Darlin'?"

"Yeah?"

"You keep doing that, and things are gonna happen."

She licks her lips. "What if I want them to? It doesn't have to mean anything."

She's horny. Well, welcome to the fucking club. Each time I rub one out is a disappointment to my dick. Nothing feels as good as being inside Bexley—her mouth or her cunt. I'd take either.

It's a bad idea. I know it. She knows it. But when you put two horny people together, poor decisions will be made each and every time.

Fuck it.

I climb on top of her and pin her hands above her head, holding them there with one hand while the other roams up and down her body. She's lost some weight, and it doesn't make me happy.

"You eating?" I ask.

"Wow. That was a mood killer." She tries to pull her hands free, but my grip is tight.

"I mean it. I can practically feel your ribs."

"That's normal. Having a layer of fat so you can't feel my ribs isn't."

"I don't like it. You're not eating enough. That means you aren't happy." I scowl at her.

"I'd be a lot happier if I was having an orgasm," she sasses. "Wanna help me out with that?"

She doesn't have to ask me twice. I fall to her side and push her top up. Thankfully she's not wearing a bra, so I'm instantly rewarded with the sight of her naked breasts. The piercings are healing nice and look sexy as fuck.

"Promise me you'll do this with me again when these things are healed," I say through a groan.

"You want to make a sex date for four months from now?"

"Assuming I'm not locked up," I clarify.

"Stop joking about that. It's not funny."

"Not tryin' to be. Just tryin' to secure a date with your titties."

"Fine. You and me in four months. I'll pencil you in." Her smile is contagious.

"Fuck that. Permanent marker that shit," I say. "They still hurt?"

"No. Not at all."

"This is okay?" I grab a handful of her breast, careful not to touch her nipple, which is easy to do given there's more than a handful.

"Yes," she breathes out.

I take turns on each, manhandling her and discovering it's not just her nipples that get her going.

"Anyone been between these thighs since me?" I ask. It's an asshole question, but if she tells me yes, I'll walk out of this room right now.

"No. No one."

"Good girl." I slide my hand into her pants and cup her sex over her panties. The fabric is soaked.

"Please, Wes," she begs.

I stroke her through the fabric as it becomes wetter and wetter with each pass. I need to taste her. It's been too fucking long. I release her and stand up.

"Clothes need to come off. Now," I order.

Her enthusiasm as she disrobes tells me she needs this as bad as I do. She removes her top first, balling it up and throwing it at my head. Her pants and panties come off next. There's a new tuft of hair on the V between her legs, and it turns me right the fuck on.

She sits up to undo the dainty buckle on her ankle, but I stop her. "Leave those on. Wanna feel those heels digging into me while I fuck you."

Her lips part, and she lies back on the bed.

I lock the door and untie my shoes before stepping out of them and stripping down. I don't miss her half-lidded eyes as she watches me. Climbing back on top of her, I spread her thighs to make room for me. My cock finds its home between her legs, nestled against her sopping wet pussy lips.

I take her mouth, and she matches my speed, nipping, sucking, and licking right along with me. My cock grows painfully hard. It would be so easy to reposition and thrust inside of her, but I don't know how many more opportunities I'll have to be with her, so I have to make it count.

And by that, I mean I need to eat her out.

I cup the base of her neck, my fingers gripping her chin. When I turn her head to the side, exposing her throat, I suck her flesh into my mouth. She's not mine anymore, but that doesn't mean I can't leave my marks all over her body.

I pull away, happy with my handiwork, and move down lower to her collarbone, where I take turns biting and kissing her. She wiggles from beneath me each time I sink my teeth into her. Her penchant for a little pain hasn't gone anywhere.

I kiss down her cleavage, leaving little bites as I go, then move to the underside of her tits. I take in a mouthful and bite down hard enough to leave an imprint of my teeth.

"Holy shit. You're going to make me come just from that."

I release her and say, "I got other plans for your first orgasm. Want your pussy juice dripping from my beard for that one."

"You're so dirty."

"Ain't seen nothing yet." I continue a path down her body until I reach her drenched cunt. Lifting to my knees, I grab the underside of her thighs and spread them as far as they'll go, then I push them up. "Hold yourself open for me, darlin'. Need to see what I'm working with."

Her pussy lips drip when I spread her with my thumb and forefinger, and I groan when I see her perfect, pink cunt.

"Love how wet you are for me. Dripping all the way down to your cute little asshole." I trail a finger down her slit, gathering wetness before tapping it against her back entrance. I've had this woman in so many ways, but I've never had her ass. I think I want to change that today.

"You're so weird." The blush I'd wanted earlier surfaces.

"I wanna fuck you here." I push a finger in up to the first knuckle, watching her reaction. Her nipples draw up tight, and her belly tightens. She wants it too.

"Will it hurt?"

"Can't say I know for sure, but I do know how to make it feel good." I push into my second knuckle with ease.

"Do it," she says.

"Gotta prepare you first."

"How do you do that?"

I smirk and lower my mouth to her pussy. Flattening my tongue, I lap at her juices, flicking the tip against her clit with each pass. All the while, I'm pumping a finger in and out of her tight, virgin ass.

She comes with my name on her lips, only making my cock throb even more. She may not want everything that comes along with being my woman, but it's me she wants to satisfy her in bed, and that's enough ... for now.

"Your arms gettin' tired? Or can you keep this position for a little longer?" I ask.

"I'm good."

I reach over into my nightstand, finding a bottle of lube still in there. "Thank fuck."

After squirting a glob of the stuff onto my fingers and spreading it around, I press two fingers in, thrusting slowly and rubbing her clit with my thumb.

"Oh, God," she pants.

"Feel good, darlin'?"

"So good."

I scissor my fingers, stretching her even wider. She doesn't even flinch, so I add a third. Her hole is tight, so I know it has to burn, but by the way her pussy continues to drip, I know she's fucking loving it.

"Not much room in here. You think you can take my cock, baby?"

"Yes. Please. I need to feel you inside me."

"Hell yeah."

Chapter
TWENTY-THREE

Bexley

What the hell am I thinking? I never imagined I'd be getting my ass fucked at a baby shower, but here we are.

He lubes up his cock, which is so hard the pierced head is an angry shade of red. He strokes himself roughly, his eyes trained on my center. Oh God, the way he makes me feel. Like out of all the flavors in the world, I'm his favorite. And he knows exactly what I like.

"Tell me if you want me to stop, yeah?"

"Yeah, baby."

He leans over to kiss me as if to reward me for using a pet name.

"You ready?" he asks, his forehead pressed to mine.

I nod, and he sits upright, widening his knees. He grips the base of his girthy cock, and the nerves kick in. There's no way that will fit up my ass. No way at all.

"Relax, darlin'. This won't work if you're clenched up tight."

I take a calming breath. He'll stop if I want him to, but I already know I won't ask. I want to give him this part of me.

Something that he knows is only his. I can't give him anything else but this.

With his dick in hand, he teases circles around my hole, the other hand playing with my pussy. He's breathing heavily, the anticipation killing us both. Then he presses in slowly. Shit, it burns. It burns so badly, but his fingers working magic on my clit help.

"Hard part is almost over. The head's almost in. You're doing so good, darlin'. You're such a good girl."

I preen at his compliment. He's the only one I'd ever let call me that. In my career, women are considered inferior—a complication the patriarchy doesn't want to deal with—so being called a "good girl" would normally push me over the edge.

But not here with Wes. I want to be his good girl. I want him to dominate me and take from my body, using me up for his own pleasure because I know he'll give it back to me in spades.

When I don't think I can stretch anymore, my body sucks in his fat head. The burning eases, and I feel so full but so good. The metal balls circling his tip feel incredible as they massage me from inside.

"Look at that ass. It was made for my cock. A perfect fucking fit." His head lulls back on his neck as he pumps into me with short and shallow thrusts, slowly easing himself deeper inside.

I close my eyes and moan, feeling euphoric as my body adjusts. It's not long before he's balls deep inside me.

"Oh, God. Oh, God." Two fingers enter my pussy.

If I thought I was full before, now I'm stuffed.

"I can feel my cock inside your ass with my fingers. Fuck, that turns me on. Gonna need you to come, darlin'. Sooner than later. What do you need?"

"More. I need more."

His thumb presses down onto my clit, rubbing little circles while his fingers hit my G-spot and his cock fucks my ass.

I grab onto the fleshy part of my tits and knead them while he works me over.

"Open your eyes, darlin'. Wanna see those brown eyes when I make you come."

We lock gazes, and he picks up the pace, overwhelming me with pleasure. The sounds we're making are obscene, and I'll play them over and over in my head when I'm alone and reliving this moment.

He leans over my body and places a hand at the base of my throat. His thumb and fingers squeeze gently, but his palm stays lax, not cutting off my airflow. He holds it for a few seconds and then releases. A head rush follows soon after, and I beg for him to do it again.

"You tell me if you want me to stop, yeah?"

I nod, and he applies a little more pressure this time. I feel light-headed, and a hot flush spreads over my body. His cock drives into me with more force, his balls slapping against my ass cheeks, adding yet another erotic sound to the playlist in my head.

I release my legs and wrap them around his waist, pulling him to me because it's never hard enough. No matter how close we get, I want him closer.

"Come. Come now," he orders, and I obey.

An orgasm takes hold, and he releases my neck, moving his hand to the underside of my breast and squeezing hard. This time, the head rush is so much bigger, and it only serves to intensify my already insane orgasm. He pounds into me, and I swear his cock swells even more, expanding my insides to the point of pain, and I fucking love every second of it.

I let out a string of curses as I come for so long, I think I'm going to explode. My legs shake, and my teeth chatter as I hang on to every second I can before slowly coming down. His hand leaves my pussy and my breast, moving to my hips, where he holds on for leverage, digging his thumbs into my pelvis.

"Yes. Harder, baby. Take it all out on my body. Punish me. Bruise me. Remind me who my body belongs to." I don't understand why I'm egging him on. My orgasm is over, but I'm still so full of emotion. Maybe if he fucks me hard enough, it'll all go away. I need him to make it go away.

"Oh, fuck." Wes pulls out and pushes in, his eyes locked on where we're joined. He does this over and over until he sucks in a sharp breath and buries himself to the hilt. His cock pulses and fills me with his cum. There's so much of it, it spills out and drips down my crack and onto the mattress.

He pushes into me one final time, holding himself as deep as he can get. He stays there for long minutes, his chest heaving and beads of sweat dripping from his body.

"That's it, darlin'. Let it out," he coos and wipes dampness from my cheek.

It takes me a second to realize what's he's talking about. I didn't even realize I was crying. Which makes my tears of release quickly morph into tears of embarrassment. What the hell is wrong with me?

He pulls out and spoons me from behind, brushing my hair from my face and pressing gentle kisses to my neck. "It's okay. You're okay."

"I don't even know why I'm crying," I sob.

"That was intense. I get it."

"I've never had anal, and I've never been choked." There are so many more reasons for all the emotion welling inside me, but I can't say any of them out loud.

"I know. It was a big day," he jokes, trying to lighten the mood. "But technically, I wasn't choking you. Just cutting off the blood to your carotid. When released, all the blood rushes back to your head, amplifying your orgasm."

"You're so good at sex," I blubber.

He lets out a full belly laugh, wrapping his arms all the way around me and holding me tight. He starts to say, "I lo—" but the words die on his tongue, and it sobers us both up.

"I should shower." I pull out of his arms and jump off the bed, collecting my clothes as I dash to the shower. After closing the door behind me, I lock it.

With cum dripping down my legs and my pussy still throbbing, I sink to the tiled floor and hug my knees to my chest. This is so hard. The hardest thing I've ever done. But I have to do it. I have to follow through. No matter how much it hurts.

I only hope he still loves me after the trial.

One month later

A knock sounds on my office door. I'm not expecting anyone. I was actually getting ready to head out for the day. I look up to see Martin walk through the door. The sight of his smug face makes my skin crawl.

The insults and threats he flung at me the last time I saw him are still fresh in my memory. He called me a slut for having Wes's mark on my neck. That probably pissed me off the most because it was all I had left of the man I love.

"We don't have an appointment," I say, feeling bold since there are people still milling about the office. "If you'd like to schedule one, Marcy would be more than happy to help you."

"That won't be necessary. This won't take long." With all the audacity in the world, he strolls in and takes a seat.

"Please, sit down," I say sarcastically.

He frowns in response. Sarcasm wasn't allowed while we were married. *"Sarcasm is the lowest form of wit,"* he'd say. I make a mental note to only be sarcastic from here and out when dealing with him.

"What can I do for you? Need a criminal attorney yet? With your history, I would've thought you'd have one by now." I rest an elbow on my desk and prop my chin up on my fist. "You know, with all your criminal activity lately."

"You had a much better attitude when you were under my thumb," he clips out.

"Some people would say I have a much better attitude now that I'm not living in fear and covered in bruises," I say, then add, "It's me. I'm some people."

His face turns an ugly shade of red, sparking memories I've kept buried for my own mental stability. I remind myself I'm not Sienna anymore. I'm Bexley fucking March, badass attorney to some of the most feared people in Nevada. That must mean something.

"If you're done." He adjusts his position. "Where are you with getting that evidence put back into play? I expected it to be done by now."

"You mean the thumb drive I destroyed? That evidence?" It's a lie. The little black stick is sitting safely next to the stack of cash I have left after relieving him of it.

"You think that was my only copy?"

There we go. That's what I was hoping he would say.

"Chill, grandpa," I say, bringing attention to his advanced age. I had thought he was a handsome man when I met him. Now he looks like a shriveled raisin. I dodged more than one bullet by leaving him. "It's safe, and I'm working on a plan."

"You're running out of time."

"I'm well aware of the trial date, thank you."

"You know, this sass is very unbecoming. That biker of yours must not know how to keep control of his women. It's surprising but says a lot about who he is." He holds his chin up high while he adjusts his cufflinks.

I hate Martin more than I've ever hated anything. If anyone deserves a painful death at the hands of Khan, it's this man.

"You aren't half the man he is. Figuratively"—I point to his dick—"and literally."

It happens so fast, I don't have time to react. He jumps to his feet and dives over my desk, putting his hands around my neck. It's a much different experience than with Wes. Martin squeezes against my windpipe, cutting off all oxygen. I claw at his hands, gasping for a breath that doesn't come.

"Listen here, you miserable bitch. I've let you get away with way more than you deserve." Spittle hits my face, and the vein in his forehead throbs. "I should've ended you when I had the chance. You're lucky the only thing I did was move to Reno and make your life a living hell. After I get this job, you better believe your career is over. I'll have you destitute, begging for me to help you, and I'll laugh in your fucking face. I've been planning that moment for so long, it's the only reason you're alive today."

With his hands still squeezing around my throat, he shoves me backward. I slam my head against the wall, tripping over my executive chair and crashing to the ground. My body contorts around the aluminum legs and leather seat as I land in a heap. All the while, I choke and cough, trying desperately to draw air into my lungs.

Spots fill my vision and I feel a trickle of warmth run down my neck before blackness takes over and I let it swallow me whole.

I don't know how long I was out, but I'm confused and in an incredible amount of pain when I wake.

"Ms. March, welcome back. Can you tell me what hurts?" A younger man in a uniform works quickly while pulling out various sterilized tools and bandages.

I blink and blink again. "Where am I?" My voice is hoarse, and it burns to speak.

"An ambulance. Your coworker found you passed out after being assaulted." He draws medication from a vial into a syringe before pushing it into the hub on the IV line in my hand.

"What?" It takes a second for me to remember what happened. Martin came in and oh, my God.

"Tell me what hurts," he repeats.

"My, my head and my throat," I croak.

He pulls up on my right eyelid and flashes a light back and forth in front of it before doing the same thing on the other side. "Safe to say you have a concussion and potential damage to your vocal cords. Do you know who did this to you?"

I can't think. There's so much at stake. If I say the wrong thing, everything will be ruined. So, for now, I shake my head.

"Your secretary said a man in a suit barged into your office and then left ten minutes later. Was it him?"

I say nothing. Whatever he pumped into my veins clouds my brain and makes me feel off.

Seconds later, the ambulance stops, and I'm taken into the emergency room. This is a nightmare. It must be.

"Female, mid to late-thirties. Violently assaulted. Ligature marks around her neck, contusion on the back of her head, and bruises, well, everywhere."

"Thanks, we'll take it from here," a woman with a kind smile dressed in scrubs says. "What's your name?"

"Bexley March," I let out in a painful whisper.

"Nice to meet you, Bexley. My name's Maddison, and I'm going to take good care of you." She wheels me into a room with glass walls and curtains all around it. She pulls them shut and goes about her business, checking vitals and injecting more of God knows what into my vein. "Can I call someone for you?"

I think for a minute. If I call Wes, he'll kill Martin, and he won't be tidy about it. He's hanging on by a thread as it is, and I can't be the reason he's sent to prison for the rest of his life. Except I'm alone and scared and there's no one else. Except maybe...

"Did my cell phone come in with me?" I ask, even though it hurts to speak.

"Was it in your purse?"

I nod.

"Then, yes." She digs around inside until she produces an iPhone. "Who can I call?"

"Birdie."

"Her name is Birdie?" Her eyebrows arch, and I nod.

Thirty minutes later, a gorgeous, panicked blonde barges into the room. "What the heck happened to you?"

She rushes over to me and pinches my chin between her fingers. She moves my head this way and that, looking for the source of my injury.

Tears well in my eyes, and I let out a choked sob. "I was assaulted."

"Christ on a cracker. I need to call Khan."

"No!" I try to yell, but I sound like a dying goat, so instead, I whisper, "No. He can't know about this."

"Are you insane? You know who he is, right?"

I nod.

Why does everyone keep asking me that?

She paces the room. "Oh my god. I will be in so much trouble for keeping this a secret. You have no idea. I don't understand. Whoever did this can be taken care of by nightfall. Why won't you let me tell him?"

"He can't get into any more trouble." I hope she's good at reading lips because my voice is done being abused.

"Honey, that's not on you. Those boys have a code that clearly says if someone messes with them, they mess right back.

Especially when it comes to their women. Keeping this a secret? I can't do it. I just can't. I'm sorry."

Tears free fall down my face as I'm reminded I'm no longer Wes's woman. It feels like a moot point to bring up, though. "Wait until tomorrow. Need time for my throat to rest."

She sighs. "That's a good compromise. Let me call Loki. I'll tell him I'm having dinner with my dad or something. That way, I can stay for a while without him getting suspicious."

She steps out of the room at the same time Maddison returns. "Okay, I've got the good stuff." She waves a syringe at me. "It's going to make you really sleepy, but you need to rest."

The second the pain meds hit my bloodstream, my body relaxes, and I feel a hundred times better. Is this what Wes was talking about when he told me about his addiction? Because I can see why. My limbs feel loose, the pain in the back of my head is gone, and my mood has improved substantially.

The problem is that it's a lie. None of it is real. But I'm happy for the reprieve anyway, as temporary as it might be.

Birdie returns and pulls a chair over to my bedside. Taking my hand, she says, "He believed it, so I have a few hours before I'll be missed. How are you feeling?"

"Amazing," I say honestly.

"Oh yeah?" She smiles brilliantly. "I see the morphine has kicked in."

"You're really pretty," I croak.

"Aw, thanks."

"Like really pretty." I reach over and twirl a strand of her hair. It's the softest thing I've felt in all my life. I want to ask what hair products she uses, but I'm suddenly sleepy.

"Okay." She takes my hand again and rests it on the bed. "Nighty-night time for you. If I'm not here when you wake up, I'll be back in the morning."

I don't have time to respond before I fall into a dreamless sleep.

I wake up a few times throughout the night. Once when they had to stitch up the gash in the back of my head. To do that, they had to shave a patch of hair. Love that for me.

The second time I woke up was when police officers wanted to question me about what happened. I thought they would wait to report it because I hadn't said a word to anyone, but I was wrong. I pray Marcy kept her mouth shut about what she saw. She knows better than to say anything to anyone without a lawyer present. I can only hope she remembered the lessons I taught her.

I refused to speak to them, claiming it was too painful. It was the truth, but even if I could speak, I wouldn't. Not yet. I haven't had a clear enough mind to think everything through.

The third time I woke up, they moved me to a CT machine, followed by an MRI because they found brain swelling. They said it was mild enough to resolve on its own but want to keep me for a few days for monitoring.

The fourth time I woke up, a different nurse was applying an ointment to the abrasions on my throat. Apparently, Martin twisted his hands while he was choking me, leaving friction burns.

The fifth time, it was morning. I was in a new room, this one with actual walls and a window. I blink my eyes open to see sunshine and blue skies.

"Thank fuck," a deep voice says from my right.

Chapter
TWENTY-FOUR

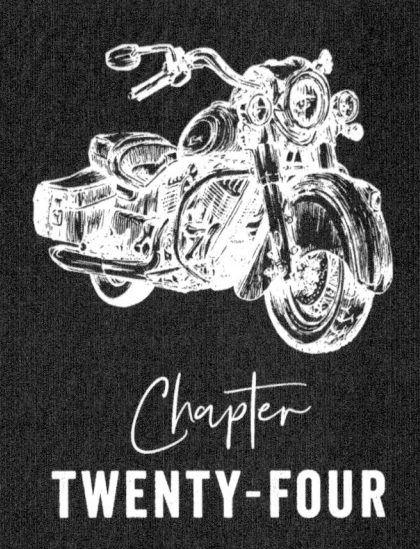

Khan
Two hours earlier

I barely get through the front door of the clubhouse before Loki is in my face, telling me Bex is in the hospital.

I don't even give him a chance to explain before I'm out the door, hopping back on my bike and riding to the hospital. I park in the ambulance lane, not giving a fuck what happens to my bike.

As I make my way through the ER entrance, fear like I've never felt before rushes through me, and I've been in some fucked up situations that would make any grown man piss himself.

Thankfully someone left my name as an approved visitor, and they give me Bex's room number. I say thankfully because there would've been some bodies on the floor if they hadn't told me.

Loki isn't far behind me, and before I can throw my fist through a wall, he clamps down on my shoulder. "Be cool, brother. We need a fuck of a lot more information before we know which way to take this. I got your back, no matter what, but we need to wait until she wakes up."

I take in his words, agreeing but not liking them.

"For right now, just worry about taking care of your girl. Looks like she's pretty fucked up. When she wakes up, it should be you she sees first. Got it?"

"Yeah. Okay." I exhale loudly and sink onto the chair next to her bed.

"I'm gonna take off and deal with some other shit. Something's going on with Coyote, and I need to get to the bottom of it. Are you cool? Am I gonna get a call about you getting locked up because you burned down a hospital?" Loki asks.

"Nah, man. I'm cool. Swear it."

"Okay. Call me when you know more."

I nod and turn my attention to Bexley. He's right. She's probably terrified and in pain. I need to be here to help her through this.

I stare over at the unconscious woman who owns me, wanting to kill whoever had the nerve to touch her. Her throat is wrapped in gauze, as is her head. Her cheeks are marred with broken blood vessels, and after lifting her blanket, I find bruises all down her legs and left hip.

I lift her hand to my lips and press a kiss there. It's one of the few spots unharmed by the dead asshole who did this to her.

I can't fucking wait to find out who I get to kill. I'll make him suffer for weeks, months even. He'll beg for a death I won't give him. My leg bounces with anticipation.

There's a knock at the door seconds before a woman in scrubs walks in. When she sees me, she stops in her tracks and reaches for the emergency call button. Her hand hovers over it as she asks, "Who are you?"

I don't blame her for judging my appearance. I could have

a shorter haircut, shave my beard, and have on a suit, and I'd still be intimidating as fuck. I'm used to it.

"Whoa, whoa. I didn't do this to her. I'm her boyfriend."

An eyebrow arches, and I realize that explanation doesn't clear me of guilt.

"This woman right here is my world, and I swear to God, the second I find out who dared touch what's mine, I'll end him." It's a risky move to threaten someone's life in front of a nurse, but she looks like she's seen some shit. Her eyes are too knowing.

The chance pays off, and she lowers her hand. "Good. It'll save me from hunting him down."

I grin. "I like you."

She gives me a returning smile. "How's our girl doing? I was here when she was brought in, but I had the night off." She flips through screens on her tablet. "Scans look okay, a little brain swelling, but the doctor thinks her body will take care of it on its own. I see she got some stitches put in on the back of her head, and they want to keep her for a few days."

"You know what happened to her?"

"She isn't talking, not that I blame her."

"What do you mean?" I ask.

"She has a strangulation injury. Right now, everything is swollen and irritated, making it hard for her to speak without incredible pain. We won't know more until the swelling goes down."

"She was choked?" I ask in a monotone voice. After this woman started listing everything off, I had to shut down my emotions. It was either that or Loki would get that call about the hospital being burned down.

Her eyes soften. "She's been through hell. Make sure when she wakes up that you're calm and gentle. She'll need it."

I nod, and the nurse works in silence, checking Bexley's vitals and whatnot.

"I'll be back in a bit," she says, then walks out.

For thirty minutes, my sweaty palm hangs onto Bex's hand like she's my only lifeline before she stirs. Her eyes flutter open, and I'm startled to see the whites of them are a bright shade of red. She focuses on the view outside the window, not seeming to realize I'm here.

"Thank fuck," I say.

Her head whips to the side, making her face pinch. Her hand clamps onto the side of her neck in obvious pain. "Ouch."

Her voice. Fuck me, her voice. It sounds like it's been put through a meat grinder and then blasted out of a cell phone with a faulty connection, the sound coming out in chopped waves.

I remember what the nurse said about being calm, so I trail a finger down her cheek and give her a smile I don't feel. "Hey, beautiful."

"What are you—"

I cut her off, knowing she should rest her voice. "Birdie told Loki what happened this morning, and then he filled me in. Got here as soon as I could."

She points to my ankle.

"It's all good. I called in and said a friend was put in the hospital."

She nods and tries to swallow. Tears gather on her lash line before falling down her cheeks.

"Hurts too bad?" I guess, and she nods. "Let me find the nurse."

I step outside the room and find the nice woman from earlier. I read off her name tag, "Maddison, she's awake and in a lot of pain."

"Okay. I'll have the doctor order more meds. I'll be there in a minute."

I return to Bexley's side. "She's bringing something."

She nods, and we lock gazes.

"Was it Martin?" I ask.

She glances away.

He's a dead man walking.

I keep that thought in my head, remembering I need to be gentle. "It's gonna be okay. I'm here for you."

When she faces me again, she's crying silent tears. I lean over the bed and hover over her. She's too broken to touch, and I don't want to hurt her, but I need her to know she's not alone. She doesn't want to be my woman, but I can't break free from her, no matter how hard I try.

It's been a month since we fucked in my room, and I haven't even thought about anyone else. It's hard to keep my distance. The caveman in me wants to figuratively whack her over the head and drag her by her hair to my cave, never letting go. But my pride stops me, and maybe I'm hanging on to hope that things will change after this trial is over.

Because then I'll no longer be tied to this tracker, and the memory of my criminal activity will fade from her mind.

That hope is the only thing keeping me sane lately.

"I can walk," Bex rasps out.

"Not gonna happen." I carry her into her apartment and lay her down on her massive bed.

This is my first look at the place she's been staying.

I look around, seeing a lot of expensive things, but nothing that tells me anything about the woman living here. There are no pictures, no personal trinkets, no mail on the kitchen counter, or even a magnet on the fridge. Nothing. It could be a hotel suite for all anyone knew.

"I'll get you some water, and it's time for your antibiotic and pain meds." I leave her to get comfortable in bed. I set out her medication and the piece of paper I've been using to keep track after they removed her IV to see if she could tolerate pills.

My woman swallowed them like a champ, probably because she was antsy to leave the hospital, but whatever.

I find her fridge stocked with bottles of water, all the labels facing one direction, and I grab two of them. When I return to her room, she's not in bed.

I find her in her en suite, leaning over her vanity and looking at herself in the mirror. She sniffles and liquid sadness runs down her cheek onto the T-shirt I brought for her to wear home, along with a pair of too-big sweats. She's also removed all her bandages. I realize this is the first time she's seeing the damage.

"What's wrong, darlin'?" I hug her middle from behind.

Lifting her tangled and unwashed hair, she points at her eyes that are still blood red. She skims a finger across the wound around her neck, then reaches around to the back of her head. I'm sure once her hair is washed, it'll mostly cover the shaved spot, but right now, the area is soaked with dried up iodine and blood.

"I'm ugly," she cries.

I hug her carefully from behind, meeting her eyes in the mirror.

"No, darlin'. Not ugly, just a bit mangled." I try for a joke, but it bombs, and she sobs harder. "I'm sorry. That wasn't funny."

"Look what he did," she rasps.

"Shh. Don't talk," I say, not only because she shouldn't be using her voice but also because I have looked and what I see makes me so angry, I can't think straight. "I don't know what it is you're seeing, but all I see is a beautiful, strong woman. Don't let him take that from you."

She wipes her nose with the back of her hand and nods. She's said more than once that she won't let him take from her anymore, so I knew that's all it would take.

"Let's take a shower," I say, and she pins me with a look. "I'll be on my best behavior."

I was good at this calm and gentle business, but the storm brewing inside keeps growing bigger and bigger. I can't do this much longer before I have to take action.

I strip her down, getting my first real look at all the bruises. A dark purple and blue one wraps around her left calf, with a matching one on that same hip. The other leg looks more mottled in random, smaller bruises, and her shoulder is also black and blue.

I turn the water on in the shower, getting myself wet because I wasn't expecting it to fall from the ceiling. After darting out of the way, I shake my head when I see a display screen that asks what temperature I'd like. Rich people solve the dumbest problems.

Not knowing what temperature a proper shower should be, I fiddle around with it until the water feels comfortable.

I get her under the spray before removing my own clothes. I'm sure she could handle washing herself, but I want to be the one to care for her. I step under the rain shower head next to her and help wet her hair before sitting her down on the built-in bench.

Skimming the bottles lined up on the shelf, I find the one that says shampoo and squirt a dollop into my palm. The doctor said it's cool if the stitches got wet but to not get much soap on them. She leans forward as I rub light circles around the area, breaking up all the crusty spots. After that, I have her put her hair over her head, and I work the shampoo through the long, thick strands.

Switching the rain shower to the detachable spray head, I rinse her hair thoroughly. I've been around enough chicks to know they like their conditioner. So I hang the showerhead back up and search out the bottle. The scent of lilac hit my nostrils.

No wonder she always smells so sweet.

She flips her hair back over, and I work the cream through her strands, avoiding the area where the cut is. She stands and allows me to wash her body. I focus, not spending too much time on certain body parts that might get my dick hard. It's not the time for bodily reactions.

She once mentioned to me that she shaves her legs every day because she can't stand the feeling of the stubble against her clothes, so I sit her back down and reach for her razor. I prop my foot up next to her on the bench and rest her ankle on my thigh.

Biting my tongue in concentration, I start at the bottom of her leg and drag the blade up her calf and all the way to the top of her thigh. She studies me while I repeat the motion over and over until I'm certain the stubble is gone. Then I do the other leg. I'm about to start my last pass when she cups my cheek.

I look up, and she leans in to give me a kiss. It's not sexual or inviting. It's a thank you, and I take it gratefully.

Her eyes close as I rinse her off before wrapping the fluffiest towel I've ever felt around her. I quickly dry myself off, tie the towel around my waist, and then help dry Bex off. I carefully apply the different ointments to the various injuries, brush her hair out, and then walk her back to her bed.

The doorbell rings, and an alarm goes off on Bex's phone. She grips my forearm, her poor red eyes widening. I fucking hate that asshole even more for putting that fear in her eyes.

"It's okay. I'm here." I type in the passcode that she gave me in the hospital to help her return emails and bring up the video feed. "It's just Miles. I'll be right back."

I open the door, and the prospect holds out two duffle bags. "Here you go. Need anything else?"

"Nah, man. Thanks."

He looks inside for Bex. "She okay?"

I'm not the only one my woman has charmed. I run a

hand through my hair, blowing out a breath. "Yeah, she's okay, considering."

Her expression turns dark. "You got a plan in order yet?"

All my brothers, and I mean all of them, have reached out to let me know they want to be there when I take that asshole down.

"Not yet. She needs me right now, and that motherfucker ain't going nowhere."

"'Kay. Let me know."

He holds out a hand, and we do the shake, back-slapping thing. "See ya."

When I return, Bex has on the T-shirt I gave her this morning and nothing else. She looks so good in my clothes, even all messed up the way she is, I still get off on seeing it.

"What?" she asks, pointing to the bags in my hand.

"I'm your new roomie," I say with a devilish grin.

Her head tilts to the side, and she points at my ankle.

"I was responsible. Don't worry. I called in and told them me and my buddy got a new place."

"I'm"—she clears her throat—"your lawyer."

"*You* aren't on the lease. Sly is."

I didn't ask her for permission to move in because I knew her answer would be no. But if I didn't do it this way, I'd have to leave her every night, and the thought of doing that all but killed me.

To my shock, she nods and scoots back against the headboard. I give her the pills I'd forgotten about and the bottle of water. She swallows them down one by one, then I tuck her in and hand her the remote.

"I need to unpack," I say.

She glares at me, and for the first time, I'm glad she doesn't have much of a voice so she can't yell. I kiss her forehead and take my bags into the closet. Three-quarters of it is full of all her stuffy lawyer things, but that's okay. I don't need much space, and there are a few shelves in the built-in storage that are empty.

Mine, now.

After I finish in there, I walk back to the bathroom and hang up the towels before scoping out what room I can take over in the cabinet. The vanity has a double sink, and she clearly prefers the right side, so I open the cupboard on the left and find it empty. I place my toiletry bag in there and stroll out, feeling pleased with myself.

It only took an assault to get my foot back in the door. That sobers me up, and I climb into bed next to Bex. We watch trashy TV, and I make her soup that she refuses to eat because anything warm burns. So instead, I bring her a nutrition drink the hospital sent us home with. Thankfully, she has no problem drinking it down.

For the next week, that's all we do. I ignore responsibilities, like Roch's build and club business, and take care of my woman.

She can deny wanting me here, but I know it's a lie. The same way I know she's lying to me about the case. All her lies will explode like a bomb one of these days. I can only hope I live through the explosion.

Chapter
TWENTY-FIVE

Bexley

"You don't have to stay," I say, twisting my hair up and securing it with a brass clip to cover the patch of missing hair. "I'm good now."

"Don't have to, but I'm going to." Khan smooths oil through his beard and uses the brush I got him months ago to tame the brown mop hanging from his chin.

I shouldn't think like that. I love his beard. I love everything about his macho man appearance. It fits him.

"We aren't together," I remind him.

"Am I in your bed every night?"

"Well, yes. But—"

"Are my things in your closet?" he asks, leaving the bathroom before I can fire back.

He infuriates me. At first, I was glad he moved in. I was scared Martin would be back to finish me off to keep me silent, but now that my injuries are healing, I feel stronger.

I go into my closet and choose a silky blouse and wide-leg trousers. I'm still not feeling my best, and it's the closest thing

I have to comfortable work attire. Wes is lounging on the bed I just made, watching TV, when I step back into my room.

I let my robe fall and dress, not bothering to hide. He's seen me at my worst already, had a front-row seat to that shit show. His eyes move from the screen to me, taking in my naked form before I have a chance to slip on underwear and a bra.

"Fucking sexy, darlin'. Yellow bruises and all."

"Perv." I stick my tongue out at him because he brings out my inner immaturity.

"Better put that thing back in your mouth before I put it to work." He blatantly adjusts his dick in his jeans. I suck my tongue back in, but not because the image he created is unwanted.

It's been hard to sleep next to him for the last week. Despite feeling like a bag of shit, his warm body holding me all night stirs up my sexual desires. Every morning I wake with his wood pressed against my crack, and it's all I can do not to back my ass into him, enticing him to take me.

But recovery time is over, and I need to put distance between us. This wasn't part of my plan, and it creates complications I don't know how to solve.

"You feeling okay about going back to work?" he asks.

Today is my first day back in the office, and I'm dreading it more than I can put into words.

"Not really," I admit.

He gets off the bed and approaches me as I struggle to fasten a necklace.

"Let me." He takes the clasps and somehow, even though he has the meatiest fingers I've ever seen, secures it.

I turn and take his hand in mine. "I don't know how these sausages can be so dexterous."

"I'm a biker, darlin'," he explains like I know what that means. My expression must give me away, and he turns his hand over and makes a motion that I can only guess is sexual. "Need dexterity to get into the small spots of the engine." He smirks, knowing that's not where my mind went. "Helps with more than putting on necklaces, too."

"Get out of here." I turn back around and find a simple pair of diamond studs to put in my ears.

"What's stressing you out about going back to work?" He hugs me from behind. It's my favorite thing he does now because it feels so protective and caring.

"A lot of things."

"Like?"

"I'm embarrassed."

"Why the fuck would you be embarrassed?" He spins me around and cups my cheeks so I have no choice but to look him in the eyes.

"Everyone is going to stare at me and whisper. I hate that."

"Let them. You're a fucking badass who survived a brutal attack. They're lucky to know someone like you."

"It's not just that. I also don't want to return to my office," I admit.

"Can't blame you there. Bad memories and shit. Can you swap offices with one of the other attorneys?"

"No. That would be something a weak person would do."

"Got that all wrong, darlin'. You can't judge the things victims do to survive." His expression turns soft.

"Maybe, but I spent my entire marriage letting him win. When I walked away, I promised myself I'd never let him win again. Moving my office because of what he did feels like a win for him."

"I hear that." He presses a kiss to my lips, his mustache tickling my nose, and I realize I never want to kiss another man for the rest of my life.

I pull away. "Okay, time to go to work."

"I'm coming with you," he announces.

"No," I say, my brows knitting together.

"Yes." He pockets his wallet and keys that now live in a dish on my dresser.

"Wes," I whine.

"Bex," he whines back.

"You're smothering me."

"Good. You can return the favor later tonight."

I drive my car, and Wes tails me on his bike. Then, as we walk into the building, he throws an arm over my shoulder, head held high.

"Ms. March, welcome back," Renata says from behind the counter in the lobby.

"Thank you."

I try to shove him off when we're in the elevator, but his arm is heavy and solid, unmoving even as we walk to my office. Marcy greets me from behind her desk with wide eyes and hands me a thick stack of calls I need to return.

She knows better than to mention what happened. I'll discuss it with her but not right now. Not while the situation is still a tender wound.

Wes finally releases me when we step into my office. Emotion bubbles up, seeing the disaster left behind. The papers on my desk are scattered everywhere from when Martin dove across it. There's a bloody circle and an indentation in the wall where my head hit. And my office chair is overturned.

Thirty seconds. That's how long it took for all of this to happen.

"Fuck," Wes says, righting my chair and then crouching to gather papers.

I should help him, but I'm frozen. Thirty seconds. If he had held me for a couple minutes longer, he could've killed me.

"You okay?" he asks.

"Yeah." I swipe a stray tear from my cheek.

He crosses the room to the bathroom and returns with wet paper towels. I watch as he scrubs the dried blood away. He's always taking care of me, and the guilt of what I have to do in two weeks hits me hard. I don't deserve his nice. Not at all.

"Come here." He pulls out my chair for me.

I round my desk and take a seat. It took longer to clean the mess than it did to make it. But I'm glad the reminder is gone. "Thank you."

He tips his head then says, "You said you didn't want to stay in this office because of the bad memories, right?"

"Yeah." I draw out the word, not knowing where he's going with this, but I'm pretty sure I won't like it.

"Then how about I give you some good memories to override the bad?"

"What do you mean?"

He walks over to my office door and flips the locks. Then he closes the blinds on both windows that look out into the hallway.

"Wes, I don't have time for—"

"Oh, you got time." He struts over to me and stands me up before crouching in front of me and popping the button of my pants.

My nipples peak, and my core clenches as he pulls my pants and panties down.

"What are you doing?" I ask.

"Making good memories." He lifts me up and sits me down on my desk before placing both of my feet on the edge of the wood and spreading me wide. "Gonna lick your pussy until you scream now."

He tugs roughly on the short triangle of hair that sits above my pussy and sits down on my office chair, taking me in like I'm his next meal. Which I am.

He licks up my seam, flicking my clit when he reaches the

top. My hand flies to the back of his head, and my fingers tangle in the hair that he's wearing down today.

Latching onto my clit, he sucks while stroking two fingers inside me. It feels so good, exactly the stress reliever I needed.

"Wes. Oh my God. Yes."

He strokes and strokes, licks and licks, sucks and sucks until I'm coming apart. I grind myself against his face, loving how his beard scratches my inner thighs. It's about time the marks on my body were from pleasure again, and a beard burn will do the trick.

I come down lazily, my limbs lax and my head floaty. "Thank you."

"No problem." He kisses my mound and stands. "Gonna use the bathroom, and then I need to talk to you right quick before I go."

"Sure. Okay." I hop off the desk and redress myself, not caring that I now have wet panties. It'll remind me of the good I've had in this office, and I need that reminder today.

I reorganize papers while he does his business, and when he returns, everything is in its rightful place.

"Are you feeling okay?" he asks, plopping down in a chair.

"Better now," I say.

"Good, 'cause we need to talk, and you're not going to like it."

"What is it?"

"I'm headed to the clubhouse this morning to put a plan in place to take out Martin."

I freeze in place. "I'm sorry?"

"You had to know I couldn't let this slide, darlin'. I know you don't understand my lifestyle, and that's okay. If I wanted a club whore, coulda found myself one real easy. But I don't want them. I want you."

My hand goes to my forehead. "You can't do that."

"Sure as shit can." He throws an arm over the chair next to him.

"No, Wes. You can't. That tracker logs every place you go. You can't do anything about it." My heart pounds in my chest. If he does this behind my back, he will destroy all my plans.

"Then I'll have the guys bring him to me. Either way, it's happening."

"Wes, look at me. I'm serious. Can you please, for me, wait until after your trial?"

He runs a hand through his hair. "You don't know how much this is killing me inside. Each breath that asshole takes is a personal attack on me. Each. Breath."

"I won't pretend to understand your code"—I throw air quotes around code—"or whatever. But I understand the law, and it would behoove you to wait until after your trial."

"You're being my lawyer right now. Need you to be my woman so you can understand."

"That's the thing, Wes. I'm your lawyer. Not your woman." It sounds like a lie even to me, but I say it anyway.

"Bullshit." He stands to his full height. "You're giving me fuckin' whiplash."

"I admit my actions have been confusing, but nothing has changed from the first time we broke up. I can't be part of this life. Look at what's happening right now, for Christ's sake. You're in my law office telling me you're leaving here to kill a man. Do you even understand how fucked that is?" I throw my hands up in frustration.

"Again, I didn't think you had your lawyer hat on."

"I always have my lawyer hat on. I know I represent lowlifes, but that doesn't mean I bend the law to accommodate them. I do my best, within the parameters of the law, to keep them out of trouble. To keep *you* out of trouble. I can't do my job when you don't let me."

"Lowlifes?" he repeats with hurt in his tone. "That's how you see me?"

I backtrack; this is going sideways. "That's not what I meant. *You're* not a lowlife, obviously."

"Sounds like what you meant." He back steps to my door. "When am I going to stop letting you hurt me?"

He shakes his head and turns to leave, slamming the door shut after him.

"Goddamn it," I shout, shoving my hands across my desk and sending the papers I just finished organizing flying.

Chapter
TWENTY-SIX

Khan

"Nice," Roch says as he walks around the house I finished framing.

It's my favorite part about a build. When there's only poured concrete, it makes the space feel small, and you don't get an accurate vision of what it's going to be. But when you can see where the walls will be, you get a better idea of how it will look.

"It's perfect," Truly chimes in, a huge ass grin on her face.

"Thanks," I say. "Should go pretty fast from here. Got roofers, electrical, and plumbers all booked. They're all friends of the club, so they'll do a good job, and they'll be quick about it. After that, I'll come in and do insulation, exterior siding, interior walls, and all that shit. Have you picked all your fixtures and paint and stuff?"

"We have. I've got it all put together on a vision board for you."

I glance over at Roch, who shrugs. Truly takes his hand and drags him from room to room, chatting his ear off.

I leave them to it and step outside. It's beautiful out here, and I can see why Roch and Loki chose this area. Our lives are so chaotic; it's gotta be nice to own a plot of land that's so calm.

My feet lead me down the hill, following a trail through the property most likely created by deer. The air smells of pine and earth, and I breathe it in before lighting a smoke and polluting it.

Haven't heard from Bex since last week when I left her office, mad as all hell. I had it in my head I was going to drive over to Martin's office and end him right then and there just to spite her. But I didn't. Instead, my bike led me home, to the clubhouse.

My brothers haven't asked why I don't have a plan yet. I'm sure they can tell I'm off, and I know this because they've all been walking on eggshells since my return. I moved back in with Loki. It's only for another week, then I'll know whether my new home will be in prison or if I'll be free to return to my room at the clubhouse.

Though that feels like a step backward to me. I've changed since all this shit started with me and Bex. I was a man-child before, not a care in the world. I was so focused on partying and plowing through as much pussy as I could, I didn't stop to think why I lived that way.

Now I know. I lived every day like it was my last because I didn't have shit to live for. Long ago, I unconsciously decided this lifestyle would take me one way or another, so fuck it. I made decisions I thought were heroic when, in reality, I was careless.

Then Bex came along, and I wanted to live. For a long damn time, too. Each day with her was a gift, and I'm a selfish motherfucker. I wanted all the gifts I could get.

Except now she's not around, and I have no desire to go back to the man I was. I want to live. And I want it to be with Bex. Then I'll plant as many babies as I can inside her and grow my own family.

Even if I'm in prison for the next five years, the second I'm out, I'll come for her. She talks a big game about not wanting to be part of the club, but I know she won't move on from me. What we have is rare.

The trees open up, exposing a large meadow covered in wildflowers. A mama deer and her two babies stand on the other side, grazing. It's so fuckin' beautiful, and even more, it's fuckin' peaceful. This is what I need.

I remove my phone from my back pocket and take a screenshot of the coordinates.

Me: I'm sending you some coordinates of a piece of land I'm interested in. Can you find the owners for me?

Sly: NP

I hit send on the coordinates and go to tuck my phone away but stop and take a picture of the meadow. I open up a text message to Bex and attach the photo. My finger hovers over the send button, but I chicken out. *I'm not letting her hurt me anymore*, I remind myself, and jam my phone back in my pocket.

"Here, let me." Sissy turns me around and undoes the mess I made of my tie.

We haven't been this close in a long time, and when we were, I wasn't exactly looking at her features. She's aging, along with the rest of us. The lines around her lips show her addiction to smoking, and the lines around her eyes and on her forehead show how much time she spends laughing at us assholes.

"Are you happy, Sis?" I ask.

She blinks up at me for a brief second before focusing back on my tie. "Why would you ask me that?"

"I don't know. You've been here for years and never had a relationship. Don't you get lonely?"

She flashes me a look I don't understand. "Tabitha and I are together, Khan. You didn't know that?"

My jaw drops. "But what about—"

"We're bisexual and horny. We knew if we didn't want to sleep with any of you assholes, we didn't have to, but contrary to what men think, some women love sex as much as men. We have no desire to only be with each other, and that's okay. At the end of the day, it's her bed I'm in, and neither of us wants that to change."

"For how long?" I can't believe I didn't know this. Though, I guess I can. I didn't give much thought to who they were as people. I was an asshole like that.

"Maybe two years after I moved in?" She shrugs.

"But there're two beds in your room."

"Yeah, and we only use one of them. Though it would be nice if you'd spring for something bigger than a full."

I make a mental note to talk to Sly about budgeting in a bed. They've taken care of all of us for so long; we should take care of them a little better.

"Do you ever think about moving out together?" I ask.

"Why? Our family is here at the clubhouse. All you guys are like brothers." She shakes her head. "No, that's gross. You guys are like cousins to us. Second cousins. Who don't share a bloodline."

I chuckle. "Well, congratulations."

"Thanks." She adjusts the tail of the tie and smooths out the fabric. "There. You're a perfectly functional member of society."

I turn back to the mirror and almost laugh. My whole life, I've never worn a suit. Not even for Pops' funeral. I knew that wasn't what was important to him. I wasn't planning to wear one today, except two days ago, someone delivered three of them to the clubhouse with a tag with my name on it. One for each day of the scheduled trial, though I'm hoping I only have to wear one of them if everything goes as planned and the prosecution is forced to drop charges.

I didn't question where the suits came from. There's only one person who could've sent them. Bex is thoughtful like that.

The suit I chose for today is navy blue, but there's a texture to it that almost makes it look like dark jean material. I know that was intentional to make me feel more comfortable. The shirt is white, and the tie is also navy blue but silky. It fits like a glove. Wouldn't expect anything less out of the woman.

"Hair up or down?" I ask Sis.

She taps a finger to her chin. "Slicked back and up."

I squirt some gel into my palm and run it through the top and sides of my hair before pulling it back into a low bun. "Good?"

"Perfect."

We walk out of the bathroom to find the main space quiet, though everyone is here. Feels like I'm walking into my own funeral.

"Why's everyone so down? Duncan, pour us some beer," I call out. My brothers pound their fists on the tables and bar while letting out hoots and hollers. That's better.

I step up to the bar and chug my glass of beer. I figured today, of all days, I deserve it. First, to calm my nerves. Second, because I don't know how many more days I'll have here with my brothers.

Goblin pounds a hand into my back. "Wish we could be there with you, but we'll all be here when you get back."

"Thanks, brother. Means a lot to me."

"And when this is all over, we're throwing you a party like the ones we used to have before I met Birdie," Loki says.

"Oh yeah?" I quirk a brow. "So we'll take shots from random chicks' cleavage and hook up with all the patch pussy we can handle?"

Loki chuckles. "I see your point, brother. Maybe it will be a little tamer."

"I'm telling Birdie you even suggested it," I joke.

"Ooo, Loki's in trouble," Moto singsongs.

"You're all assholes." Loki waggles a finger.

I know what they're doing by distracting me, and I love them for it.

"All right, I better go. But there better be a party when I return." I slam my glass down.

One at a time, my brothers approach me to give back-slapping hugs and words of encouragement. Not since I was locked up with Goblin's dad has a brother been in prison, so all this fanfare is awkward for everyone.

I grab my cut on the way out the door and tuck it into my saddlebag. With any luck, I'll be tossing this suit coat and wearing this home.

I ride off alone. My brothers weren't happy when I banned them from coming, but Bex texted yesterday to say it might not look good for me if the courtroom was full of outlaw bikers. They understood, but I know it hurts them to not be there for me.

The ride to the courthouse takes fifteen minutes, and I spend that time getting my head right. The prosecutors still haven't called to say their key evidence is missing, and I have no idea why. Though the shady way Bex was talking about it, I have my suspicions.

Before last week, I wasn't nervous. I trusted Bex when she said she had my back. But now, after everything that's happened, I'm not sure.

I push that away and focus on the piece of land I put an offer in on. The owners weren't selling, but my offer was good enough that they said they'd consider. Of course, if I'm locked up, it won't matter. But if I'm not, I have that little piece of calm to look forward to. And my brothers would be my neighbors.

All too fast, the courthouse comes into view. I park out front and enter the building. Despite the metal detector not buzzing when I walk through, the officer still pulls me aside to scan me by hand.

"Want me to bend over and cough?" I ask.

"Not necessary," he replies, waving me off.

Before the trial, I'm meeting Bex to discuss any last-minute details. I get to the room assigned to us and find her already seated, papers strewn all around the circular table she's commandeered.

She hardly glances at me before saying, "You're here. Perfect. Take a seat."

She's got her lawyer hat on today. Great.

"No news on the missing tapes?" I ask.

Her hands which had been shuffling papers, freeze. "No."

"Isn't that weird?"

"Not necessarily." Her shuffling resumes.

"What aren't you telling me?" I slam my hand down in front of her, stopping her fidgeting.

"I'm telling you everything you need to know." She yanks the documents from under my hand and stacks them before placing them in her briefcase. "Are you ready? It's just about time."

"Sure, Bex. I'm ready."

She stands, and I notice she's wearing a blue turtleneck under her white suit, and her hair is pulled up.

"You don't have to hide your marks, you know?"

"They're distracting, and we don't need distractions. Now let's go."

The courtroom is bigger than I thought it'd be. It's an old Art Deco building, and the architecture reflects that. There are marble baseboards and paneling, burled walnut wainscoting, and the original Art Deco lighting fixtures. If I weren't here for a trail, I'd be in awe of how beautiful it is.

We take our seats at the front of the room, the prosecution already seated. Bex and I don't speak as we wait for things to begin.

The jury enters, and their eyes go right to me. Bex assured me she made good choices during selection, but I'm not so sure with the way they're staring me down.

I wonder what they're thinking. That I look like a lowlife in a monkey suit? Probably.

A door opens behind where the judge sits, and he walks out. My jaw clenches and my hands ball into fists.

I steal a glance at Bex and whisper, "Did you know he was the presiding judge?"

She shushes me and keeps her eyes forward.

What the actual fuck is happening?

Judge Martin Alexander takes a seat, and the bailiff positions himself front and center.

"All rise." Everyone stands. "Court is now in session. Judge Alexander presiding."

I black out, my mind spinning too fast to concentrate. She obviously knew. Why would she work so hard to keep him alive when she knows he's itching to screw me over? This isn't a fair trial. Maybe the jury is the deciding factor, but he's the one who will sentence me, right?

The extent of my trial knowledge comes from TV shows and movies. I realize I don't know shit about how this all works, and Bex did fuck-all to prepare me. Was that intentional? Does she want me out of her life this badly?

The prosecuting lawyer, who looks like he has a stick a mile long up his ass, walks in front of the jury. He yaps shit about how I'm in a gang and what I did could've killed people and that I was lucky no employees were working late that day.

Bexley's **BIKER**

I want to jump to my feet and tell them we made sure no one was there. The reason we blew it up in the first place was that the fuckin' Corsettis were planning to use it to house women and children being trafficked for sex. Bet they wouldn't be looking at me like I'm a murderer if they knew that bit of information.

Bex places a hand on my knee to stop my leg from bouncing and whispers, "Trust me."

But I don't. I don't fucking trust anything that's going on right now. This feels like a setup, and I can't figure out why.

What he says next is the blow I knew was coming, but it doesn't soften it. "We have video evidence proving Mr. McMillen stole the van."

I see red.

Before I know what's happening, it's Bex's turn to give an opening speech. She's confident as she strolls around the courtroom. She speaks, not that I hear what she says. She crushed my heart when she ended things this last time, but she obliterated my soul by not destroying the one piece of evidence that would ruin my life.

If it were anyone but her, I'd be imagining all the ways I could torture her. I'd fantasize about making her pay for daring to betray a Royal Bastard. But that's not the case, and there's no way I could ever hurt her the way she's hurt me. I love her more than I hate her.

Judge Motherfucker calls a recess, and I bolt out of the courtroom. The way I feel right now—if for some reason I don't go down for the theft and explosion—I'll definitely go down for killing a judge in the middle of his courtroom.

Heels clack against the marble hallway. "Wes, wait."

I don't wait. I leave the courthouse, ready to walk away from everything, become a nomad hiding out from the law. I joined the Royal Bastards to be part of a family, not to roam alone.

Sure, I'll still have my RBMC patch, but my VP rocker will be replaced by Nomad. Something I never wanted.

Fuck all of this. I tried to make a life for myself. I worked damn hard, all for everything I ever tried to build to be yanked away from me by some bitch.

"Wes. Stop," she shouts and tries to catch up, but is no match for my long strides. "Please. Give me just a minute."

I whirl around and charge, stopping only inches from her. "What, Bex? You want to look me in the eye when you tell me you fucked me over? You want to see the devastation on my face? Well, here it is. Fuckin' happy?"

Her lower lip trembles, and her eyes turn glassy. "I-I—"

"I gave you all of me. Every last bit. There's nothing left." I pound my fist on my chest, then turn to leave.

"Where are you going?"

"Far away from you."

"You can't leave. Please," she pleads, her voice quavering.

"You'll never see me again," I say under my breath.

I throw my leg over my bike, the plastic around my ankle knocking against the bike. Needing to get the thing off me right fuckin' now, I open my saddlebag and find one of my knives. I unsheathe it and slice through the band. The device falls to the ground and cracks open.

I leave it there in the parking lot along with my whole heart.

Chapter
TWENTY-SEVEN

Bexley

I dash into the bathroom to dry my eyes, but for every single tear I wipe away, three more appear. I knew it would be bad. I knew there was a chance he'd hate me forever, but I thought he'd at least stick around to see why I did what I did.

I check my texts, seeing a new message from Stephen.

Stephen: All set. Get ready for the fireworks.

I quickly shove my phone into my purse and reenter the courtroom. I feel as empty as the seat next to me is. He'll never forgive me.

Martin appears through the doors and takes his seat. He immediately notices the absence of my client and smirks. He thinks he's won.

He ruined my chance at true love, but I'm about to ruin his life.

FBI agents enter from the back of the courtroom. The one leading the charge holds up a piece of paper. "Judge Alexander, we have a warrant for your arrest."

He stands from behind the bench, looking nonplussed. "There must be a mistake."

"No, sir. There isn't."

"What are the charges?" He still thinks this is a joke.

Well, this is embarrassing.

"Tampering with evidence, obstruction of justice, and assault." A female agent pulls a set of cuffs out and skillfully brings Martin's hands behind his back to secure them around his wrists. He struggles as she escorts him down from the bench and through the center aisle of the courtroom.

"Was this you?" Martin shouts as he passes me. "You'll pay, you bitch."

After they're gone, the prosecuting attorney looks to me and says, "To be continued, I guess?"

"I doubt it." I gather my things and walk outside.

Standing on the steps is Stephen Sullivan, the man running against Martin for district court judge. He's leaning against a pillar, hands in his pant pockets. "Thanks for the tip."

"No problem. Run into any issues?"

"Nope. Though I was surprised to find you filed assault charges against him this morning." He pushes off the pillar and steps closer. "You okay?"

"I am," I say, then correct myself. "I will be."

"I'm proud of you," Stephen says, grinning. "I got something for you."

I hold out my hand, and he drops a black plastic rectangle into it.

I grip it in my palm and hold it to my chest. "Thank you."

I promised myself after stealing Martin's money and illegally obtaining my new identity, I'd never break another law. So this should feel wrong and unethical. Instead, it feels like redemption for my man. Assuming he'll take me back after everything I've put him through.

"Now we're even." He winks at me.

He's a handsome man, and in another life, his grin might've made me swoon. But this man is too put together, too proper, and my tastes have changed since college. Now I prefer only one man—a big, burly oaf with a long beard and longer hair. A man who smacks my ass and uses a knife for foreplay.

"Thank you. I'm sorry, but I have to run."

He holds up his hands. "Don't let me stop you."

"Thanks again for your help," I say as I dash to my car.

I use my car for what it was built for, speed. I don't know what's going through Wes's head right now, but it's not good, and I have no idea what he's capable of. Actually, I do, and that thought scares me more.

Ten minutes later, I'm skidding to a stop in front of the iron gate at the clubhouse. Ford recognizes my car, and the gate opens. I park and jump out.

"Is Khan here?" I shout to Ford.

"Not sure."

He's no help. I barge through the front door, finding the main area empty of anyone. Looking to my left, I see the Church's door closed. They must be in there. I swing it open, and nine pairs of eyes shoot in my direction, including an older man I recognize but can't place.

I scan the faces until I find the one I'm looking for. Thank God.

"Not a good time, Bexley," Loki warns in his authoritative tone.

"I have something to say."

"It's over, Bex," Wes says, his eyes cast down at the table.

"What do you mean?"

Goblin stands and crosses his arms over his chest. "He means because of you, we just voted to approve Khan's motion to go nomad."

"Nomad?"

"He's no longer part of our chapter or anyone's chapter. You basically exiled him," Loki says.

"What? Why?"

I don't understand why he would do that. This is his family.

"Because I'm assuming there'll be a warrant out for my arrest because I skipped the trial. So I'm leaving. No one will hear from me again. It'll be too risky for the club." Khan stands, still not meeting my eyes.

Everyone here is pissed at me. I broke up their family.

"Wait. That's not necessary." I don't want to cry, but the tears fall anyway.

"It is. Now go back to your perfect life and leave me the fuck alone," he says through a clenched jaw.

"He was arrested," I say. "Martin was arrested."

All nine eyes are back on me.

"Gonna have to explain, doll," Loki says.

"I couldn't tell you why there was no information about the video because I was working with another judge to bring charges against Martin. Had I told you, I know you'd have killed him before he was arrested." I try to explain, but I know I'm not doing a good job. There are so many layers to the story, I can't get them all out with everyone staring at me, expecting answers.

Wes grips my upper arm roughly and yanks me down the hall to his room.

"Sit down," he orders through gritted teeth.

I obey, placing my hands on my lap.

"Start from the beginning."

"I didn't destroy the thumb drive," I say.

"No shit," he bites out as he paces back and forth, hands in his front pockets. The suit is long gone, and his jeans and white T-shirt are back.

"Stop being so mean to me. I can't take it."

I deserve his harsh treatment, but my emotions are all over the place. I want to feel relief knowing this is all over, but the anxiety over what will happen when Wes finds out the truth is overpowering it.

"Then tell me what the fuck is going on."

I'm not going to get what I want until I tell the story, so I start again. "I didn't destroy the thumb drive. At first, I didn't understand why I was holding onto it. But the more I thought about it, the more I wanted revenge. And I didn't tell you he was presiding because it wasn't an issue. My plan was going to be to take him down long before the trial. But then he assaulted me, and my plans got put on hold." I'm skipping forward, so I take a deep breath and try again. "By downloading this copy, he was tampering with evidence. I wasn't sure it would pan out since, regardless of his tampering, the video still existed. Then I remembered Stephen Sullivan, who's running against Martin for district court judge—"

"You're rambling, Bex."

"I know. I'm sorry. Stephen is a client of mine. I recently helped him through some stuff," I say cryptically. I may have recently broken the law, but I refuse to go against attorney/client privilege. "And he owed me. So I called him up and told him everything."

"About you and your past?" He looks shocked. He should be. Wes is the only other person in the world I've told my truth to. Until Stephen.

"Yes. He was sympathetic and probably more than that, he wanted Martin gone so he could be the only name on the ballot come November. He agreed that the tampering might just get him a slap on the wrist, but if we could get something else on him, it would show a pattern of behavior. I got to thinking about all the whispers I heard about him back in New York."

"Like what?"

"Like him demanding sexual favors in exchange for charges dropped. I couldn't imagine him changing just because his address did."

"You looked into those allegations?"

"Stephen did. There hadn't been anything official, but a bunch of names came up, and Stephen gave me those names. I contacted the twenty-two women and explained what I was trying to do. Out of twenty-two, only seven would sign a written statement. After all, by doing so, they'd be setting themselves up to have their charges reinstated, and there wasn't enough time to work out an immunity deal."

"How did you get seven women to agree?"

"Martin got rough with those seven. Really rough. One of them had a broken arm, one had a broken nose—most were black eyes and bruises—but he choked one of them," I say quietly, their stories still playing on repeat in my head. "At the time, they were just words on a paper. A statement. But then he attacked me, and it made it so much more real. I wanted to get your charges dropped, but even more, I had to get justice for those women."

He sinks onto the mattress next to me and runs a hand through his hair. "And you did all of this by yourself?"

"Stephen helped but yes."

"Why didn't you tell me?"

"I'm getting to that part. After I had the statements and I knew we had enough, I was going to tell you. After what happened with Martin, you were so mad. Put yourself in my shoes. If I told you he beat the shit out of seven other women, what would you have done?" I ask, knowing the answer.

"I didn't have to know about those other women. What he did to you was enough to end his life." His jaw ticks, and he rubs his hands together.

"Exactly. I have another question for you, and I want you

to answer honestly. If you were Martin, what would be a worse fate for you? Spending twenty to forty years in prison, knowing you're fifty-five years old and your life is over, even if you live long enough to be released? Or being tortured, then killed?"

He thinks on it for a while before saying, "Prison."

"Exactly," I say again. "You can see why, instead of telling you, I had to make you mad at me. So mad, you wouldn't feel the need to kill him."

"You hurt me bad," he says, and it feels like a knife to the chest.

"I know."

"Is there a reason it took until the trial for him to be arrested?"

"There was a lot of boring, behind-the-scenes stuff. We had to find the right FBI officials to bring the information to. Ones who weren't corrupt and wouldn't use this to advance their own careers or pad their pockets. Then we needed a warrant for his personal computer so forensics could get the evidence. That happened this morning," I say. His hands are still rubbing furiously together, so I reach over and cover them with one of mine. "And I had to work out a deal for you."

"What?"

"I had to make sure the charges against you would be dropped. It was a much easier task than I thought since there was no evidence against you. But there was an obvious trail leading from Martin's IP address that showed him breaking into the system and downloading the file." I smile and hold out my closed hand. He extends his palm, and I drop both thumb drives into it. "There are no other copies. Stephen was with the FBI when they raided Martin's house. He discreetly stole the second copy of the footage."

"Why wasn't the prosecution ever told their smoking gun

had gone missing?" he asks, crushing the drives in his fist. No, really. He crushed the plastic *with his fist*.

"Martin convinced Evidence that he'd get it back. That sounded like a better idea to them than saying they lost it."

"Is that it?"

I run through everything in my head. "Yeah. I think so. Honestly, it's all a blur. I've been so busy. Oh wait, there is one more thing."

"What's that?"

"I filed assault charges against him this morning, so he has that going for him, too. I had the nurse take photos and scrape my nails for DNA after it happened, and I allowed Marcy to give her statement about who she saw leaving my office."

"That was brave of you."

"Thank you." With nothing left to say, I stand. "For what it's worth, I'm really sorry. I never meant for it to go this way, and I didn't mean anything I said."

He nods but says nothing.

"I'll go now." I open the door slowly, giving him every opportunity to stop me.

"Bex?"

"Yeah?" I turn around, expecting an epic moment where he forgives me, and we ride off into the sunset. That's not what I get.

"What happens when he outs you to the first person who'll listen?"

I cock my head to the side. "What do you mean?"

"He knows who you are. What if he tells someone who cares enough to look into it?"

I shrug. "I don't know. If it happens, it happens, and I'll deal with it."

That was the last thing on my mind through all of this. Especially since I have enough money to last me a long time. Martin's left-over money is at the casino, and I have well over a million in the bank that I've accumulated since opening the law office. Representing high-powered criminals who have a lot to lose is lucrative.

If it comes down to it, I can run. I'm good at that.

He nods, and I leave. The second I get out the front door, everything hits me, and I break down. I climb behind the steering wheel and start my car, but I can't see through my tears enough to drive. I gasp for air, clawing at the stupid turtleneck I wish I hadn't worn.

My heart pounds in my chest, and I'm certain I'm having a heart attack. I can't get enough oxygen into my lungs, and my whole body shakes at the realization that he's not coming back to me. The pain I caused him is too deep. He'll never be able to look at me again without hearing the words I said to him. Words I wish I could take back.

I scream and beat on my steering wheel, wishing things were different and wishing I didn't choose to have this meltdown in front of the clubhouse.

A fist raps against my window, and I look out to see Wes. He motions for me to roll down my window, reminding me of the time I picked him up from jail. Things were so much better when I was the one who hated him.

"Take a ride with me," he says.

"Where to?" I say through rough gasps of air.

"Does it matter?"

"Not really."

"I'll give you a minute. Meet me over by my bike."

I nod and roll the window back up. Blasting the air on high, I take calming breaths, feeling my heart rate slow. When I've regained control of myself, I flip down the visor and look.

Black lines streak down my cheeks, my entire face is swollen, and my eyes are bloodshot. I dig a makeup wipe out of my purse and clean myself up the best I can. Finding a bottle of water on the floorboard, I guzzle it down, not caring that it's been sitting in a hot car for God knows how long.

I press the ignition button, shutting down my car. I leave my purse where it's at. The security around the compound is so tight, a mouse couldn't pass through without them knowing, so leaving my purse is no big deal.

I find Wes where he said he'd be, straddling his bike and waiting for me. He has a blue bandana tied around his head, and he's wearing his cut. It looks really good on him.

He holds a helmet out to me. "Put it on."

I let my hair out of the clip and use a hair tie to pull it into a bun at the back of my head. Then I slip the helmet on and secure it to my head. "I'm wearing heels and a white suit."

"Hook the peg with your heel. And I don't know what to say about your suit. Afraid of a little dirt, Ms. March?" The faintest hint of a tease has my stomach doing cartwheels.

I'd agree to roll around in the mud, effectively ruining my two-thousand-dollar suit, if it meant I'd get more of that from him. Plus, he's never asked me to ride on the back of his bike before. It feels momentous.

He offers me a hand, and I take it, lifting onto the peg with my right heel and swinging my left leg over the bike. We must look a sight. An uptight lawyer on the back of a Harley being driven by the VP of the Royal Bastards.

"Hang on," he shouts over the roar of the engine.

I wrap my arms around him tight, and he takes off down the road. The ride is exhilarating. I'm so close to the road, it's terrifying, but it's also the most fun I've had in a long time.

He turns onto the freeway toward Tahoe, and I wonder if we're going to Loki's. But why? I push the questions away and instead enjoy the ride.

I get it now. He's explained what it feels like to ride, but I didn't understand before experiencing it myself. I feel part of the world around me. The wind blowing across my face makes me feel free. I see so much more, too. Things I wouldn't have noticed before. Like the wild horses out in the hills and the hawks flying over our head. It's as close to a religious experience as I've ever had.

We don't make it as far as Loki's street, Wes turns off a few miles before. He takes me down a dirt road and comes to a stop in the middle of the forest. He throws down the kickstand and hops off the bike before helping me to do the same. We remove our helmets, and without a word, he starts walking.

My heels are not meant for this terrain, so I trip and stumble behind him. Out of nowhere, he stops, gazing out in front of him. I continue to struggle my way over to him but freeze when I look in the same direction. There's a clearing in the trees. A meadow full of orange and purple flowers is nestled in the middle of the forest.

"It's beautiful," I say.

"It's mine."

I stare up at him. "You bought a meadow?"

"No, darlin'. I bought this land. From the road to here and fifteen more acres past here." He motions to the distance.

"When did this happen?"

"I made an offer last week. They called to tell me it's mine right after you went to your car. Roch's property line butts up against mine. And Loki's is only two miles past his."

"Aw, besties," I sass.

"Missed that smart mouth," he says.

"I missed using my smart mouth on you."

"I love you, Bex. That's not the issue." He tucks his hands in his pockets and turns back to his property.

"What's the issue then?"

"You still don't trust me. Rule number three was your problems are my problems."

My mind travels back to when he made rules for me. Rule number one, as long as we're both into it, we do it. Rule number two, no more freaking out and trying to escape after we fuck. And rule number three, my problems are his problems.

"I remember," I say. "You're right. I wasn't trusting you, and that was wrong of me. But you have to understand my point of view."

"What's that?"

"Martin ruined my ability to trust. He gaslit me until even I was convinced that no one would believe me. I married a man who beat me and belittled me. I didn't even trust myself after what he put me through. Then, after I ran, I only had myself to rely on. I couldn't confide in anyone in case it somehow made it back to Martin about where I was. All of that created the ill-adjusted person I am today."

"I see your point, but it still doesn't solve our problem." He squints up at the sun streaming between the trees.

"What's our problem?"

"I'm in love with someone incapable of trusting me."

Chapter
TWENTY-EIGHT

Khan

"I'm in love with someone incapable of trusting me," I say.

Her hand flies to her forehead. "I don't know what to say. I can't lie and say I've changed—I haven't. That will take time and patience. I guess our problem is bigger than just trust."

"Goddamn it." I kick the dirt and walk in a circle. "I fucking love you so much I feel like I can't breathe without you. But I'm terrified you'll never stop pushing me away when things get tough. What if next time you freak out, we have a kid together? You gonna leave him behind too?"

Holy shit, if that isn't the crux of the issue. I'm worried Bex will turn into my mom.

"I wouldn't do that," she says quietly, resting a hand on my arm. "I know I haven't been stable lately, but having a child is one of the most selfish things a person can do, and I'd never make a kid's existence their problem. I grew up being passed around from family member to family member. All of them made sure

I was reminded every day that I was a burden. If I brought a child into the world, I would never abandon them."

"You never told me that before." I realize I told her all about my childhood, but I never asked her about hers.

"It's not something I enjoy discussing. I never knew who my dad was, and my mom wasn't good at being a parent. Neither were her parents or siblings. But that's who I spent my childhood with. I didn't get to make friends because I switched schools so often. I didn't want to end up in a single-wide in the middle of nowhere New York, so I worked hard to save money. Despite all the moves, my grades were good enough to get me a scholarship."

"Thank you for telling me that. I think I understand you a bit better now."

"I'm sorry I'm not the most open book." She bumps her hip into my thigh since she's so much shorter than I am. "So what do you say? You have any patience left for me?"

I'm torn. I need to choose between taking a risk and being with the woman I love or self-preservation. Before Bex, I always chose myself first but now, I'm not certain that's any way to live.

"I don't know. You have any other exes who could come to town and nearly ruin my life?"

"Nope." She pops her P. "Only the one."

"Then I guess there's not a choice to make." I grip her around the waist. "I choose you."

"I choose you too," she says.

"Do you love me, darlin'?" I've told her as much but she has yet to say it back.

"What?" Her expression is unreadable, and I don't know how to take it.

I rest my forehead on hers. "Do. You. Love. Me?"

"How could you not know that? Of course I do."

"Need to hear the words," I say.

"I love you so much, I don't know what to do with myself. You're all I've thought about for months. I'm annoyingly giddy inside every time I see you. When I'm alone at night and touching myself, it's your body I'm fantasizing about. Yes, I love you, Wes." She tips her head up in an invitation.

Our lips meet, and I bend down and grab the backs of her thighs, lifting her to straddle me. Her arms wrap around my neck, and she locks her ankles behind my back. I carry her down to the meadow, our lips tangled together the whole way, and I lay her down on the ground.

Nuzzling our noses, I say, "Any objections to being fucked outdoors?"

She looks around. "No."

I thrust my tongue in her mouth. She tastes like candy canes and coffee. Our lips move together while I work to remove her blazer. I get that off and remember she has on a goddamn turtleneck of all things. She must be hot since it's nearly ninety out today.

I release her, and we wrestle with the damn thing until I'm convinced she sewed it onto herself this morning. I grab my pocket knife and flip out the blade. Without asking, I cut the fabric from the bottom hem all the way up. It falls to either side of her body, revealing a lacy bra that's so thin I can see her piercings through the material.

"Did you wear this for me?" I trace a finger over each breast.

"I was hoping it would end this way." She sucks in a sharp breath when I tease a finger over her areola. "I'm pretty sure they're healed."

"Hasn't been six months."

"They don't hurt, and they're so sensitive. Even more now. Please," she begs.

"Fine, but if you get a flesh-eating bacteria, I'll be really pissed. I love your tits."

"I'll be fine. I promise."

She ain't a doctor, so it's a promise she can't keep, yet I pull down the cups of her bra and lower my mouth to the closest nipple I can reach. I flick my tongue against the stiff peak and swirl it around the cold barbell. Her whole body shivers. God, I've missed how responsive her nipples are.

"More," she breathes out, and I latch on, sucking hard. She moans and rubs her legs together. I pluck at the nipple my mouth isn't on, then give the barbell a tug.

Her legs wrap around my thigh, and she grinds herself against me. She's going to make herself come one way or another. Might as well be with my dick buried in her cunt.

I release her long enough to get her pants off and push mine down over my ass. After rolling her onto her stomach, I pull back on her hips and kick her legs wide with my knees.

"Gonna be hard and fast. You down?"

"Yes," she hisses.

In one thrust, I'm balls deep inside her sopping wet pussy. I rise higher on my knees and pound into her at an angle I know will hit her G-spot.

Her breasts sway, and her head falls forward. I have the urge to wrap her hair around my fist, but I don't know how bad her scalp still hurts, so I save it for next time after I can ask.

I slap a palm down her ass, causing her to clench around me. The added squeeze feels so good, I do it again and again, watching her ass redden with my palm prints.

"Oh my God. Harder," she shouts, and I'm glad the nearest neighbor isn't close enough to hear.

I increase both the intensity and the speed of my slaps, never landing in the same place more than once. By the time she screams my name, her entire ass and both sit spots are hot and bright red.

It turns me on so much that I come right along with her, blowing my load deep inside while chanting, "Mine, mine, mine."

Someday I'll do this, and she won't be on the pill. I'll fill her with my cum every day until she's pregnant with my baby. While I think Bex and I have some growing to do before that happens, it's a dream that I hope we can make come true.

We both fall back onto the wildflowers that are now crushed from our knees.

"So this thing with Martin is really over?" I ask.

I think I feel an ant crawling up my ass, so I pull my jeans on. She must have the same concern because she quickly dresses too, except with no shirt now, she sits down in just pants and a bra.

"I think it's only the beginning. There will be a trial that I'm certain the seven women will have to testify at. I've already agreed to cover their representation because Martin only fucked with women who couldn't defend themselves. Then there are my assault charges he'll have to answer to. I'll probably have to testify for that one."

"How long will it take to be done with all this?"

"Years," she says matter-of-factly. None of this is new information to her, but I don't know the law.

"Jesus. Can't get rid of that asshole no matter how hard I try."

"I'm sorry." She picks an untouched purple flower and tucks it behind her ear. "I don't have to tell you about it all so you don't stress."

I throw her a look of irritation.

"I know. Rule number three, my problems are your problems."

"She can be taught," I call out into the forest.

She giggles and says, "I'm happy."

"Me too, darlin'. Me too."

An hour later, we return to the clubhouse. Not able to wear a slashed shirt, Bex was forced to make the ride in just her buttoned blazer. I like the look since it puts her tits on display, but she's self-conscious about it and keeps a hand over the top of her chest. We both have grass stains on our clothes, and she's still picking twigs out of her hair.

We walk inside, hand in hand, and I yell out, "Prez, I'd like to move to strike the vote for me to become nomad from the records."

My brothers bang fists and rush over to give me our signature back-slapping hug, starting with Loki.

"Wouldn't have been the same without you, brother," he says.

Bex moves off to the side to observe, but I can tell she's feeling embarrassed after everything she put me through.

"Let's get a round of beers," I yell over to Duncan. He nods and starts pouring, lining them up on the bar.

I raise my glass in the air. "To Bexley, the best goddamn lawyer a biker club could have. Because of her, all charges against me are being dropped."

The guys cheer, and Goblin lifts Bex up in a bear hug. Her smile returns as she pats his back placatingly.

"Now let's fuckin' party," Loki says.

"I need to go clean up," Bex says, still covering her top.

"Make it quick." I slap her ass as she walks away.

"Glad to see you got everything squared away." Loki taps his glass against mine.

"Thanks, neighbor."

"Huh?"

"I bought the land next to Roch's. Gonna start building in the spring."

Loki smiles. "That's fucking awesome news."

"Thanks, man."

"Bexley's gonna be moving into this new house with you?" he asks.

"Sure as shit hope so."

People start to arrive, mostly friends of the club who want to show their support for me being a free man. I realize Bexley still hasn't come back, so I seek her out. Opening my bedroom door, I find her curled up on my bed, asleep, a towel wrapped around her wet hair and my T-shirt covering her body.

This whole thing must've been so stressful. I doubt she was able to sleep at all. Not wanting to leave her alone, I climb in next to her.

She stirs, and her eyes open. "Oh, no. Did I fall asleep?"

I chuckle. "Sure did."

"I'm sorry. I guess I'm more tired than I thought I was." She covers a yawn.

"Let's get you home."

"But the party," she says through yet another yawn. "I'll be fine. You go have fun."

"Not how it works, darlin'. You're in here sleeping, but all I can think about is being in bed with you."

"Fine. Then I'll come out." Her eyelids sag, and I know she's seconds from being pulled back under.

"Nope. We're leaving." I climb off the bed and scoop her up. She reaches down and tugs my shirt under her ass to cover it.

I hold her in my arms through the main area where everyone is having a damn good time. The music from the basement is pumping a different tune than up here, and I'm proud that I could give something back to my brothers, who have always been there for me.

"We're out of here," I say to anyone who's listening as I walk out to Bex's car.

Bex giggles, her face pressed into my neck. I set her down

in the passenger seat of her Mercedes before climbing into the driver's side.

"How come you never took me on your bike before today?" she asks.

I shrug. "Wanted to make sure you were mine before I put you on the back of my bike. It means something to me."

"Does that mean you're sure about me now?"

"No," I scoff, and her face falls. "I was sure about you the first time I laid eyes on you. I was just waiting for you to be sure."

I kiss her full on the lips and drive away into our future.

EPILOGUE

Khan

I pull the hood off the old fuck's head. He's still passed out from the blow to the temple I delivered in his living room. Martin Alexander was released on a million-dollar bond two days after he was charged. The man doesn't have much, but he's got money.

Had money. He had money. Sly and Moto broke into his safe while me and Loki roughed him up and got him into the van. They found over two million in cash before wiping cameras the paranoid asshole had over every inch of his mansion.

It took less than ten minutes from the time we pulled into his driveway until we drove away. He lives out in the hills, so there were no neighbors to worry about. And pretty soon, there'll be no Martin to worry about either.

I work quickly to secure the chains around his wrists and then use the winch to hoist him up until only the very tips of his toes can touch the ground below. I enjoy watching my prey dance around like a fuckin' ballerina.

I use one of my knives to slice through his clothes until

they're a pile of scraps on the floor. Men don't like being vulnerable in front of other men, especially a man like Martin, who lives for the rush of power. How's he going to feel when he wakes up and realizes he'll die powerless? That thought makes me smile.

I take him in, trying to understand what Bex saw in him. After leading a life of luxury, he's overweight with no muscle mass to speak of. He's inferior to me in every way.

Out of sheer curiosity, I glance down lower, and I'm not impressed with that either. His small, shriveled-up dick looks like a turtle hiding in its shell. No wonder he has a complex.

Lighting up a cig, I fill a glass of water from the faucet and toss it in his face. He gasps and sputters, his eyes flying open.

"Wakey, wakey," I say, inhaling the nicotine.

"Where am I?" he asks.

"My kill room."

He scans the space, his eyes widening more and more as he takes it all in: cement walls, drain in the middle of the floor, table with various knives laid out, and a big motherfucker standing next to him with homicide in his eyes.

He yanks on the chains and screams for help, but it's no use.

"You're an even bigger psycho than I thought," he says, saliva dripping down his chin.

"You're one to speak."

With my lit cigarette dangling from my lips, I put on a pair of latex gloves and pick up my favorite knife. It's a beautiful horn-handle, fixed-steel blade. "Usually, I tell people I'll make their death quick if they answer my questions. But I don't have any questions for you, and there's no way I'll make this quick."

"I have money. I can get you a lot of it. Clean cash, too."

"We found your clean cash already, and now it's in our safe instead of yours."

"You took my money?" he asks incredulously.

"You won't need it where you're going." I set my blade down

and move behind him. He dances on his toes, trying to turn around to see what I'm doing.

Dance ballerina, dance.

Gripping my cig with one hand and holding his left eye open with the other, I push the cherry into his eyeball until it fizzles out. His head lulls back onto my shoulder and I bask in the loud cry of pain he lets out. It's like music to my fuckin' ears.

"You're insane," he spits out. "You can't do this to me."

"Can't I?" I ask, relighting the cig.

The flavor is off. Gathering the saliva in my mouth, I spit it out onto the ground. *Gross.* I move to the next eyeball and stamp the cherry completely out into the white of his eye.

His head lulls forward, and he squeezes his eyes closed. He's blubbering now, like the weak pig he is. Picking back up my blade, I fist the back of his hair and jerk his head up.

"Bex was an impressionable nineteen-year-old when you, a grown-ass man, ruined her life. You made her trust you, made her dependent on you, then you let her see who you really were. You abused her, mentally and physically." It fucks me up to think about who she would've been if she hadn't met Martin Alexander. Though I'm glad it led her to me, I don't enjoy thinking about the path she had to take to get here. "This is for that nineteen-year-old girl."

I make a quick slice down the center of his face, effectively cutting off his nose. Blood oozes down his face, and only a hole with leftover cartilage remains. His shriek is otherworldly, but no one hears it but me. This room is soundproof.

"You could've stopped after she left. You could've taken the opportunity to look inside yourself and realize what you did was wrong. But you didn't, did you? Instead, you abused other women, all while plotting your revenge." I grip his rubbery ear, letting out a disgusted noise when I see he has wiry dark hairs growing out of it. "This is for all those women you manipulated and hurt."

I whack his ear off and toss the useless flesh to the ground before moving to the other side and carving off the other one. Bright red blood gushes down his shoulders and drips to the floor. Penance can look like a lot of things. Some people pray, some people apologize. Martin Alexander is paying for his sins in blood.

"You couldn't get Bex out of your head, could you?" I walk circles around his dangling body. "I get it. She has the same effect on me. That sassy mouth, her independence, and those tits, am I right?"

He blubbers something I can't understand.

"What was that?"

"Fat bitch," he spews.

Acting out of anger always ends a kill too quickly, so I try not to let the fury of his words get to me, but they do anyway. He's dying tonight, and instead of asking for redemption, he's choosing to insult my woman further. Fuck that.

I walk over to my knives and pick up a pouch full of the needles that body modification artists use for piercings. I use them to cause pain. I pry his mouth open, which isn't hard to do since he's growing weaker by the minute, and he wasn't a strong man to begin with.

"This is for coming here to ruin her life for a second time."

Guessing what I'm about to do, he holds his tongue back as far as he can, making it difficult for me to get ahold of it, but not impossible. I stab through the tip and stretch his tongue out as far as I can get it. Then, with my knife, I hack the damn thing off.

Blood pools in his mouth and spills from his chin. That should shut him up. His face goes white, and he passes out, hanging lifelessly from the chains. That won't do. I'm not finished, and he needs to hear what I have to say. I get another glass of cold water and dump it over his head.

He makes a pained sound but doesn't lift his head or try to stand up. I'm losing him before I've gotten to the best part. I need to speed things up.

"As if moving to Reno and blackmailing her wasn't stupid enough, you took it one step further. You chose to hurt her. Do you have any idea what it does to a man like me when someone hurts their woman? Any fucking clue?" I dig around between his legs until I get a grip on his pencil dick. "Never had to work this hard to cut off a cock before. Does this thing even work?"

His toes attempt to gain purchase, but where does he think he can go even if he was strong enough to lift himself up? This is the end of the line for him.

"This is for the trauma you inflicted on Bex when you choked her, slammed her head through a wall, and left her for someone else to find." I slash his dick clean off. My face pinches as I hold it up. "Jesus, man. This is smaller than a little smokie. Embarrassing."

I toss the bit of dick next to his ears and nose. I'm collecting quite the stack of parts. The prospects are going to have fun cleaning this one up.

He's minutes from bleeding out, and I'm still not finished, so I hurry to get the last of it in.

"The rest of this is for me. For the moment I had to walk into a motherfucking hospital and see my woman covered in bruises, head split open, and your handprints around her neck." I slice off his saggy, hairy ball sack, adding it to the pile.

For my final scene, I saw into his chest and use the bone end of my knife to crush his ribs. An incredible amount of blood pours out of him, and I push away the bone fragments to find what I'm looking for. His heart. It's not beating anymore, but it's warm in my hand.

Using my boot to his torso as leverage, I roar a battle cry as I yank his heart from his chest. It's not easy—the aorta and whatever is connected to it are surprisingly tough, and the heart itself is slippery—but I manage. I hold it above my head, putting on a show for an audience of one. This shit was personal, though, so I'm the only one who matters.

I hurl the fucking thing at the wall, and it lands with a splat.

But I'm not done. I release his chains and he falls to the ground with a thud. Back at my table of implements, I pick up my pruning shears and snip off each of his fingers for daring to touch what's mine.

"I never make a promise I don't keep, motherfucker." My chest heaves, and I'm suddenly exhausted. The relief I feel is immeasurable. It's over. He's gone. And he'll never hurt Bexley again.

I stroll through the front door of our apartment. *Our* apartment. The day after Martin was arrested, I took Sly off the lease and put Bex and me on it. Everything in our lives from here on out won't be hidden from the world.

"Hey, babe. How was your day?" Bexley's on the sofa. Her hair is piled on her head, and she's dressed in one of my T-shirts with her shapely legs crossed in front of her. Papers and her laptop are on the coffee table, and a medical drama plays on the TV.

"Fuckin' fantastic," I say because it's the truth. Killing Martin this afternoon was the most satisfying thing I've done in a long-ass time.

I sit down next to her and bring her to my side. She does me one better and straddles my hips. Her hands move to my hair, freeing it from the bun it was in and combing through the strands.

"That's good. I missed you today."

My hands slip under her shirt and settle on her hips, where I find the thin strip of fabric holding up her thong. "Missed you too, darlin.'"

Her nose scrunches. "I need a pet name that's only for me. You call every woman you meet darlin.'"

I smile and let my head fall back onto the cushion. "What do you want me to call you then?"

"How about honey?" she suggests, and my eyebrow quirks. "Don't like that one?"

I shake my head.

"Sweetie?" She realizes right away that's a bad one and shakes her head. "Sugar?"

"How 'bout wifey?" I ask.

"But I'm not your—" The words die on her lips and make a beautiful "O" shape instead.

I reach into my cut and pull out a diamond ring I'd been holding onto since before she broke up with me the second time. Or was it the third? I lost track. I didn't intend to give it to her today since we're still working through shit, but our future is brighter than ever with Martin gone.

"We don't need to get married tomorrow or next week or even next year. But I'm gonna marry you, and then I'm going to knock you up every chance I get."

"Romantic," she jokes, but her eyes are brimming with tears. I usually break down at the sight of them, but these are happy ones, which makes me happy.

"You're a pain in my ass, but I love you. Will you marry me?" I slip the ring on her finger. It's nothing too fancy, just a princess-cut solitaire set in gold.

She holds her hand up to the light of the setting sun streaming through the apartment. "It's beautiful."

"That a yes, *wifey?*"

She cups my cheeks and bounces up and down on my lap, making my cock stiffen. "Yes! Of course, I will."

I wrap my arms around her middle tightly and stand up.

"Where are we going?" She giggles, burying her face in my neck.

"I need to fuck my fiancé."

"I have work to do," she complains.

I slap her ass, loving the way it jiggles under my palm. "The only work you're doing tonight is with your mouth on my dick."

"Dirty." She slaps my chest playfully, and I toss her on the bed.

"You ain't seen nothing yet." I spread her legs, my eyes zeroing in on the small scrap of fabric covering her pussy. I rub up and down her seam, remembering I have one last question to ask. "Am I marrying Sienna Alexander or Bexley March?"

She grins. "Which one of us do you want to marry?"

"Which one is sluttier?"

She laughs, and the sound is pure magic. "Considering Sienna's only experience with sex was the missionary position, I have to say Bexley is a lot more fun in the sack."

"Bexley it is then."

THE MOTHERFUCKIN' END

Need more Coyote and Riley? This series continues in *Riley's Biker*. Out now!

Preview of *Riley's Biker*

PROLOGUE

Coyote
Five years ago . . .

"Let's do another shot." Loki, the prince of the Royal Bastards, slaps one hand on my shoulder while the other forms a fist and pounds on the bar. The prospect on the other side of the wooden bar scrambles to do his bidding.

"One more, then I'm out." I swivel on my barstool and take in the chaos and debauchery going on around me.

I grin and tuck my head when I see Trucker, Prez of Reno's Royal Bastards, making out on a leather sofa with his ol' lady like they're teenagers. Boar, the VP of this chapter, has his face buried in some young girl's chest—who is not his wife, but we don't talk about that—while the younger members are screwing patch pussy like their peckers are going to fall off.

I swivel back around. This ain't my scene. I pick up my shot glass of God knows what and clink it against Loki's.

"Cheers," Loki says and tosses the shot down his throat without a flinch. When you grow up in the clubhouse of a motorcycle club, booze and women are early lessons learned.

"Cheers." I throw back the shot and set the glass down.

Mmm. Mezcal. The prince has good taste.

"What're your plans when you leave here?" he asks, wrapping an arm around a blonde wearing a shirt low-cut enough to see the tops of her areolas. She blatantly cups him over his jeans, startling a reaction out of him. He leans into her and whispers, "In a minute."

I shift my gaze to the peanut-shell-covered floor, and I scratch at the back of my neck. "Meetin' back up with Dunk and Mac. Gettin' to be cold out, so we'll probably head south."

He quirks a brow. "Or you could patch in here and stick around."

"Nah. You know me." I chuckle as if my inability to stay in one place is a personality trait. It's not, and we both know it. Reno is a fine place to rest, but there's no settling down for a man like me.

"Don't be a stranger. We'll catch you next time." He takes his bottle of beer and leads the blonde over to a quiet corner.

I leave my half-empty bottle and head out to the backyard. The second the door closes behind me, it's quiet and serene. The air is easier to breathe, and my heart rate slows the further I get from the clubhouse and the closer I get to my pup tent.

I strip down to my underwear before climbing inside to lie down. I need some sleep before I meet up with Mac and Dunk tomorrow. My nomad brothers skipped our stop in Reno in favor of hitting up some Vegas casinos with plans to reunite in Northern California before riding down the coast.

My eyes have almost shut when I hear a sniffing. I scan the area through the mesh walls of my tent, but I don't see anything.

Wild horses, bears, and coyotes all live out here in the high desert. Normally, I wouldn't go inspect, except it didn't sound like any of those things. What I heard was more human.

I pull on my faded black jeans and leather boots before stepping outside. At first glance, there's nothing to see. It's dark, and the lights from the house are too far away to light up the area.

Then I hear it again. My eyes scour the fence line until I see it. Or rather, see her. A girl is hunched over on the ground. Her back is leaning against the fence post, and the light of her cell phone illuminates her face as her thumbs work fast and furious to type out a message.

"Hey," I call out. Her eyes go wide as saucers, her mouth drops open, and she freezes. I chuckle to myself and shake my head. "I can still see you, little owl."

She slowly rises to her feet. Her jean shorts are cut off at the tops of her thighs, and her tight black tank top is cut low. She's young for a club whore, but I've seen all types show up looking to bag a biker.

"You okay?" I ask because it's the polite thing to do.

"Do you know why every Uber driver cancels my pick up?" she asks. Her voice is sweet and thick like syrup.

My cock hardens, and I talk myself down. If she hangs around the club, she's probably fucked every single one of my brothers just so she can run home to her girlfriends to tell them all about her walk on the dark side. Not into that shit.

"They won't come anywhere near the club. Walk a few blocks away and try again."

Her face falls. "Damn it. Can nothing go right tonight?"

"Not sure what else went wrong, but it's an easy solution." I point in the direction she should start hoofing it.

"Do you have a bike?" she asks.

"Yeah." I don't like where this is going. I don't let chicks on the back of my bike.

"Can you take me to the airport?"

My brows lift. "Nope."

"But I have a flight to catch." She walks over to me, and I get my first, up-close look at her.

I'm six foot four, and she barely reaches my chest, making her no taller than five foot three. She's tiny, too. I'll bet my biceps are thicker than her thighs.

Her soft, creamy complexion contrasts with the sharp points of her Cupid's bow lips, the high arch of her dark eyebrows, and her defined jawline. Her eyes are swollen, and her cheeks are red from crying, but it doesn't take away from her beauty.

"Like I said, a couple blocks that way." I point again.

"It's dark, and I don't know the area." She twists a strand of her hair around a finger.

I roll my eyes. "Not gonna work on me, little owl. But go inside; one of my brothers would be happy to service you again."

"Again?" she scoffs, her hand falling to her side. "I didn't go in there, and I wouldn't"—she glances away, embarrassed—"do that with any of them."

"Then why are you here?" I ask.

Her gaze meets mine, and her cobalt eyes go icy. "It doesn't matter."

The little owl has some bite. Maybe she isn't a sweet butt.

"Look. I'll walk you to the street, but after that, you're on your own." I turn and walk back toward my tent.

"Where are you going?" she asks, trailing behind me.

"To put on a shirt." I reach into my tent and pull out my pack.

"Do you live out here?" She folds her arms across her chest, propping up her bite-sized titties.

"Don't live anywhere." I find a black tee and pull it over my head.

"What does that mean?" She watches me closely with a focused interest I don't like.

"Means I'm a nomad."

"Nomad?" Her brows furrow.

I sigh. "I'm a Royal Bastard, like all those guys in there, but I don't belong to a chapter. I'm on my own. I help out if someone needs me, then I'm back on the road."

She walks a circle around the tent, taking in the contents inside. My pack. My cut. Bedding. Nothing special. "Interesting.

Why is your tent made from mesh? That can't protect you from the weather."

It's not the question that has me closing my eyes and taking a breath, it's the answer. Something I haven't told a soul, and I'm not about to start with a girl I don't know.

"Have a tarp in case it rains, but I don't see much weather 'cause I ride south for the winter." I tie the laces on my boots to give me an extra second to avoid her scrutinizing gaze.

"Don't you get lonely?" She stops in front of me and knocks her tennis shoes against my boots. I look up to see her hands on her hips.

"No." I'm done answering questions, so I turn the table on her. "Why are you going to the airport?"

The sky suddenly becomes interesting to her. She's avoiding, like me.

"I need to catch a flight home."

"Still not gonna tell me why you're here?" I ask.

"Nope."

"When's your flight?"

"Tomorrow morning at eight." She sinks to the ground in defeat. Guess we're not going anywhere anytime soon. Not that I entirely mind. I like talking to her, and I like hearing her voice. My cock's interested, too, now that I know she wasn't in the clubhouse making the rounds.

"Oh yeah?" I sit down next to her, one leg outstretched and the other bent.

"I didn't plan this out well. I thought I'd show up, and things would be . . . different." She scoops handfuls of sand, then spreads her delicate fingers wide so it all falls to the ground again. "But that's not what happened, and now I'm stranded in a place where Uber drivers are too scared to venture. How is this my life right now?"

She's talking to herself more than me, and her story is

nothing but a garbled, vague retelling I don't understand, so I say nothing. Then she hides her face with her hands and the tears return. I pat her back awkwardly, not knowing how the hell I got myself into this situation.

"You could stay the night here. It ain't much, but at least you don't have to sit in an empty airport all night."

This is my dick talking. Not me. It's been too long since I've found a woman who sparks my interest, and, for whatever reason, this one does.

"I'm not having sex with you," she says.

"Not interested in that with you, little owl." It's a lie. Now that I have the idea in my head, all I can think about is her tight little body riding me until the sun comes up.

She peers over at me, her face pinched in irritation. "Why not? What's wrong with me?"

I chuckle, then lean into her and, in a lust-thick voice, say, "Ain't nothing wrong with you. If it were up to me, I'd strip you down and fuck you so hard you can't sit down on your flight home tomorrow."

"Oh." Her eyes home in on my lips. "Then why don't you?"

I pull away. "You said no and I don't force myself on women."

"Okay. I guess, in that case, I'll stay here and catch an Uber in the morning."

"Whatever you wanna do." I kick off my boots and stand. "I'm going to bed."

"I'm coming too."

Those big owl eyes watch as I strip off my pants and shirt, leaving me in a pair of boxer briefs. I smirk. She's more interested than she lets on.

She kicks off her Chucks, and we climb inside. As she pointed out before, the walls of this tent are made of mesh, so even though we're inside, it feels like we're still outside.

I only have one pillow, so I offer it to her. Likewise, I only have one sleeping bag, so I unzip it and spread it over the top of us. The blow-up mattress pad keeps us from feeling the rocks underneath, but for us to both be on it, we have to get close. Real close. Close enough I smell the patchouli and mint from her shampoo.

We lie on our sides, both facing the same direction but not touching. It should be awkward. We know fuck-all about each other, but for whatever reason, I don't feel uncomfortable.

"What's your name?" she whispers.

"Coyote."

She flips over, her face coming within inches of mine. "Your momma named you Coyote?"

The mention of my mom is like a stab through the heart, but I'm used to the pain. "No. What's your name?"

"Way to change the subject, but I'll let it pass. I'm Riley. It's nice to meet you." She holds out her hand, which barely fits in the space between us. I shake it slowly and intentionally.

"Nice to meet you too."

We stare at each other for a long moment, our warm breaths mingling between us. The tension builds and builds, neither of us turning away.

"Are you going to kiss me, Coyote?"

"No."

"What if I ask you to?" she pouts.

"Sorry, little owl. I'm a man. I don't make out with girls anymore."

"What if I want *more*?"

Maybe I'm pussy deprived, but her boldness turns me right the fuck on.

"How old are you?" I assume she's of age, but I make it a habit to ask when there's even a question.

"Nineteen."

"Then all you have to do is ask." I reach over and grip her by the hip, tugging her against me. Those owl eyes widen impossibly big when she feels the result of her words against her belly.

She swallows hard. "Ask?"

"Need your words."

Her lips purse as she decides. "Coyote, will you fuck me?"

The curse sounds wrong in her saccharine voice, but it doesn't stop me from crushing my lips to hers and snaking an arm under her head. I feel her pebbled nipples through her thin tank top telling me she's not wearing a bra, and thank fuck for that. Reaching under the sleeping bag, I snake a hand under her shirt and am met with bare flesh.

Her tits are barely a palmful, but I love the way they feel in my hand. I pinch her nipple, and she lets out a choked sound that is all pleasure.

"Feel good, little owl?"

"Yes," she says on an exhale. Tentatively, she places a hand on my chest and drags it lower. Reaching the band of my underwear, she teases the elastic with the tips of her fingers.

Tossing the sleeping bag off us, I roll on top of her and shove her tank top up. My mouth wraps around her tit, sucking the whole thing in before releasing it with a *pop*. "What about that?"

She wraps her legs around my waist and rocks her pelvis against me. "So good."

I continue to suck and bite on her tiny nipples, working her up into a frenzy.

"Need to taste the rest of you." I sit up and help her out of her shorts and panties.

I wish I could see her pussy, but it's too dark, so I'll live with the next best thing. Touching her. Swiping a finger through her folds, I find her wet, sopping really. I can smell her arousal from here, and it's an addictive scent I'll never forget.

Lowering my mouth to her cunt, I lick her up and down,

eliciting a sexy moan from her. "How do you like it? Fast and hard or soft and sweet?"

The question perplexes her for a moment before she says, "Fast and hard."

"My kind of girl." I flick my tongue against her clit, inserting a finger into her tight hole. It's gonna be a stretch for her to take my cock, but I'm willing to put in the effort.

It only takes a few more minutes before she's coming, her channel pulsing around my fingers and her hips grinding against my face. Her sweet cream coats my tongue, the flavor like a freshly picked tomato after it's been sitting in the sun all day.

I've never wanted anyone like I want her. If she changed her mind right now, I'd have blue balls for a month.

I coax her down from her orgasm before reaching for my pack and digging out a condom. Riley watches me intently as I push my boxer briefs past my ass and roll the rubber down my cock.

"You ready?" I rub a hand up her pussy, feeling how wet she still is for me.

She doesn't respond, and I can't make out her expression. As much as it will pain me, I'm not about to do this if she doesn't want it.

I lean over her body and kiss her sweet lips. "I'll ask again. Are you ready?"

"I feel like I should tell you something."

"What?"

"I'm a virgin." She locks her arms around my neck, preventing me from pulling away. "I'm not saving it out of some purity culture obligation. It just hasn't happened, and I want it to. With you."

"Don't fuck virgins, little owl." Despite my words, my cock is like a heat-seeking missile, aligning itself at her entrance.

"Please," she begs. "I want it to be you."

I want it to be me too, but I'm not sure what the right thing to do is. I'm too old to be fucking virgins. Hell, I wasn't even with a virgin when I was fourteen and losing my own virginity. That was sixteen years ago, and I don't know if girls still feel the same about their cherry as they did back then.

"I won't be sweet and gentle."

"I don't want sweet and gentle," she spits out as though I offended her.

My answer is to grip the base of my cock and thrust into her in one fluid motion. God, she's tight. So tight there's no chance of me lasting long. She sucks in a sharp breath, and her fingernails claw into my neck. The pain spurs me on, and I lift onto my knees, tossing her legs over either shoulder and reaching under her ass to take two handfuls.

I use her body to fuck my cock, pushing and pulling on her elevated hips. Her chest heaves, thrusting those gorgeous bite-sized tits into the air. Her heels dig into the back of my shoulders, helping me to move her body back and forth on my hard length.

To my surprise, she cries out with another orgasm. Her cunt bears down on me, strangling me in the best way. Beads of sweat gather on my brow and lower back from the exertion. My muscles will be sore tomorrow, but I don't give a shit right now.

"Damn, little owl. Your cunt is so good, you're going to make me come. You ready?"

She nods vehemently, her hands reaching between her legs to dig her nails into my abdomen. The image of the claw marks she's leaving behind spurs me into an orgasm.

I come with a roar, burying my cock as deep as I can get. I don't ever remember it lasting this long or feeling this good, but with Riley, it does.

I pull out and toss the used condom outside. I'll deal with it in the morning.

"That was . . . well, it was incredible," she gasps out, her breaths still coming fast.

"Hell yeah, it was." I flop back down onto the mattress and encourage her to her side.

I'm not much for cuddling, but I'm also not an asshole, so I'm going to hold her all night. She melds into me, letting out a satisfied sigh.

I don't mean to fall asleep so quickly, but I do, and when I wake the next morning, she's gone. Every trace of her. If it weren't for the used condom I find when I climb out of my tent, I'd think I dreamed the whole thing.

Guess it's for the best, though I wish I could've gotten a look at her in the daylight.

I'm up later than I planned, so I quickly pack up. It's not until I'm walking through the clubhouse that I feel like something's missing. I dig through my backpack and come up empty-handed. It's then I realize something.

The bitch stole my cut.

Need more Coyote and Riley? This series continues in *Riley's Biker*. Out now!

ROYAL BASTARDS MC SERIES THIRD RUN

Winter Travers: *Monk*
K.L. Ramsey: *Ratchet's Revenge*
Chelle C. Craze & Eli Abbott: *Cocked Hammer*
Nikki Landis: *Hell's Fury*
M. Merin: *Diesel*
Kristine Allen: *Chains*
KE Osborn: *Seeking Shadows*
Scarlett Black: *River*
Erin Trejo: *Bleed for Me*
Crimson Syn: *Afflicted with Desire*
J.Lynn Lombard: *Torch's Torment*
Glenna Maynard: *Taken by the Biker*
K Webster: *Dragon*
Khloe Wren: *Flood of Bravery*
Rae B. Lake: *Chaos and Paradise*
Misty Walker: *Bexley's Biker*
J.L. Leslie: *Worth the Pain*
Nicole James: *Climbing the Ranks*
Ker Dukey: *Carnage*
Deja Voss: *Steel Resurrection*
Elle Boon: *Royally Inked*
Jessica Ames: *Into the Flames*
Shannon Youngblood: *Sex and Candy*
B.B. Blaque: *Southern Ballz*
K.L. Savage: *Raven*
Izzy Sweet & Sean Moriarty: *Broken Lines*
E.C. Land: *Spiral into Chaos*
Jax Hart: *Desert Heat*

Royal Bastards MC Facebook Group
www.facebook.com/groups/royalbastardsmc

Website
www.royalbastardsmc.com

ABOUT THE AUTHOR

Misty Walker writes everything from dark and delicious, to sweet and spicy. Most of her books are forbidden in some way and many are age-gap, because that's her jam.

She's lived quite the nomadic life, never staying in the same place for long until she met her husband. They've recently settled in Reno, NV with their two daughters, two dogs, and two hamsters, because everything's better in pairs.

Misty is fueled by coffee and the voices in her head screaming for their stories to be told. Which is why the coffee is necessary, because there are only so many hours in a day and who needs sleep anyway?

If you'd like to keep up to date on all her future releases, please sign up for her newsletter on her website. You can also order a signed paperback of this book, or any of her releases, there.

Connect with Misty:

www.authormistywalker.com
authormistywalker@gmail.com
Instagram: www.instagram.com/authormistywalker
Facebook: www.facebook.com/authormistywalker
Twitter: @mistywalkerbook

Turn the page for a list of all of Misty Walker's books.

ALSO BY MISTY WALKER

Standalones:
Vindicated
Conversion (also available on audio)
Cop-Out
Crow's Scorn: Diamond Kings MC

Royal Bastards: Reno, NV:
Birdie's Biker
Truly's Biker
Bexley's Biker
Riley's Biker
Petra's Bikers

Brigs Ferry Bay Series:
Kian's Focus
Kian's Focus (also available on audio)
Adler's Hart
Leif's Serenity
Doctor Daddy
Brigs Ferry Bay Omnibus

ACKNOWLEDGMENTS

Kristi, sometimes I think about us being grandmas, still writing filthy books, and it makes me smile. Love you to pieces.

Ty-bot, someday I'll make you my bitch. Thanks for everything, babe. Love you.

Ariadna, Sarah, Sara, Elizabeth, Lauren, Rhonda, and Jayce, thank you for being my beta team. I'm equally grateful and mortified that you see me in my rawest form and continue to stay!

Sarah Goodman, it's an absolute treat to have you on my team. Your input is vital and I'm so glad you love my characters as much as I do!

Molly Whitman, thank you for having a better memory than I do and using that talent to close all those pesky plot holes I open up. You make my words better!

Stacey Blake, thank you for making the pages of this book as badass as the bikers themselves.

Mom, your friendship means more to me than you'll ever know. It's a pretty darn good feeling knowing you're out there believing in me more than I believe in myself. I love you!

To my readers & my reader group, Misty Walker's Thirsty Readers, thank you the most! You guys rock my world and motivate me to keep writing. I love nothing more than to get your messages and read your reviews. It's a great big book world, but you choose to read my books, and that means everything.

Lorelai and Mabel, don't ever read this book. I love you.

Printed in Great Britain
by Amazon